# A Slay
# Ride Together
# with You

## The Sherlock Holmes Bookshop Mystery

*The Sign of Four Spirits*
*The Game Is a Footnote*
*A Curious Incident*
*There's a Murder Afoot*
*A Scandal in Scarlet*
*The Cat of the Baskervilles*
*Body on Baker Street*
*Elementary, She Read*

## The Lighthouse Library Mysteries (writing as Eva Gates)

*Death Knells and Wedding Bells*
*Death by Beach Read*
*Deadly Ever After*
*A Death Long Overdue*
*Read and Buried*
*Something Read, Something Dead*
*The Spook in the Stacks*
*Reading Up A Storm*
*Booked for Trouble*
*By Book or by Crook*

## The Ashley Grant Mysteries

*Coral Reef Views*
*Blue Water Hues*
*White Sand Blues*

## The Klondike Mysteries

*Gold Web*
*Gold Mountain*
*Gold Fever*
*Gold Digger*

## The Ray Robertson Mysteries

*Blood and Belonging*
*Haitian Graves*
*Juba Good*

## The Year Round Christmas Mysteries

*Have Yourself a Deadly Little Christmas*
*Dying in a Winter Wonderland*
*Silent Night, Deadly Night*
*Hark the Herald Angels Slay*
*We Wish You a Murderous Christmas*
*Rest Ye Murdered Gentlemen*

## The Constable Molly Smith Mysteries

*Unreasonable Doubt*
*Under Cold Stone*
*A Cold White Sun*
*Among the Departed*
*Negative Image*
*Winter of Secrets*
*Valley of the Lost*
*In the Shadow of the Glacier*

## The Tea By The Sea Mysteries

*Trouble is Brewing*
*Steeped in Malice*
*Murder Spills the Tea*
*Murder in a Teacup*
*Tea & Treachery*

## The Catskill Summer Resort Mystery

*Deadly Director's Cut*
*Deadly Summer Nights*

## Also Available By Vicki Delany

*More than Sorrow*
*Murder at Lost Dog Lake*
*Burden of Memory*
*Scare the Light Away*
*Whiteout*

# A Slay Ride Together with You

## A YEAR-ROUND CHRISTMAS MYSTERY

## Vicki Delany

**CROOKED LANE**

NEW YORK

Published in the United States by Crooked Lane Books, an imprint of The Quick Brown Fox & Company LLC.

Crooked Lane Books and its logo are trademarks of The Quick Brown Fox & Company LLC.

Library of Congress Catalog-in-Publication data available upon request.

ISBN (hardcover): 978-1-63910-879-4
ISBN (ebook): 978-1-63910-880-0

Cover design by Elsa Kerls

Printed in the United States.

www.crookedlanebooks.com

Crooked Lane Books
34 West 27th St., 10th Floor
New York, NY 10001

First Edition: September 2024

10 9 8 7 6 5 4 3 2 1

To my mother, still going strong as her 100th birthday approaches.

# Chapter One

Spring in Rudolph, New York, is a time to relax. A time to welcome the long-awaited arrival of soft rains and longer days. A time of a warming sun, when the fields turn green almost instantly, and the first of the green shoots struggle to push their way out of the cold, dark soil.

Rudolph, New York, calls itself "America's Christmas Town," and to the relief of everyone in town, spring—and the celebration of Easter that comes with it—is a long way until Christmas rolls around once again.

Not that we don't love Christmas. We do. It's the entire reason behind the success of our town and the prosperity of its residents, and we celebrate the season with all the joy it deserves.

Joy—and a heck of a lot of hard work.

We don't even get a break in the summer, as Christmas in July is almost as big an occasion as the holidays themselves. Old Saint Nick arrives by boat for his vacation by the lake, and he's escorted into town by a full-scale nautical Santa Claus parade.

Easter, by contrast, is a lower-key time. Not a lot of tourists come to town in the early spring, and some shop owners take the opportunity to enjoy their own vacations. The end of winter is a time for me to close my store, Mrs. Claus's Treasures, early; to do inventory; to read design and houseware catalogues, and order what I'll need for the busy summer and holiday seasons.

Time to spend with my boyfriend, Alan Anderson. Alan's a woodworker. He handcrafts furniture and many of the toys sold in stores throughout Upstate New York. He also acts as Santa's head toymaker at public events, so for Alan, Easter's also a time to sit back and take a breath. My parents will be hosting Easter dinner this year, but it won't be anything near the over-the-top event they put on at Christmas.

Oh, and did I mention that my own father, Noel Wilkinson, is the official town Santa? Needless to say, in America's Christmas Town that's almost a full-time job at certain times of the year.

Easter was late this year, and it was still a just under a month away, but some of the stores had started filling their shelves and windows with decorations featuring bunnies and colored eggs and chicks peeking out of baskets. Tonight, the lights in the big tree in the bandstand at the town park would be switched on in a blaze of pale blue, soft green, and bright pink. The week prior to Easter itself, the town's horse-drawn Christmas sleigh would be converted to an Easter wagon, taking excited kids and indulgent parents from one side of town to the other. And back again.

I'd taken advantage of the midweek, pre-Easter lull to take an extra-long break, and I was enjoying a leisurely lunch across the table from my best friend, Vicky Casey, owner and head chef at Victoria's Bake Shoppe.

Only a couple of weeks ago, Vicky had told me in a burst of excitement, not at all untypical of her, that she and Mark Grosse had gotten engaged. After I'd squealed and jumped up and down and hugged her until she struggled to breathe, I'd asked the most logical questions, which were when the wedding would be. And could I be a bridesmaid.

"We haven't set a date yet," she said, "and we're planning a pretty low-key affair. Immediate family, close friends." She gave me a wink. "I suppose I can squeeze you in. If I must." This time her hug was as enthusiastic as mine. I liked Mark a great deal, and I thought he was a good match for the woman I'd been best friends with since the first day of school.

At first, I'd thought she'd suggested today's lunch so we could talk wedding plans, but I soon realized something was off, and I wondered if she was getting cold feet. She should have been relaxed today, without the hordes of tourists lining up for breakfast, lunch, or take-out meals and treats, but instead she was noticeably on edge as she fidgeted in her seat, alternately watching everything happening around her with a vacant expression and pushing pieces of chicken pot pie around her plate.

I tore a hunk off one of Vicky's bakery-made whole-wheat buns, dipped it into my curried butternut squash soup, and munched happily. I said nothing. I didn't ask her what was wrong. She knew I was here for her and she'd tell me—or not—in her own time.

The bakery wasn't Christmas-hordes crowded, but it was busy with Rudolphites enjoying their own lunch, and the occasional confused tourist who'd wandered into Christmas Town three weeks prior to Easter.

Like the other owners of most of the shops and restaurants in town, including me, Vicky had made an effort to add some seasonal touches to the usual Christmas decorations and fare. Hot cross buns were displayed in the bread racks, and baked ham and scalloped potatoes were featured on the catering menu. A row of paper cutouts colored to look like Easter eggs hung in the window, and a pair of stuffed Easter bunnies stood on the shelf above the serving counter, next to the trophies for the winning float in last year's Santa Claus parades. Vicky's bakery wins the prize almost every year—twice—and Mrs. Claus's Treasures never has. I put that down to the fact that Vicky bribes the judges with hot cider and homemade mince tarts before the parade begins.

I try not to let it bother me. In that, I fail.

"Mom's going to Italy next month," I said around a spoonful of soup. My mother, Aline Steiner, is an opera singer. She was a major star in her day, soloing at the Metropolitan Opera as well as at some of the best opera houses in Europe and Asia. A young singer Mom had taken under her wing shortly before she retired was having his first solo performance in *Madama Butterfly* at La Scala, and Mom was excited about attending.

"Hmm." Vicky speared a slice of chicken. She stared intently at it twirling in the air on the end of her fork. Her sleeves were pulled back, and I could see the tattoo of a gingerbread cookie (the specialty of Victoria's Bake Shoppe) on her thin wrist. A line of silver rings ran up both ears, and a long pink lock of hair fell over her right eye. Pink, in honor of the season. The rest of her jet-black hair was shaved almost down to the scalp.

"She's decided to run for pope and needs to get better known before the current pope dies," I said.

"Good idea," Vicky said.

"Vicky."

Her head jerked up. "What?"

"You are not listening to me. Obviously, something's on your mind. Want to share?"

She let out a long sigh. I ate my bread and finished my soup and contemplated having something for dessert.

"Yeah. You're right, Merry, as you usually are."

"As I always am," I said modestly. "Are things okay with you and Mark?"

"Yeah, we're fine. It's not that." She put down her fork and looked at me. "I've a big decision to make. Actually, change that: I've *made* a big decision."

My heart missed a beat. Was Vicky going to tell me she and Mark were moving away? Mark was head chef at one of the fanciest restaurants in the area. He should be able to get a good job just about anywhere. Would Vicky go with him? Leave Rudolph? The first day of kindergarten, Vicky, already looming over me at five years old, stood in front of me, hands on her nonexistent hips, and informed me I would be her best friend. Shy, nervous little me, not thinking I had much choice in the matter, agreed.

Best friends we still were.

It would break my heart if she left Rudolph. It would upset the natural order of things. I was the one who'd gone away. I'd sought the bright lights and the big career and true love in the big city. But I'd eventually realized that bright lights aren't as good as Christmas lights, and the big career didn't measure up to owning my own beloved store. And true love was waiting for me here at home all along.

I put down my spoon and said nothing. I waited. She had her own life to live, and I'd support her in whatever she decided.

"Mark's found a house he wants us to buy."

"He's been talking about that for a while. Alan told me he isn't having a lot of luck. In some ways Rudolph's been a victim of its own success; it's increasingly difficult for people who work here to find a place to live at a price they can afford. I heard he was considering going as far afield as Muddle Harbor." I suppressed a shudder. "Did he?"

"Buy in Muddle Harbor? Thankfully not. No, we have found something we can afford in Rudolph. Not all that far from your place, close to the lake."

I mentally scanned a map of my neighborhood of grand Victorian-era homes on large pieces of land. Houses built for prosperous businessmen and shipping magnates with big families and a fleet of servants in the days when Rudolph was a vitally important Great Lakes port. In recent years, some of the big houses had been broken up into apartments or office suites. I myself occupied half of the top floor of one of those houses. Over the long years of the town's decline, many of the grand old houses had been torn down or allowed to fall into disrepair, eventually replaced in the 1960s or 1970s by small bungalows on enormous lots. In turn, those houses were being bulldozed, and bigger and more modern houses plopped down on the large lakeview lots.

"I'm glad you found something," I said. "What street is it on?"

"Lakeside Drive."

I blinked. Mark must be doing better than I'd thought at his chef's job. Either that or he was trying to convince Vicky to take on a mortgage they couldn't comfortably afford.

"The house isn't directly on the lake front path, though. It's at the end of the street, tucked up against the hill."

"Those are still mighty nice houses and a great location. Which is entirely beside the point. You're obviously not entirely comfortable with it. Don't you like the house? It's a big step. Don't let him talk you into something that's not right for you."

"I like the house fine. Good location. Big lot. It's sure to appreciate in value. I'll still be able to walk to work, which is important to me."

"But?"

"I don't know if Sandbanks will be okay with the move."

I laughed. Sandbanks was Vicky's increasingly ancient golden Labrador. "Sandbanks will be fine. All he wants in life is a comfy rug, a full food bowl, and a piece of grass where he can relieve himself. Besides, you told me the other day the lease on your apartment is up at the end of this month and you'd decided not to renew it, in anticipation of the upcoming nuptials. Are you using Sandbanks as an excuse? If so, you don't need an excuse. You need to tell Mark no. If he doesn't understand, then that's an answer in itself."

The edges of her mouth lifted. "Not an excuse. I worry about the old guy."

"Mark or Sandbanks?"

Vicky laughed. "I should have come to you in the first place, soon as he asked me about the house. Mark loves Sandbanks, and it'll be even easier managing him when we're together. I work mornings and afternoons, and Mark's at the restaurant mostly late afternoons and evenings, so the dog's needs are covered. The house is a good investment, Merry. And it's not as though Mark wants to move away. Which I don't, so that would be a problem."

"Obviously it's your decision. Buying a house is a big step, but if you're sure the investment is sound, you can always sell the house later. Right? Maybe even make a nice profit to get a place you two like better. By the way, Mom doesn't want to be pope."

"Huh?"

"Never mind." I had a thought. "Just make sure you're not overcommitting yourself financially."

"Mark . . ." She smiled to herself, and I knew before she said anything that she'd made up her mind. "I'll admit to being a bit hesitant, but Mark loves the house. He's so excited about us starting our lives in it together." She leaped to her feet and ran around the table, then bent over me and wrapped me in an enormous hug that had the breath shooting out of me. "You are the best, Merry."

"I know that," I said when I could breathe again.

"I'm going to phone Mark right now!" She spun around, fumbling in her jeans pocket for her phone, heading for the door.

"Wait!" I said. "Hold on. One minute."

She turned back. Her face shone with joy. "Yes?"

"I'm happy for you. For you both. But I have to ask. Oh, never mind. None of my business."

She skipped away.

I pushed my empty bowl to one side and unhooked my purse from the back of my chair. I'd intended to ask her how, if Mark was earlier complaining he might have to go all the way to Muddle Harbor to find something he and Vicky could afford, they could then turn around and buy a house on Lakeside Drive. But that truly was none of my business, right? Maybe he'd come into an unexpected inheritance; maybe his or Vicky's parents had offered to help the newlyweds with the down payment.

I decided to celebrate Vicky's news with a lemon tart. My favorite thing Vicky bakes is her mince tarts, but she only makes those in the holiday season. Lemon would have to do. Mince or lemon or anything else, Vicky's were the best I've ever had. By far.

I joined the line for counter service. Two women were in front of me. The smaller was on her phone, gasping in shock as she heard some piece of news. Her friend nodded politely at me in recognition. They were locals, about seventy years old. I didn't know their names, but I often saw them around town or enjoying a glass of lemonade on the front porch of my own house, in the company of my landlady.

The shorter one put her phone away and turned to her friend with a satisfied expression. "You were right, Dottie. The news has been positively confirmed by none other than Mabel D'Angelo herself."

"Hard to credit. After all these years."

"Incredible, isn't it? I suppose it was bound to happen sooner or later. You heard Emmeline died recently?"

"I did," Dottie replied. "I also heard no one went to the funeral. No one except her lawyer and a few people from her charity groups. So sad."

"Such a tragedy. The poor thing."

The line edged forward. Maybe rather than a lemon tart, I'd have a raspberry one. They did look delicious. Perfect little jewels.

"It's true then," Dottie said. "Some fool went and bought Cole House."

"Whoever it is must be a complete outsider. No one who knows a thing about that place would want to live there."

I sucked in a breath. "Excuse me. I couldn't help but overhear. Are you talking about that old house on Lakeside Drive?"

"Good afternoon, Merry," Dottie said. Her friend nodded enthusiastically. "That we are. Marlene Jones is the realtor. I assume they gave her that listing because she's at the absolute bottom of the pile in the realtor's office. I heard she was about to quit and go back to teaching, she's such a bad salesperson. She'll be overjoyed to get that dump off her hands so quickly."

"I suppose," her friend said, "the new owner will tear that heap down and build another from scratch."

"Won't help. Everyone knows the grounds are as cursed as the house."

# Chapter Two

O nce Vicky and Mark had made up their minds, things happened quickly. As the house was currently unoccupied and the owner recently deceased, the closing took little more than a week.

"The real estate agent is going to hand over the keys to us at three." Vicky phoned me on Friday, only a week after she'd given me the news about Mark and her buying Cole House. "Want to come with me?"

"Wouldn't you rather it be just you and Mark? The first time inside as the owners?"

"We did a final walk-through a couple of days ago, after we put in the offer and secured the financing. He didn't exactly carry me over the threshold"—she chuckled deep in her throat—"but it was still nice. Except for that woman following us from room to room in case we intended to steal something. Not that there's anything we'd want to steal. Never mind. Today, it will be our very own house."

"In that case, I'd like to see it." I hadn't seen or spoken to Vicky since our lunch, although I'd received a steady stream of excited texts to do with meeting with lawyers and bankers and signing documents. Vicky might have had her initial doubts about buying the house, but as usual, once she'd made up her mind, she was in all in with everything she had. "I have to ask, Vicky, are you talking about the place at the end of Lakeside Drive? The one that stands all by itself and is . . . somewhat overgrown."

"Yup. The garden's a jungle, and the house needs a lot of work. That's the only reason we could afford it."

"Is Mark skilled enough? Is he planning to renovate it himself?"

"He can do some of the work, as time permits, and we'll save for the bigger stuff that we need help and licensed contractors to do. I'm so excited." I heard the sound of clapping hands. "I'll pick you up at five to three. Bring Mattie. He'll enjoy exploring the yard." She hung up. I turned to see my shop assistant, Jackie O'Reilly, watching me, her ears standing at attention. She shook her head. "I would never listen in on a private conversation, Merry—you know that—but considering you took that call standing right there, I couldn't help but overhear. Everyone's talking about it. Mark Grosse and Vicky Casey bought Cole House. The general consensus around town is that they've lost their minds. Then again, he's an outsider, and chefs are said to be temperamental, so maybe he didn't know any better. But you'd think Vicky Casey would. Do you think that's wise?"

"I think," I said, "it's none of your business, Jackie."

"Sure it is," she said cheerfully. "Everyone in town will be talking about nothing else by nightfall, if they aren't already. And I have the inside scoop." She rubbed her hands together. Her eyes gleamed in anticipation. Jackie wasn't exactly the ideal employee; she generally considered me to be more of an obstacle to the efficient running of the store than the actual boss. And she had no hesitation in letting me know it. But she was unfailingly cheerful and good with the customers. Men liked her small-town pretty looks that might almost (and incorrectly) be called wholesome, and women liked her bouncy personality.

Unfortunately, at the moment the shop was empty, leaving Jackie with nothing to distract her. "Vicky must really be in love. I mean, Mark wouldn't necessarily know any better, but for Vicky Casey to even consider living in Cole House! She's got stronger nerves than I do."

"Come on, Jackie. We're not in high school anymore. Cole House might be a run-down old dump, but there's nothing a bit of TLC can't fix."

She shook her head sadly, the expression ruined by the gleam of excitement in her eyes. "I'm not so sure, Merry. It's not only high school kids—"

"I hear Mattie calling me," I said. "I'd better check up on him." I ran for the back, followed by Jackie's cries of "Only last month, Kyle—" She was cut off in mid-sentence as the chimes over the door tinkled and customers came in.

My Saint Bernard, Matterhorn, commonly called Mattie, opened one eye when I came into the office. I dropped into a chair. He closed the eye and rolled over. When Mattie—all one hundred and seventy pounds of him—rolls over, it's a seismic event.

I glanced at my watch. Two forty-five. I had ten minutes to wait until Vicky picked me up.

One of the problems with the off season in Rudolph, is that the townspeople have far too much time on their hands. More than a few of them would spend that time gossiping. Cole House had been the subject of a lot of that gossip over the years.

\* \* \*

13

Every small town has its haunted house. Usually, it's nothing but an old house, maybe a place where one night years ago some kid saw a plastic bag caught on a tree branch and fled in terror, thinking a ghost was after him. Made-up stories were told by older kids to younger kids on dark winter nights, in the hopes of scaring someone. Perhaps the stories circulated as a warning to the unwary to stay away from a poorly maintained property.

Cole House was the haunted house of Rudolph, New York.

Unlike most other "haunted houses" in other towns, it truly looked the part.

I couldn't help a small shudder as Vicky pulled the bakery van up to the property. On Lakeside Drive, we'd driven past turreted and gingerbread-trimmed Victorian houses with wide, pillared verandas, refurbished to their former glory, next to huge new homes of glass and concrete with sharp lines and flat roofs. Spacious gardens were springing to life, and the huge old maples and oaks lining the street were bursting with the first sign of buds. To our left, Lake Ontario caressed the lush green lawns leading down to the public path along the shore, and to the right, houses on the small rise enjoyed expansive lake views.

The paved road ended abruptly where a wire fence marked off the last property on the street. A large, heavily graffitied sign, warning "Private Property. No Trespassing," hung at an angle on the fence. The tall metal gates stood open. Carriage lamps, all rust and flaking black paint, drooped on the gateposts. A tangle of wires hung uselessly from one, and the glass was shattered on both of them, the lightbulbs long gone. Beyond them lay an ill-maintained gravel track.

Vicky drove through the gates and onto the grounds of Cole House.

I closed my eyes and took a deep breath. From the back of the van, Mattie woofed softly. I glanced at my friend. Vicky's hands rested lightly on the steering wheel, and she was smiling to herself. I was about to say, "Don't you remember?" when I remembered she hadn't been there, and I'd never told her what happened the only time I'd ventured onto this property.

It had been a hot, sticky summer night, and I'd been all of fifteen years old. The town had been in full celebration for Christmas in July. Mom was out of town, touring with *Carmen* (in which she sang the titular role), and Dad was busy presiding over the festivities as Santa Claus. A group of kids from my school had declared their intention to break into Cole House after dark. Vicky would have told them they were idiots and we'd have no part of it, but that year Vicky had gone to Nova Scotia to spend most of the summer with her maternal grandparents. I was on my own. Adrift without my best friend, I didn't know how to say no, and so I went.

Even sixteen years ago the house had been firmly boarded up, and we never did get inside. For which I am eternally grateful. Just walking through the grounds, across the weed-choked grass, beneath heavily leafed trees and broken branches, stumbling over cracked paving stones, with only the poor lights from a couple of flashlights to guide the way, was enough to have us all on edge.

I don't remember much about what happened. Muffled noises, the wind in the trees, the waves in the distance, the distant sounds of festive merrymaking coming from the town park, boards of the old porch creaking, footsteps behind me. Weak light slipped between the plywood boards nailed over the windows, and someone screamed that she'd seen a shape moving across the light. When we heard a low, indeterminate moan coming from the house, our nerve broke and we ran for all we were worth, a mad tumble of girls tripping all over themselves through the woods and fleeing down Lakeside Drive, heading for the lights of the town park and the cheer of the holiday festivities. I think I remember laughter following us as we clambered over the fence. I do remember that I tore my best jeans.

Now, with the benefit of sixteen plus years and a lot of experience, I know a group of older kids must have heard us planning the expedition, and lain in wait with the intention of frightening us. At which they succeeded.

"You okay, Merry?" Vicky asked me.

"Me? Yeah. Yeah, okay. Fine." I'd never told Vicky what happened that night. I suppose I was afraid she'd laugh at my naivety. "Here we are."

The driveway was maintained well enough that no saplings were pushing themselves through the gravel, but the rest of the property was as I remembered it from that long-ago night: vine-choked shrubs, huge trees draped with dead branches and withered leaves, lawns of weeds and crab grass, rose bushes that were nothing but thorns and shriveled flowers, a few scraps of perennials struggling to survive in the spots where they'd been planted all those years ago.

The house loomed in front of us. Trees crowded against it, and on a sun-filled spring day, the house was wrapped in semi-darkness. Two stories of red brick, multiple chimneys, a wide wrap-around porch, tons of broken and crumbling gingerbread trim. The windows were covered in plywood, but incongruously, the porch was swept clean of debris, and the front door stood wide open in welcome.

Two cars were parked in front of the house. I recognized Mark's car, and I assumed the shiny black SUV belonged to the realtor. The garage was more of a carriage house, with doors that had to be opened rather than rolled up. Those doors were open now, and I could see that the space was jammed full of bits of furniture, boxes, and assorted construction equipment and tools.

"It's not as bad inside as it looks from the outside." Vicky said, having read my mind.

"That's good to know. I mean, how long will it be before you can actually live here?"

"Didn't I tell you? We're moving in over the weekend. I hope you and Alan are free to give us a hand."

"But—" I said.

Vicky opened her door and got out. "Come on in and I'll show you around."

When Vicky made up her mind to do something, she wasted no time in doing it. She'd only decided to move here a week ago. *No,* I said to myself. *She knew all along she was going to do it.* She just needed to say it out loud to someone.

Three people stepped onto the front porch: Mark and our friend Russell Durham, editor in chief of the *Rudolph Gazette,* with a woman in her mid-forties whom I assumed was the relator. Vicky jumped up and down, clapping her hands, and then she skipped lightly up the steps. Mark held out his arms and she jumped into them. He swung her around, both of them laughing. Russ and the woman smiled. I cringed, hoping the planks beneath their feet wouldn't give way beneath them. Over our heads, the eaves troughs were either nonexistent or full of holes, and the roof above the door, designed to shelter visitors from the rain, would achieve nothing of the sort.

"I'm glad you're with me," I said to Mattie. "You can frighten any ghosts away." I got out of the van and called for the dog to come. He considered whether or not he wanted to do that, for a few seconds, and finally he made up his mind, leaped over the seat, and clambered to the ground. He immediately started taking stock of his surroundings, and his nose twitched as he followed a trail only he could see, tail rapidly moving. Mattie, like most of his breed, isn't known for being a high-energy dog, but the strange smells around here soon had him running from one bush to another, to the wheels of the cars, to the overgrown flower beds next to the porch and the base of the front steps.

The woman with my friends held out her hand to me. "I'm Marlene. Marlene Jones."

"Merry Wilkinson," I said, as we shook.

"I know who you are well enough," she said with a laugh. "You and the famous Victoria, she of the mince tarts and the gingerbread."

"Famous," Vicky said. "That's me."

"Shall we go in?" Marlene stepped back. Arms around each other, still laughing, Vicky and Mark entered the house. Marlene followed.

I waited outside for a moment, under the pretext of letting Mattie explore. I put my hands on the porch railing, taking care not to lean too heavily on it. Russ stood next to me, and we watched the dog.

I gave Russ a look. "Have you been inside?"

"Oh yeah. It's not as bad as it looks, but bad enough. I know what you're thinking, Merry. When Mark told me he was considering buying this house, I did some poking into its history. Sort of a rite of passage for kids from Rudolph High to spend a night here. Did you?"

I suppressed a shudder. "A whole night? Perish the thought."

Perhaps I didn't suppress the shudder as well as I thought I had. "You've been here? As a kid?"

"Once. And that was enough. The place has a reputation. Teenagers, overactive imaginations, dares, and pranksters—you know what it can be like."

"Being from New Orleans," he said in his deep rolling drawl, "I know from haunted houses. We should go in. Vicky and Mark are anxious to show us the house. Try to sound pleased for them, Merry. It's not as bad as you think."

I called Mattie, who tore himself reluctantly away from the in-depth inspection of a thorny bush; then I plastered on a pleased expression and followed Russ into Cole House.

*   *   *

It wasn't as bad as I'd expected. But bad enough.

"This house has been in the Cole family for a hundred and forty years," Mark explained to us. "The last surviving member of the family, Miss Emmeline Cole, passed away a few months ago. Emmeline was almost eighty, and she was living in Rochester. She's been away from Rudolph and this house for—what, Marlene? Forty years?"

"The house was last occupied in 1983, when Emmeline moved to Rochester. From what I heard, she never married and was considered a recluse. Folks say that once she left, she never stepped foot in the house again."

"Why didn't she sell it?" Russ asked. "If she didn't want to live here herself. Or at least rent it out."

We stood in the front hall. A heavy glass chandelier, thick with dust, hung over our heads; cracked black and white marble tiles were at our feet; and a wide staircase with oak banisters and mouse-chewed red carpeting swept up into the gloom of the second floor. At least the electricity had been switched on, and a forty-watt bulb above the stairs illuminated the foyer.

"The terms of her father's will stipulated that the house was to remain in his family until no direct descendants of his remained," Marlene explained. "The will was written when Emmeline's two sisters were still alive, so with three daughters it was natural Mr. Cole expected to have descendants."

"What happened to the sisters?" Russ, ever the newspaperman, asked. "I know they died quite young. I tried to find out the details, but all I could dig up in a hurry was their dates of death and the word *accidental*."

Marlene ignored the question. "Emmeline could have overturned that clause in her father's will if she'd wanted to, I'm sure, but for reasons I don't know, she never did. As she was the only surviving child upon her parents' death, she was left with the entirety of their estate. She might have simply decided it was too much trouble to try to fight the will." She turned to Mark and Vicky. "Ms. Casey, Mr. Grosse, this is your house now. Do you want to show your guests around? I see the dog has already started doing so."

Mattie, likely following a mouse trail, was heading off down the long corridor to the back of the house.

"The old Grosse place they'll call this in years to come," Vicky said. "Children will whisper about miserable old man Grosse chasing them out of his yard and shaking a meat cleaver at the clouds."

Mark gave her an affectionate smile.

"They'll also talk about the sweet, lovely, eternally young Ms. Casey, who made up for the cranky old grump with her magic gingerbread cookies."

"Sorry to interrupt your dreams for the future," I said, "but I have to ask. The electricity's been switched on and that's good, but . . . how livable is this place?"

"Let's show you," Mark said.

We walked down the corridor, following Mattie. Doors were open, and I peeked inside as we passed. I saw furniture draped in sheets, and heavy curtains pulled back behind plywood-protected windows. Living room with shrouded couch and chairs, small low tables, cold, dark fireplace full of cobwebs. Dining room—another fireplace, more cobwebs, a large table surrounded by at least twenty chairs, and a long, low sideboard. A library with draped chairs, reading tables, and bookshelves full of books. A large, round object, which I took to be a globe under a sheet, stood on a table.

"The place comes fully furnished?" I asked.

"Yes, but most of it will be headed straight for the dump," Mark said. "Forty years of mice and mold and damp isn't good for furniture. Those books you were admiring will crumble to dust at a touch."

"We might be able to salvage some things," Vicky said. "I'm going to ask Alan to take a look and let me know if he can reclaim the wood tables, at least."

The kitchen came as a big surprise to me. It looked like a still-used, working kitchen. It was clean—relatively clean; as clean as my kitchen, anyway. The decor was hideously out of date, with wood-fronted cabinets, linoleum flooring, Formica countertops, but the shining steel fridge matched the dish-washer, and it hummed quietly in a corner. The countertops were scrubbed, the floor washed and swept, the induction stove polished. The big glass-topped table in the center of the room was surrounded by four chairs. A huge bouquet of peach roses in a glass vase occupied the middle of the table.

"This is . . . surprisingly nice," I said.

"The kitchen was originally designed as a place where servants would work, out of sight and completely out of mind. Certainly not a room for the family and their guests to gather and enjoy." Mark ruffled Vicky's short hair, and she smiled up at him. "As the only servants in this house are us, I intend to have those walls knocked down, which will open up the kitchen to the dining room, and we should be able to widen the windows. Maybe put in French doors opening out to the garden. I'm thinking a kitchen garden close to the house. For vegetables and herbs."

"My granddad was the Cole family lawyer for many years," Vicky said. "My dad now looks after what's left of their affairs. Charles Cole left money specifically intended to be used for the upkeep of the house, regardless of which of his daughters was living here. Or none of them, as it transpired. The amount dwindled over the years, and things got a lot more expensive. That fund soon didn't have enough to maintain the entire house and grounds, so rather than doing bits and pieces here and there, the money, under Granddad and then Dad's administration, went to maintaining the gate and fence as and when needed, ensuring the bushes didn't encroach onto neighboring property, and keeping the kitchen and ground-floor bathroom in working order, along with what used to be the morning room, which is big enough for our bedroom until we can renovate the rooms upstairs. The stove, fridge, and dishwasher got here yesterday, and there's a freezer in what used to be the pantry. Neither Mark nor I would be able to last long without top-of-the-line appliances. Mark needs his knives"—she nodded to the wooden block on the counter on the far side of the room—"and I prefer to test my recipes for the book at home rather than in the bakery, where something's always interrupting me, even when we're closed."

Along with everything else she had on the go, Vicky was working on a baking book. Tentatively titled *Year-Round Holiday Favorites from America's Christmas Town*, I was almost as excited about it as she was. I figured it was a guaranteed bestseller, with not only Vicky's skills with flour, butter, and sugar, but the Christmas Town theme. I was encouraging her to put a formal proposal together. When she had that ready, I'd contact people I know in the publishing industry in New York. I'd once been a props stylist and then a design editor, at *Jennifer's Lifestyle Magazine*, and we'd run many features highlighting recipes from new (and old) cookbooks. I'd worked closely with editors and publishers as well as the authors and their agents, to get that done. I hoped someone—anyone—would remember me.

Thus," Vicky said, beaming, "we can move right in."

# Chapter Three

By the time we left Cole House, I felt fractionally better about Vicky living there. The house was, to put it mildly, in poor repair, but some of the rooms were livable. Vicky and Mark were busy people, but they were also young and in love and full of enthusiasm, with good incomes and supportive families. They intended to initially put a hunk of money into the most important thing, which was getting a new roof, and they planned to start working on the garden themselves. They confessed that neither of them knew anything about gardening, but you didn't need to be a horticulturalist to know that the tangle of vines choking the bushes and trees needed to be cleared out, fallen branches hauled away, weeds dug out of the perennials, and the lawn exposed to the sunlight.

As we drove through the gates onto Lakeside Drive, I looked at the houses ahead of us. Large, prosperous, well looked after. "The neighbors have got to be overjoyed, having that eyesore cleaned up."

Vicky chuckled. "They will be. Dad says there've been attempts to have the property condemned or to get Emmeline Cole to sell, but as long as the place was maintained to some degree, there was nothing anyone could do. It was her house and if she chose not to live there, that was up to her."

"I wonder what the story is there," I said. "I bet there is one. She lived in Rochester—not exactly the other side of the continent—but she never came back?"

"Bad memories, maybe," Vicky said. "She had two sisters who died young."

"That's probably it." We drove down Jingle Bell Lane, past the lakeside park.

Mattie stuck his big head between the seats and dripped drool down my left shoulder. Fortunately, I'm always prepared for that, and I keep a spare sweater in the store office.

Vicky pulled into a parking space in front of Mrs. Claus's Treasures. Margie Thatcher, owner of Rudolph Gift Nook, the store next door, was standing on the sidewalk, watching the traffic pass, and she gave us a wave.

"Never thought I'd live to see the day," Vicky said.

"The power of Christmas," I said. Margie, Rudolph's very own Grinch, had been so overcome by the message of last season's amateur theatrical production of *A Christmas Carol* that, although she didn't exactly have a complete Scrooge-type conversion, she'd mellowed considerably. Witnessed by the fact that Vicky and I got a wave and not a scowl today.

"Before I go, one thing," I said. "This is none of my business, but that's never stopped us before, has it?"

"Go ahead."

"Okay. I will. You said you and Mark have bought the house. I hope that means you are co-owners, and you're not just paying him rent. Is your name on the papers, Vicky?"

"It is."

"That's good. And, if I may say, things would be easier in case . . . of unanticipated events if you two are legally married."

"As usual, I'm way ahead of you."

"That's good. I think. How are you way ahead of me?"

"I hope you've got nothing on for Easter Saturday."

"What?"

"My dad agrees with you. He's been pretty insistent that Mark and I marry before I make any substantial contributions to the house, financially or otherwise. There needs to be no uncertainties, Dad said, or things can get complicated in case something happened to one of us. With work on the house to do and all the cost involved, Mark and I've decided to just go ahead and have a low-key wedding soon as possible. No fuss. No bother."

"You've sure had a busy couple of days. Is your mom okay with a no-fuss, no-bother, sudden wedding? I hope you remembered to tell your parents."

"Yes, Merry, I remembered. They're totally okay with what we want. You know my family, Merry. I've got second and third cousins, and second and third cousins once removed, coming out of the woodwork, all of them having big, splashy weddings. Aunts and uncles getting remarried and having another round of big, splashy weddings. Scarcely a month goes by there's not a Casey wedding in Rudolph and environs."

That, I knew, was true enough.

"Sometimes I get invited to a wedding of people I don't even know how I'm related to. I can usually beg off on the grounds of work, but I always feel I have to send a gift." Her face twisted in thought. "Maybe that's why I get invited to weddings of people I don't know. Because they expect a gift. I'll have to think about that. My mom's got three younger sisters, and she was the head

26

bridesmaid at their weddings, so she got that out of her system. She's fine with me having a super low-key wedding." She studied my face. "I hope you are too. I won't have a pack of bridesmaids and the like, but I want you to be there with me. We're having the service at Uncle Roy's church. He'll officiate, and then we'll gather with a small group for dinner at the Yuletide."

"I'd love to," I said. "Is Alan invited?"

"Natch."

"What about Mark?"

"He's invited."

"Yes, Vicky. I got that. I mean, are his parents okay with this plan?"

"You know Mark's been married before, right?"

"No, I didn't know that."

"To his high school sweetheart. It didn't last a year. Turns out she wanted to be a movie star more than she wanted to be married to a guy from her hometown. They had no kids, and she's totally out of his life now, so that's all okay. Anyway, his first wedding was a huge, over-the-top thing at which he was completely and totally uncomfortable, as were his own parents. The bride wanted to be the star of the day, and having a groom tagging along was sort of a necessary afterthought."

"She sounds lovely. *Not.* You said she's an actor. Might I have seen her in anything?"

"Her acting career was as successful as her first marriage. Mark's mom tells him she soon came back home and got married again. Her parents refused to fund another big wedding, and I gather she had a major hissy fit about that. Now she has two kids and works in a hardware store. Anyway, beside the point. After that experience, Mark's mom does not want him to have a big wedding. She thinks it's a curse. Mark and I visited them last month. He told me his parents liked me. I hope that's true."

"How could it not be? Do you want me to come shopping with you?"

"Shopping for what?"

"A wedding dress, you ninny. You might want a low-key wedding, but you can't be married in the jeans you wear to work."

She winked at me. "Oh, right. Let's talk later, set up a day and time. My mom will want to come with us. Is that okay?"

"As long as you don't keep putting it off."

"Would I do that?"

"Yes, Vicky, you would."

\* \* \*

The next day, Mark arranged for a junk removal company to come to the house. They carted away the most obviously ruined things, including carpets and beds, chewed books, and stuff he and Vicky didn't want, such as fifty-year-old kitchen appliances and tools. The next day, Alan and I, along with our dogs, Russ, and a couple of guys who worked with Mark at the Yuletide Inn, helped the happy couple move. While Ranger, Alan's Jack Russell, cavorted around the property thrilled at all the new scents, Mattie sniffed at everything before resting in the shade of a stately oak, and Sandbanks promptly fell asleep on the porch, we carried boxes and electronics and furniture up the steps and into the house. Vicky and Mark were initially only occupying three rooms, so Vicky'd arranged for some of her many young cousins to help out on Sunday by taking some of her and Mark's bigger possessions, such as excess furniture and winter clothes, into storage, to be retrieved as the house was gradually renovated. We were finished not long after lunchtime. Before we gathered in the kitchen to dig into the sandwiches and beer Mark provided for the hard-working gang, Alan examined the major pieces of furniture—the bookcases, the dining room table, and sideboard—and said they were in surprisingly good condition. "The mice have gotten into the cushions of the chairs, but they're easy enough to replace. Some sanding and polishing to the other stuff, and it'll be as good as new. Better than new. Not a lot of that sort of handcrafted furniture is made anymore."

"I never thought I'd want a house full of antique furniture," Vicky said, "but it suits this place, doesn't it?"

I pulled a cobweb out of my hair and said nothing. Sandbanks had followed us and was enjoying another snooze under the kitchen table. Ranger was upstairs, running from one room to another, and Mattie sat next to me, hoping for some lunchtime tidbit to drop. It never does, but he never gives up hope. A lesson for us all, perhaps.

I was still not entirely comfortable here. The kitchen was clean and welcoming. One of Vicky's staff had given her a housewarming gift of a six-foot-long metal fork to hang on the wall next to a row of cabinets. Vicky and Mark had made the morning room into a cheerful bedroom and sitting room with colorful cushions piled in the window seat overlooking the back garden, sparkling mirrors, and brightly colored art. Plywood had been ripped off some of the downstairs windows, and the windows cleaned so light once again streamed into the rooms, but the house still gave me that creepy feeling.

Mark was like a kid in a candy store. He loved absolutely everything about this house. He shouted with glee when he found a wicker basket of apples so wrinkled and desiccated, they were almost unrecognizable in what had once been the pantry. "From our own apple trees, I bet. I can't wait to get them producing again."

As for Vicky, she was obviously happy as long as Mark was happy, but I caught something in her expression as she walked down the long, dim hallway and glanced into the library before hurrying past or turned quickly from the bedroom window.

I said nothing, and she didn't tell me if something was bothering her.

# Chapter Four

Like all business owners in any seasonal tourist town, competition for good staff can be intense. I don't need extra help in the off season, but I do when we're busy. I was disappointed, but not at all surprised, when my reliable part-timer, Chrystal Wong, informed me she would not be returning this year. Chrystal had started working for me when she was in high school, and kept on during vacations once she'd begun her studies at the School of Visual Arts in New York City. As well as working in the shop, she made much of the jewelry we sold. Her stuff was so popular, she was now able to devote herself full time to her jewelry business while she finished her education.

Jackie had told me Kyle Lambert, her boyfriend, was looking for a job. I had a difficult time keeping the horror off my face at the very idea of Kyle being around not only my delicate ornaments, but my customers. "He's not planning to go back to the ice-cream parlor this summer?"

"Nah. He didn't like the way the owner yelled at him all the time. I mean, it wasn't Kyle's fault that kid dropped her cone. Although, I suppose Kyle shouldn't have laughed the way he did. And then the kid's dad got mad, and Kyle threw the ice-cream scoop at him. It wasn't Kyle's fault the metal scoop hit him in the eye, and the guy had to go to the hospital. I mean, the eye was saved, okay? No harm done."

Not a ringing endorsement for Kyle's customer relationship skills. If the incident hadn't been Kyle's fault, I couldn't imagine whose it had been. "How about the hotdog stand outside the butcher shop?"

"He hasn't worked there since the cart exploded that time."

"Oh yes. I remember that."

I eventually hired a young woman named Melissa Grantham. She was newly married, new to town, and over-the-top excited about the whole Year-Round-Christmas thing. Melissa would start by filling in for Jackie and me a few hours a week, working up to full-time starting in June.

Vicky, I knew, was also having trouble finding good seasonal staff.

I dropped into the bakery one afternoon shortly before closing. It was a cool and rainy Monday, and business had been slow at Mrs. Claus's all day. It was Jackie's day off, so I put a "Back soon" sign in the window, grabbed my umbrella, and dashed through the puddles forming on the sidewalk of Jingle Bell Lane.

I shook my umbrella off, furled it, and walked into the warm, scented bakery. Marjorie waved to me from behind the counter. "We're closing in a minute, Merry."

"Any sandwiches left?"

"I've got ham and Swiss on rye, hummus with pita, or tuna salad."

"Tuna please. And a nonfat latte to go. Vicky in?"

"She's interviewing."

Marjorie handed me my order, and I passed her the money. A young woman came out of the back. Early twenties, late teens maybe, of average height, slim without being skinny, gently curving in all the right places. She was strikingly pretty, with clear pale skin, large brown eyes lined by thick lashes, red lips, and a pert chin. A river of heavy black hair cascaded down her back. All that was wrong with her looks was the expression on her face. She was, to put it mildly, not pleased. She ignored me, threw Marjorie a poisonous look, and stormed out of the bakery. The door slammed shut behind her.

"That was a prospective employee?" I said to Marjorie.

"I'm guessing the interview didn't go as well as she might have hoped."

Vicky came out of the back, shaking her head. "Talk about entitlement."

"What happened?" Marjorie and I chorused.

"She answered my ad for a waitress and barista. Didn't take long to find out she doesn't want to be a waitress and a barista; she wants to be a pastry chef. I told her I'm the pastry chef here, and I already have an assistant. That's Janelle."

"She got mad at that?" Marjorie said. "Weird."

"She didn't get mad right away. She launched into her job experience, which consists of—and I kid you not—making cakes and pies at the Muddle Harbor Café."

I laughed heartily. I caught the look on Vicky's face and said, "Oh. You're not kidding."

"I almost feel sorry for her. Her name's Brittany Pettigrew, and if she wants to get ahead in the baking world, good for her. I'd be more than happy to show her the ropes, and I started to say so. I told her we get powerful busy in here in the summer, and I need waitstaff who work hard, keep smiling, stay on their toes, and can switch tasks on the fly. This year the staff might be busier than usual if I need to take time to work on the cookbook, presuming I get any interest from a publisher. If so, she might get a chance to help in the kitchen, but that's not guaranteed in the job I'm hiring for. She doesn't want to learn the ropes; she wants to be my assistant pastry chef. Right now. Today."

"Obviously your well-intentioned advice wasn't well received."

"If she's prepared to cut that many corners building her career, I'm pretty sure she'll cut corners with her time and the quality of her ingredients, so even if I had room in my kitchen for another full-time assistant, I wouldn't want her. When I told her about my cookbook project, she hurried to tell me she's working on a baking cookbook too, when she can find the time. Like I don't have to carve out every second I can find to get done what I have to do. Never mind. I have a few other people to interview tomorrow. What brings you here, anyway?"

I held up my sandwich bag. "Lunch. What else?"

# Chapter Five

Two weeks passed and I didn't see Vicky, although we texted regularly. She sounded upbeat, starting to get excited for her wedding, so I put my misgivings about her house aside. She'd hired some part-time staff for the busy season at the bakery and was trying to get work done on her cookbook. Although, she admitted reluctantly, with everything else going on in her life, the book wasn't coming on as well as she'd planned.

Hoping to give her a reason to get the book finished, I called some of my previous contacts in publishing. Most of the people I phoned remembered me, to my surprise, and told me they'd be more than happy to see my friend's proposal when she had it ready. "Don't wait too long," everyone told me. "Baking's super-hot right now. Doesn't mean that's going to last."

I finally managed to get Vicky to set a date for us to go dress shopping, and the following Monday we met in the park outside the library on Jingle Bell Lane, as arranged.

The first thing I said to her was "Are you okay?"

"Me? I'm fine." Circles the color of bruises lay under her eyes, and her eyes were dull, the whites tinged red. Lines of strain radiated from the edges of her mouth. She'd allowed the lock of pink hair to fade to a dull beige without recoloring it.

"You don't look too good. Are you coming down with something? We can postpone the shopping trip if you want to go home and rest."

She ran her fingers through the short hair at the back of her head. "I'm fine, Merry. Really, I am. You're the one who keeps telling me not to put this off any longer."

"Buying your wedding dress shouldn't be a chore, Vicky."

She gave me a bright smile that went some way, but not all the way, to taking the tiredness out of her eyes. "It's not a chore. I'm excited about it. Let's go."

I plonked myself down on a park bench. "Best friends' time. Sit."

She sat.

"If you're not sick, then something's bothering you. Are you having doubts about the wedding?"

"No, not that. I'm not sleeping well, Merry. I don't think I've had a good night's sleep since I moved into that house. Not because I'm worrying about anything but . . ." She let out a choked laugh. "My imagination is running away with me. I imagine I hear things in the night. When I'm in the yard, I have the feeling someone . . . or some*thing* is watching me."

"What sort of things do you hear?"

"Floorboards creaking. Knocking and scratching at the windows."

"That's natural in an old house, particularly one that's not been looked after. My parents' house sounds like it's possessed when the wind blows."

"Yeah, I know. I'm being silly, right?"

"No. Not silly. What does Mark have to say?"

"Nothing. He sleeps like a baby, with a silly smile on his face all night long. And I know that because I'm awake. When I'm not hearing noises, I'm lying there wondering if I'm about to start hearing noises."

We watched the traffic moving on Jingle Bell Lane and pedestrians passing on the sidewalk. People walked in and out of the library, laden with books. The bakery was located next to the library, before the walkway leading to the town hall. As we watched, Marjorie stepped out, locked the door behind her, and headed in the other direction.

"Cole House is supposedly haunted," I said. "Did—"

"It is *not* haunted. There is no such thing. I'm not hearing ghosts, Merry."

She'd shot that suggestion down so quickly, I knew I'd hit the mark. "Not ghosts themselves, but is it possible you're thinking, even subconsciously, about ghosts?"

She thought for a while. "Maybe. Hard to say what I'm thinking subconsciously, right?"

Vicky was anything but a fanciful person. She was about the last one, other than my father, I'd suspect of imagining ghosts.

"Have you told Mark?"

"I decided not to. He'd worry I'm having doubts about getting married. About living in that house. About being with him. I don't want him to think that. I just need to get the wedding over with, the house business settled, and my book finished. Then I'll be okay." She sprang to her feet. "Best friend session over. Thanks, Merry. I'm glad I got that off my chest. All will be okay now."

I wasn't so sure. I thought about asking her what "house business" she was talking about. They'd knowingly and willingly taken on renovations that would take years; was Vicky only now understanding what an all-consuming chore that would be? It was possible she'd heard a mouse in the ceiling or squirrels in the attic; branches rubbing against the eaves troughs or the loose bricks of the old chimneys on a windy night—throwing her imagination into overdrive. Vicky was levelheaded and thoroughly practical. I like to think I'm all that too, but Cole House gave me the creeps. Even in broad daylight with my friends around me. I couldn't imagine being alone there at night.

I decided to say nothing more, and we set about prowling the dress shops of Rudolph. Not that there are a lot of nice women's wear stores in Rudolph, but Vicky, as a proud supporter of local businesses, refused to go out of town. That, plus the fact that her aunt owns Jayne's Ladies Wear, and word would get around fast enough if Vicky went someplace else.

Jayne's Ladies Wear sounds as though it sells the sort of garments your grandmother would wear to a church tea, but it's unexpectedly well stocked with fun, modern clothes.

Vicky might want a low-key wedding, but if there is one thing Vicky Casey herself is not, it's low key.

"Nothing white," Vicky said as we waited for the light to change, to cross the street. "I look hideous in white."

"Rubbish. You look marvelous in everything." And she did. The so-short hair worked on her because it accented the fabulous bone structure of her pale, heart-shaped face. As for clothes—everything looks good on her. At five foot eleven, Vicky is a good six inches taller than me, and because she's nothing but a ball of energy, she's rail thin. Whereas I, who don't bake all day for a living, am not rail thin. Her makeup is always dramatic: a slash of deep red lipstick on her full lips, and thick black mascara and liner that emphasize her expressive blue eyes.

The little man in the traffic lights appeared, and Vicky and I hurried across the intersection. I'd left Mattie at the store. Lots of businesses allow dogs inside these days, but not many would be pleased to admit a full-sized, drooling, male Saint Bernard, no matter how friendly he might be. It was a Wednesday and we were unlikely to be too busy, so I reluctantly left Jackie to supervise Melissa, my new part-time assistant. Reluctantly, because although Jackie was a great store clerk, she could have delusions of grandeur when it came to her rank in the hierarchy and attitude toward new employees.

"I'm thinking two outfits," Vicky said as we entered the store. "Something sedate, cream and lace maybe, to wear in church. And then a party dress for dinner."

"That would be great." I glanced at her, pleased to see that some light was coming back into her eyes and the tired heaviness leaving. I told myself that Vicky had a lot on her mind. We were in our early thirties, and Vicky had lived on her own in a miniscule apartment since college. Living with someone else, in a large, strange old house, would be a big change for her. I considered having a quiet word with Mark later, to let him know what was going on, but I decided not to. Not yet, anyway. She would not thank me for interfering.

Vicky's mother ran in a couple of minutes after us, bubbling over with joy. I take after my father far more than my mother, but Vicky and her mom could be twins except for the age difference. Michelle isn't quite as tall as her daughter, and the extra years have added a couple of pounds, but the eyes have identical sparkles, the smile is as infectious, and she excludes the same excitement and energy.

She took one look at Vicky and said, "You're not getting enough sleep. I hope you're not working on that house at all hours."

"We're not. Don't worry, Mom—I'm fine."

"You don't look fine. Merry, tell her to slow down sometimes."

"As if anything I say is going to help."

"True enough. No one knows that better than I do," Michelle said. "How's the cookbook coming?"

"Slowly but steadily."

"I might think you're taking on too much, but you're young and healthy. You can recover fast enough."

"I seem to recall," Vicky said, "stories of you burning the candle at all ends when you were in nursing school and Dad was trying to start his practice. On top of that you had two kids."

Michelle and Vicky smiled identical smiles at each other. "Sometimes," Michelle said, "I still think I'm burning the candle at all ends. Particularly with all the cutbacks at the hospital."

"As for the book," I said, "when it comes to nonfiction, publishers and agents don't want to see the final result. They want a proposal. I'll send you an email on what that entails. Get it done first, and we can start sending it out while you continue working on your recipes."

"Already started," Vicky said. "Yet another thing on the to-do list."

I wandered off to check out a row of dresses. As I moved away, Michelle lowered her voice and said, "Your dad told me about that issue regarding the house. Have you heard anything more?"

"I'm not getting involved, Mom. Mark's handling it."

I'd turned to ask what they were talking about, when Jayne swept up with a bundle of clothes in her arms. "This is so exciting. I'm sure we'll find the perfect thing for you, Vicky."

We had a fun couple of hours. Michelle and Jayne had good taste and a good eye for dressing Vicky. We carefully pointed out that the seafoam green dress she originally wanted to wear to the church might, with its thigh-revealing length and curve-clinging outline, be not entirely appropriate. "My darling brother, Roy," Michelle said, "has a relaxed attitude to what people wear to church these days, and he's welcoming to everyone no matter how they appear, but . . ."

"But," I said, "that one's a firm no."

Eventually we settled on a knee-length, off-white dress with elbow-length sleeves and a cropped silver jacket for the church, and something much more "Vicky" for the dinner: a candy-cane concoction with a tightly fitted pink bodice and a multicolored skirt made up of layers of tulle petticoats. Vicky twirled in front of the mirror, and Michelle, Jayne, and I applauded. "Mark's tall enough that I can wear those stiletto heels I haven't gotten much use of yet to church," Vicky said. "And then something with a flatter heel for dancing at the dinner. But not too much flatter."

Michelle insisted on paying for the dresses, and Vicky gave her mom a huge hug. Jayne and I joined in. "I'd like to say this was such fun we should do it again," Michelle said when we'd separated, "but I hope you won't need to go wedding dress shopping again, dear."

"I won't," Vicky said firmly. Michelle and I exchanged smiles. That's what every bride says, but I sincerely hoped in this case it was true.

"Will your parents understand that Vicky wants to keep the guest list down?" Michelle asked me as we left the store, Vicky swinging her bags.

"Not a problem. My mom and dad know just about everyone in town. They can't go to every celebration." Although my dad tries to.

"I'm on night shift this week," Michelle said, "so I need to get home for a short nap. Talk to you later, dear." She gave Vicky a quick kiss and hurried away. Michelle was an ER nurse at the hospital.

"Time for coffee?" Vicky asked me.

"Better not. That new girl I hired to replace Chrystal started last week, and I dare not keep her under Jackie's supervision for long."

We were about to go our separate ways when an angry shout had us turning around. "You there! Mrs. Grosse!" A man was heading toward us with angry, determined steps. He was in his early sixties, wearing badly fitting jeans and a far-from-new New York Giants T-shirt. It wasn't a particularly warm day, but drops of sweat dripped from his thinning hairline, and his round face was red with rage. He was not much taller than me and sported a belly the size of a basketball. He shoved his finger in Vicky's face.

She swatted it away. "Who are you and what do you want?"

"You're Mrs. Grosse, right?" He spat out the words.

"As it happens," Vicky said calmly, "I am not."

His shoulders slumped, some of the anger faded from his face, and he took a step backward. Then he focused his attention on me. "You?"

"Nope."

He took another step back and held out his hands. "Sorry, ladies. I must have made a mistake. I asked at a couple of the shops, and they described a woman a lot like you. Do you know her?"

"If I did," Vicky said, "I'd be unlikely to send you after her. What do you want with her, anyway?"

"Nothing. I've no argument with her, but I've been leaving messages for her husband, and he's not returning my calls."

"I wonder why?" I said under my breath. He gave me a filthy look. I stood my ground.

"Mr. Cole, I presume," Vicky said.

I threw her a look.

"Got it in one," he said. "Jim Cole. If you know Mrs. Grosse, you can tell her I need to talk to her and her husband. And soon."

"Other than Mark's mother, who doesn't live anywhere near here, I know no Mrs. Grosse." Vicky stood a bit taller; she pulled her shoulders back. She loomed over the man, staring him down. He shifted nervously, sensing something he didn't like in her demeanor. I put myself on alert, although I didn't have a clue what was going on. "I'm glad we ran into each other, Jim. Now you're here, perhaps we should have a chat after all. I am not Mrs. Grosse, but I know you've been bothering Mr. Grosse. I know he told you he'd talk to you through his lawyer. As that lawyer happens to be my father, I know you're not doing that. So, I'd like to ask you, as politely as possible, to get lost and leave us alone."

His eyes turned toward me. I attempted to look as stern as Vicky did.

"I only want what's mine," he said.

"No, Jim," Vicky said. "You want what's *mine*. Mine and Mark's. Allow me to assure you, you are not going to get it."

"Don't be so sure about that, whatever your name is. I've been asking around town about Grosse. He's a cook at a hotel. Whether you're his wife or not, you're a baker. I doubt you two have the money to put up a fight in court. When I win, as I will, I'll be asking for expenses and damages. Think it over," he said. "Talk it over."

He turned around and walked away, full of righteous indignation. The image he was trying to project was spoiled

43

somewhat when he turned to give Vicky one last malicious glare and ran full on into none other than my mother, coming down the street with her own shopping bags. He stepped on her foot, and she yelped in pain.

"Excuse me," she said in that voice that once carried to the upper balconies of the great opera houses of Europe. "Can you not watch where you are going, sir?"

"Sorry, sorry." He slipped away.

We all watched him go.

"From where I stood, that confrontation appeared to be tense," Mom said. "I decided to step out of the wings and hurry him on his way."

"Nicely done, Aline," Vicky said. "Thanks, but we're okay. Nothing but a miserable little man trying to make himself sound important."

"Miserable little men can cause a lot of problems. Hopefully you've seen the last of him. May I congratulate you on your engagement, dear?"

"You most certainly can."

"I'll look forward to Noel and me receiving our invitation to the wedding." Mom's eyes dropped to the heavy bags Vicky was carrying. "Doing some shopping?"

"No time to talk, Mom," I said. "We're going for a coffee. Catch you later."

I half dragged Vicky down Jingle Bell Lane. I glanced in the window of Mrs. Claus's as we passed, and was pleased to see both Jackie and Melissa interacting with customers. Vicky and I went into Cranberry Coffee Bar, mostly empty in the late afternoon, and I grabbed a table by the window. "Sit," I ordered for the second time that day.

Vicky sat.

"Okay, first, don't worry about my mom expecting a wedding invitation. I can convince her it's nothing personal."

"I'd like to have her and your dad. They've always been like second parents to me. She stepped into that guy's path deliberately—did you notice?"

"I did notice, but that's not the point here. Obviously, there's something you didn't tell me. What's going on and what's that about lawyers? You called that man Cole; is he related to the late Emmeline? And what is it Mark and your dad are handling? Is that why you're not sleeping? Nothing to do with noises in the night?"

Vicky shrugged. "The noises are happening, yes. I think so, anyway, although I will admit I've been lying awake with other things on my mind, so I might be overreacting. As for the Cole issue, I'm leaving it up to Mark and Dad to sort out. Jim Cole is, so he says, a descendent of the man who built the house. Our house. He claims he should have inherited on Emmeline's death, and her lawyers had no right to sell the house out from underneath him. His words. Because according to him, the house rightfully belongs to him."

"Does he have grounds for that claim?"

"Dad says no. Jim's trying to make a nuisance of himself, hoping to get something from an out-of-court settlement."

"What's his relationship to the family?"

"His grandfather, Henry Cole, built the house. Jim is a grandson of Henry. Meaning he's a cousin of Emmeline, not a descendent of her father, Charles. Charles Cole's will specified that the house was to remain in the family until his own line ended. Which it did with Emmeline's death. Jim claims his father was much younger than his brother, more the age of a son, and when he said descendent, Charles meant for his brother's children to be included."

"I don't know much about the laws of inheritance, but it sounds pretty iffy to me. Does Jim have anything in writing?"

"No. Which is why Dad says the claim is completely without merit. Charles Cole died when Jim was a small child. He can't know what his father and uncle intended, and he has no letters between them recording Charles's thoughts on the matter. Dad doesn't expect it will even get to court. In Emmeline Cole's will she left everything—and it seems all she had, other than a bit of cash and a few stocks, is the house—to charity. She instructed that the house be sold and the money received be given to the charities she specified. Notably, Jim Cole was not mentioned anywhere in her will. Not even given a pittance or a memento. My dad, as the lawyer and executor of her estate, will argue, if it comes to it, she didn't mention Jim because she saw no reason for him to have anything of hers. Including the house. From what information Dad's been able to get, Jim had no contact whatsoever with his cousin Emmeline for years. Decades. As for whose fault that was, or why, it doesn't matter."

"Merry and Vicky," the barista called. "Can I get you something?"

Vicky shook her head, and I said, "Sorry, no. We needed a place to talk. Is that okay?"

"Stay as long as you like."

"You need to tell Mark and your dad he accosted you," I said.

"Yeah. I do. Mark'll have a fit. He considers the whole thing to be a minor irritation, but it's not good that Jim's come to town."

"Not just 'come to town,' but he's been asking about you guys. That must mean he's taking this seriously. Does he live in the area?"

"I've no idea, Merry." She stood up. "I'm going back to the bakery. I need to get some prep done for tomorrow. I'll call Dad and Mark from there. I'm sorry our day got spoiled."

"It wasn't spoiled," I said. "It was great fun, and you got two fabulous outfits to wear on your wedding day. Never mind that minor hiccup at the end. We might never see him again. The look on my mother's face when he stepped on her foot would be enough to scare anyone out of town."

She gave me that Vicky grin, and I was pleased to see it.

"Don't keep anything else from me, okay? Anything else bothering you, let me know."

# Chapter Six

M y father's family has lived in Rudolph for as long as there's been a town here on the southern shores of Lake Ontario. He was the mayor for many years, and he's still on the town council. Plus, he's Santa Claus.

He knows just about everything that is happening, or has happened, in town.

He also, I sometimes suspect, can read my mind.

I wasn't entirely sure Jim Cole would turn out to be as harmless as Vicky seemed to think. I wasn't all that sure Vicky believed it either. Even if he had no rightful claim to their house, he could make a darn nuisance of himself. After our chat in Cranberries, I decided to find out what I could about the Cole inheritance. My dad would be a good place to start.

As I said: he reads my mind. Even from the other side of town.

Jackie and Melissa had finished work for the day, and I was getting ready to close up when my father came in. "Hey, honeybunch." He was dressed in a pair of well-loved jeans and a plain oatmeal sweater over a blue shirt. Even out of "uniform" Dad looks like Santa, with his bushy gray beard, mass of gray curls, red nose and cheeks, cheerful blue eyes, and substantial round belly.

"Dad. Hi. What brings you here? I'm about to close. Can you flip the sign on the door and turn the lock?"

He did so. "Good day?"

"Good enough for this time of year. Spring's come early, and the weather's been nice, so we've had people from the cities, venturing out for a day by the lake. Browsers most of them, but a few shoppers."

"You mother tells me you and Vicky were involved in an altercation earlier."

"Hardly an altercation, Dad. An annoying man said some annoying things to Vicky. He was leaving when Mom interfered. What did she tell you?"

"She might have embellished her role a tiny bit."

"My mother, embellish? Perish the thought."

We both laughed. Aline Steiner Wilkinson had been an opera diva. She might be retired now, but she remained every inch the diva.

"She told me the man was yelling at you and Vicky, and she feared he'd turn physical. She was about to whack him over the back of the head with her shopping bag, when he turned around. So instead of whacking, she stepped directly into his path. I've seen what she had in that shopping bag, and it might well have done some damage. She bought two pairs at an end-of-season sale on winter boots. So, what was it about?"

"Let's go into the back. I've been in and out all day, so Mattie hasn't had much of a break from the office." Even when the store was closed, I never let the dog into the front. He's not quite the size of a bull, but close enough, and I do own a china shop.

Mattie doesn't get excited at much, but he loves my dad and is eager to prove it. After enthusiastic greetings were exchanged, I snapped the leash on his collar, and we went into the back alley. We strolled up and down while Mattie checked every garbage can and doorway and followed a zigzagging trail only he could see.

"The man in the street," I told my father, "is named Jim Cole. Nephew of Charles Cole, of Cole House on Lakeside Drive. You know the one?"

"Of course I do. That place was once the glory of Rudolph. No longer. It's been an eyesore for years. Neighbors are always petitioning the town to do something about it, but our hands have been tied, as they've kept the electricity and water connected and done regular, although minor, maintenance. Enough to keep the place from falling down or spontaneously bursting into flames. I'm well aware that high school kids have been known to climb the fence on dark nights and party on the grounds. I am, of course, mentioning no names. If I were a few years younger, I would likely have done the same. I also know Mark Grosse and Vicky Casey recently bought the property. They've moved in and have long-term plans for renovating, reconstruction, and reclaiming."

"As usual, you pretty much know everything."

"First, I've heard of this Jim Cole character, though. I'll have a word with Tom Casey. We can't have angry people accosting visitors or residents on our main street in the middle of the afternoon. We can't have people accosting people anywhere at any time, but you get my point, honeybunch. What's his problem?"

"He claims he's the rightful heir to Miss Emmeline Cole, and thus the house belongs to him."

"Unlikely, but as I said I'll check with Tom."

We continued down the alley. Rachel McIntosh from Candy Cane Sweets came out with a bag of trash and called, "Good afternoon, Noel."

"Rachel. How's business?"

She tossed the bag into the bin. "Can't complain. Fortunately, kids like candy as much at Easter as at Christmas, maybe even more. My handmade chocolate eggs are a big hit with their mothers too."

"Save a few for me," Dad said.

"Already done, Noel. Already done." She went back inside. Mattie took his time checking out the fresh scents, and then he lifted his back leg to give the trash bin his seal of approval.

"Tell me about the Cole family," I said to my dad when we were moving again. "The history, I mean. I know Charles Cole intended the house to be handed down through his descendants, and then he never had any from his daughters. I don't know why the house was abandoned for all these years. Why didn't his surviving daughter sell it if she didn't want to live in it?"

Dad grimaced. "It's a sad story, honeybunch. It's also a long one, so why don't we have a drink at A Touch of Holly and I'll tell it to you."

"I can do that," I said, and I called to Mattie to turn around.

* * *

"The Cole family, like several others at that time and in this place, made a lot of money in Great Lakes shipping in the nineteenth and early twentieth centuries. They probably, like several others, enjoyed a nice bit of extra income during Prohibition from smuggling rum over from Canada. Henry Cole built the house we're talking about in 1893. He had two sons, names of Charles and Robert, and two daughters, both of whom left

Rudolph on their marriages and whose names are largely forgotten."

"As women's too often are."

"You're right about that, honeybunch—I mean Merry. Henry's first wife died when Charles and his sisters were young. Henry remained unmarried for a long time, but eventually he did remarry. The second son, Robert, was a good deal younger than his half-siblings."

"Jim must be Robert's son then, or claiming to be so." I sipped my wine. I'd taken Mattie back to the office, promising him I wouldn't be long, and Dad and I crossed the street to A Touch of Holly. We were comfortably settled in the bar, at a table for two overlooking the street, with drinks in front of us. "The Charles Cole we're talking about is Emmeline's father? The one who wrote the will we're talking about?"

"Yes. Charles was the eldest child in Henry's family. Henry died in 1945 after making even more money manufacturing munitions for the war. Charles took over the businesses on his father's death, as well as becoming master of the house. Charles married a woman from, of all places, Muddle Harbor, which was not the shocking incident it would be if it happened today. I believe her name was Ethel, but I don't recall her original surname. They in turn had three children. All girls.

"At this point the sad part of the story begins. The first girl fell out of a tree on the property when she was around fifteen years old, and she died as a result of head injuries suffered in the fall. The second daughter was killed in a horse-riding accident when she was in her early twenties. I should mention that, at the time, the Cole House property was far more extensive than it is today, including a substantial piece of lakefront. The house had stables and plenty of land for the girls to ride on. Charles himself died a year before the second daughter did, and Ethel sold the horses and much of the land, including what the stables were on, after the death of her second daughter. She likely was in need of the money.

"By that time the family fortunes were dwindling considerably. The heyday of Great Lakes shipping was at its end. No one needed to run rum anymore, and although there's always a market for munitions, Charles's declining health in his later years meant control of the company had largely passed out of his hands. It was sold on his death, and his family—meaning his widow and sole surviving daughter—had no more involvement. Charles's younger brother, Robert, left Rudolph for college, never came back, and as far as I know was never involved in the family business."

"Emmeline and her mother were left rattling around in that big old house."

"Yes. Eventually, only Emmeline remained. Her mother died in 1980, when Emmeline would have been a bit over thirty. Now, obviously this isn't that long ago in the scheme of things, but the Coles were a very traditional family. Emmeline and her sisters had a good education at private boarding schools. I forget where they went, but they were never intended to have proper careers. After the death of her mother, Emmeline remained in the house, on her own. It was only forty years ago, and plenty of people remember her well. Or rather, don't remember her well. She was young, just over thirty, but she rarely mixed with townspeople and isn't known to have had much in the way of friends locally. She'd gone out of town to school, remember. She had a maid or two who did most of her shopping. She wasn't entirely a recluse, though, and she did occasionally come to charitable functions or help out at fundraising events."

"I suppose that might explain why she left Rudolph," I said. "If she didn't have any friends or any prospects here. Doesn't explain why she didn't try to sell the house, though. It was worth a lot of money; she could have used that money to provide her with a fresh start and a full life. Instead, she moved all the way to Rochester? Not," I added quickly, "that there's anything wrong with Rochester."

Dad sipped his beer. "Emmeline herself got engaged in the spring of 1982 to a man from New York City. Something about his sister having gone to school with Emmeline, and the sister putting them in touch. He brought Emmeline out of her near seclusion. I have vague memories of them coming to the Easter dance at the community center. That was before Rudolph truly got into the whole Christmas Town thing, and the dance was a fundraiser for the hospital." My father looked into the distance, and his thoughts were momentarily lost in memory. "I didn't pay a great deal of attention to Emmeline and her date, because it was the first time I brought your mother to a Rudolph function."

I smiled to myself. I could just imagine a young and incredibly glamorous Aline Steiner, already making an impact in the world of opera, attending an Easter dance at the Rudolph Community Center. My parents were total opposites in almost every way, but their love for and devotion to each other remained complete.

My father pulled himself back to the here and now and continued. "The date was a good-looking man, as far as I remember, and Emmeline— I didn't really know her—looked so happy and so beautiful that spring."

"Let me guess," cynical me said. "The guy stole what was left of her money and dumped her."

"He died."

"Oh no. What happened?"

"The wedding was scheduled for the day after Christmas. It was going to be a small private affair. Emmeline's parents were dead, as were her sisters. She had no relatives on her mother's side, and on her father's there were aunts and an uncle, but they'd moved away and had little to no contact. The fiancé arrived in Rudolph to spend the holiday with Emmeline prior to the wedding. He fell down the stairs on Christmas Eve. Broke his neck."

I gasped. "That poor woman. All that death surrounding her. Was there any suggestion of foul play? That someone might have pushed him?"

"Not that I heard. He was apparently sneaking downstairs to put Emmeline's special present under the tree. They'd been to a restaurant for dinner, and he'd had a lot to drink, and then, so the autopsy said, several more when they got back to the house, before turning in."

I twisted the stem of my wineglass in my hands. A sad story indeed.

"Emmeline left town Christmas Day, leaving the house exactly as it was, Christmas tree in the front hall, decorations up. She took a small suitcase and never came back. She never sent for anything either. She never stepped foot inside Cole House or its grounds again. She initially went to a friend in Rochester, and then she bought a small house in that city. Which, so rumor goes, she never left other than to venture into town for some grocery shopping. Even that stopped when online delivery became a thing."

"You remembered all of this?"

My father smiled at me. "No. When I heard Mark and Vicky were moving into Cole House, it got me remembering. I had to look up many of the details."

"I can see why that house has a bad reputation. Two young daughters died in accidents on the property, and then the fiancé of the sole remaining Cole had a tragic accident in the house. Why is this story not better known, Dad? I've always known the house was supposedly haunted, but never the details of why. Never thought to ask, now that I come to think of it. It was enough for us that it looked haunted."

"Hard to say, honeybunch. Maybe people just wanted to forget. Not long after the death of the fiancé and Emmeline leaving, we hit on the idea of trying to revive the fortunes of the town by taking advantage of the name and marketing Rudolph as a Year-Round Christmas destination. We didn't want any negative thoughts associated with Christmas, so the story of the Cole family was swept under the rug." By *we*, my dad meant *I*, but I didn't bother to correct him. The whole thing had been his idea, and it was his hard work to make it happen that was responsible for the prosperity our town enjoys today.

My dad stared into space. "Perhaps Emmeline would have eventually returned had we not taken on the Christmas Town idea. They say she never celebrated the holidays again. That her house in Rochester was wrapped in shadow all of December, and a wreath with a huge black bow hung on her door every Christmas Eve."

I ducked my head. What a tragic story. I wondered if Vicky knew this about her new house. I'd overheard the women in the bakery saying the grounds themselves were cursed. Was that what was bothering Vicky's sleep?

# Chapter Seven

"This movie's terrible," I said to Vicky.

"Isn't that the point?" she replied.

"There's bad movies and there's terrible movies. I say we give up on it."

Vicky picked up the remote, pointed it at the screen, and the room was plunged into near darkness. We hadn't had a "bad movie" night for a long time, so when Vicky suggested I come to her house to drink wine, eat pizza, talk, and watch a movie, I'd eagerly agreed.

Sandbanks and Mattie snoozed contentedly on the floor next to the coffee table. Vicky had brought a small table and a sofa into what had once been some sort of study or office at the back of the house, next to the morning room they were using as their bedroom. No curtains covered the windows, which didn't matter as the rear of the house looked out onto dark, shrouded woods.

Without exchanging a word, we'd passed on selecting a horror movie for tonight.

Vicky reached for her wineglass, curled her legs up underneath her, and said, "So, as long as we're not watching a movie, we have to talk. You start."

"I last saw you yesterday, so I don't have a heck of a lot to talk about. Did you show Mark your wedding dresses?"

"Of course not. I don't have a scrap of respect for tradition in my body, as you are well aware, never mind wedding traditions, which are the worst of them all, but even I know it's bad luck for the groom to see the bride's dress before the ceremony." Her face crinkled. "I might have to give that more thought. I bet his first wife kept her totally over-the-top wedding gown a secret, and look how well that marriage turned out."

An empty cardboard box and two plates containing nothing but scraps of crust were all that remained of our pizza dinner. I reached for a lemon lavender tart Vicky'd brought home from her bakery. As an Easter touch each perfect little piece of pastry had a tiny chocolate egg piped on the top. I took a bite: it tasted as wonderful as it looked.

"My mom was going to invite you and Mark to their house for dinner on Easter Sunday. It'll be the usual collection of whoever Mom gathers up at the last moment. That was before you made your sudden wedding plans. Would you still like to come, or are you going on your honeymoon?"

"I'd like to come, but I'll be on my own. We're taking Saturday off to get married, but then straight back to the routine. We're having brunch at my parents', and then Mark's going in for dinner shift. Easter Sunday's a big day for treating the grandparents to a fancy dinner out."

"He's working the day after his wedding?"

"Yes. I won't be, because the bakery'll be closed, but I'll be in on Monday, bright and cheerful. We're putting our money into the house, as well as any vacation time we manage to get."

Mattie woke with a start. His big head jerked up, and his ears stood at attention. He bounded nimbly (as nimbly as he is ever inclined to do) to his feet. Old Sandbanks was almost completely deaf, but he felt Mattie moving and was startled awake. He gave a woof of surprise.

A second later we humans heard it too. A loud knock, sounding like someone rapping on a door. Vicky and I exchanged glances. Her eyes were wide, and the color had drained from her face. It sounded again.

"Someone's at the door," I said.

"It's coming from inside the house." Her voice shook.

I jumped to my feet. "Nonsense. I'll get it."

I ran down the long dark hallway. Mattie passed me. I felt Vicky behind me, and old Sandbanks trying to keep up. The bulbs in the enormous chandelier hanging above the front hall had not been replaced, but a small light burned above the stairs leading to the second floor.

I threw the lock, turned the handle, and opened the door. No one was there. I peered out. It was dark now; most of the trees were not yet in leaf, but there was no moonlight for them to block. Lamps lining the driveway weren't on, and we were too far away from the street for the streetlamps to be visible.

I stepped onto the porch and looked around. Nothing and no one appeared out of the darkness, and all was quiet.

Mattie woofed softly. I looked down at him. His hackles were standing on end and his ears were up. I laid my hand on the top of his head, feeling the strong, solid warmth beneath.

"Hello?" I called.

"Come inside," Vicky said. "Quickly."

I did so and called to Mattie. He didn't move. "Mattie. Matterhorn. Come here." I reached out, grabbed his collar, and pulled him after me. He came, although reluctantly. He was a well-trained dog. At his size, he has to be. If he didn't want to

59

move, Matterhorn did not move, and there would be nothing I could do about it.

Vicky slammed the door.

Almost against my will I looked at the stairs leading up into the darkness of the unoccupied second floor. Then I looked at the cracked black and white tiles at my feet. Emmeline Cole's fiancé had fallen to his death down these stairs. He would have landed near where I was standing. Maybe on the very spot. It had been approaching midnight on Christmas Eve, and he'd been on his way to playfully place a gift for his loved one under the tree. Perhaps he hadn't wanted to wake her by turning on the light, and so he'd stumbled in the darkness. Fallen from the top of the steps maybe. The steps were steep, and there were a great many of them. Had Emmeline heard him fall, or had she woken bright and early on Christmas morning, full of the joy of the season, and . . .

The knock sounded again, this time coming from the rear of the house. One. A pause. Two.

I abandoned thoughts of Emmeline Cole and her lost fiancé and ran back the way I'd come, fumbling in my pocket for my phone. I burst into the kitchen. A single light burned above the sink. I threw the kitchen door open to be greeted by, once again, nothing. I switched my phone's flashlight on and swept the light back and forth across the crumbling and broken concrete steps and the weed-choked grass beyond. All was dark and still. The solid trunks of trees and their sweeping branches edged too close to the house.

Mattie stood beside me, sniffing the air.

"I wish," I said, not for the first time, "you could tell me what you're sensing out there."

Vicky grabbed my arm and pulled me back into the house. She reached around me and slammed the door shut.

"You've got a floorboard loose upstairs," I said. "Maybe some tiles on the roof are flapping in the wind."

"There's no wind tonight, Merry."

"Squirrels playing on them maybe. Is this the sort of thing you've been hearing in the night?"

She nodded.

In our friendship, Vicky's the brave one, the impulsive one. I can usually be found following cautiously behind, swept up in the waves of her enthusiasm for life. Tonight, I took one look at her pale frightened face, at an expression I'd never seen before, and decided I'd have to be the one in charge.

"Okay. We're two strong young women. We have phones to call for assistance if we need it. We have two dogs." I threw a look at the animals in question. Sandbanks scratched under his chin. Mattie gazed up at me, wondering if we were going to play. "Okay, neither of these creatures are attack dogs, but they are dogs, and in Mattie's case size is all that matters. We're going to get to the bottom of this."

A wooden block bristling with Mark's set of professional kitchen knives stood on the countertop. I took three determined steps across the floor and pulled one out. I held it up. "We have defensive weapons if needed. Not that they will be. Let's go."

"Where are we going?"

"To search the house."

"No. I'm sure you're right. A board's come loose over one of the upstairs windows maybe. Let's go back to the TV room. There's still some wine in the bottle."

"You're frightened to be in this house, and that can't continue, Vicky, not if you want to live here and be happy here. Do you believe in ghosts?"

"No," she said in a low voice. "I mean *no*! I do not."

"Neither do I. Therefore a ghost can't be haunting this house. Let's go. Stay with me and keep the dogs close. Neither of us are too stupid to live."

When I look back on that night, I wonder if I'd temporarily lost my mind. Or maybe it was that the time had come for me to be brave for Vicky. I was determined to be so, and so I was. I took a firm grip on the knife in my right hand (feeling rather foolish as I did so) and carried my phone in my left. I turned lights on in every room as we entered, pleased that many of them still worked. We checked the downstairs first, pushing aside torn and dusty curtains to shake the plywood coverings on the windows, stomping hard on worn carpets and uneven and shifting floorboards to check they were secure. As we moved, I kept one eye on Mattie and Sandbanks. Something had definitely caught Mattie's attention when we were standing at the open doors, but now we were back inside, he'd returned to his regular calm self. He accompanied me on the search simply because where I went, he did too. Sandbanks did the same with Vicky.

They say animals are sensitive to the supernatural, don't they? Perhaps it was that matter-of-fact way Mattie moved through the house that helped to make me brave.

"Have you been upstairs since showing us through the house?" I said to Vicky when I was satisfied nothing was to be found on the ground floor. In that, I was disappointed. I was desperate to find something I could show Vicky as proof her nighttime fears had a rational, physical explanation.

"No, I haven't," she said. "Mark and I want to get the ground floor fully livable before starting work on the upstairs. You saw what it's like up there, Merry. A mess, to put it mildly."

I agreed. Half the spider population of New York State must live in this house.

"We'd better go and check it out then." I led the way up the staircase. Steps creaked under our weight, and I wondered how secure these stairs were. "Is this what you're hearing?" I said as a board let out a low creak when my foot touched it.

"I suppose it could be, but Merry?"

"What?"

"These stairs aren't going to make any sounds unless someone. . . . something . . . stands on them."

Had Emmeline's fiancé tripped on a broken step? I pushed thoughts of him aside and said, "Mice maybe?"

"Must be mighty fat mice," she said.

"Do ghosts have weight? They're usually depicted as floating through the air, feet above the ground." I bit my tongue as another thought came to mind. *If not a weightless being, then what?*

"Ask Mark to hammer this firmly into place tomorrow. Doesn't have to be a fancy fix—a couple of good nails should do it." I glanced at her face. "If you don't want to tell Mark you're concerned, I can ask Alan to come around."

"I can fix a loose board myself, but that's not the real issue here. It's time I talked to Mark."

"I think you should. Come on—let's finish what we've started."

As bad as the ground floor was, the second floor of this building could have been used to film Miss Haversham's house in *Great Expectations*. Minor structural repairs had been done over the years, but thick, sticky cobwebs hung from every corner, and mice droppings were scattered across the floors, along with chewed-up fabric I guessed had come from bed coverings or seat cushions to be used for nesting.

I brushed a spiderweb off my cheek with a shudder and swung my flashlight across the upstairs landing. Vicky and I jumped at the sound of retreating feet. Mattie ran forward, head down, nose moving, heading directly for the bottom of the two-foot-high baseboards. He gave the wood a scratch and a sniff before giving up pursuit and returning to my side. Sandbanks sniffed at him and then yawned.

"That sound I've heard," Vicky said. "Mice in the walls, and likely other creatures too. You cannot tell me that sounded like the knocks we heard."

"No," I admitted. "It didn't."

The junk collectors had taken away almost all of the furniture that was too damaged to reclaim and the soft coverings. Vicky had told me Emmeline's clothes, now nothing but chewed tatters, had still been hanging in the closets. The rooms were empty, but I went into each of them anyway, checking closets and window latches, stamping on floorboards. Nothing but the occasional soft creak and the sound of more mice fleeing for their lives.

The bathtub was an old-fashioned claw-footed thing. If it could be cleaned up, it would be quite beautiful. I turned on the taps. Pipes clanged, but no water came out.

"Water's been switched off to the upper floor," Vicky said.

"Attic?" I asked.

"Let's not go there. The dogs can't get up there."

"I'd like to check it."

Vicky sucked in a breath. For a while, we'd managed to stop being frightened, or even concerned. We were just two friends having fun exploring an old house. But some of the hesitation returned to her face as she threw a worried look at the ceiling over our heads.

"No point in searching," I said, "if we don't search everywhere."

"Okay. The staircase is behind that trapdoor." She pointed to the end of the hallway and up. A rope hung from the ceiling. It looked fairly new. No doubt it had been maintained over the years to give access to the attic if necessary. I reached up, grabbed the rope, and gave it a solid tug. A door in the ceiling slid open, making surprisingly little noise, and a ladder smoothly descended. It was also in good shape.

I was still holding the knife in one hand and my phone in the other. I handed Vicky the knife. She slipped her phone into her pocket, took the knife, and lifted her hands, one blade in each.

"You look like a pirate about to storm aboard a prize ship," I said.

"Avast," she said with a soft grin and the slightest trace of humor.

I took a firm hold of the ladder with my free hand and climbed up into the darkness. My head popped through the hole in the floor, and I checked out my surroundings before venturing the rest of the way. The weak beam from my phone threw shifting shadows into the corners. I took a moment to feel my feet firm on the ladder, and then I swept the light across the room. The floor was thick with dust, and I could see no trace of human footsteps. Plenty of other footsteps, but from no creatures that wouldn't be as frightened by me as me by them. When nothing moved and no one sprang out at me, I climbed the rest of the way up and stepped into the crowded space. The attic had not yet been cleared out. It was full of years—decades—of family mementos and junk. More cobwebs and mouse droppings. The floor was made of wide-planked bare boards, heavily worn;

the roof descended from a center peak to half height. A big steamer trunk stood against one wall. A cluster of suitcases, some modern enough to have wheels, many not, were stacked in the middle of the floor. Piles of rolled-up carpet were covered in damp and mold. A baby's cradle stacked full of scraps of faded and unrecognizable cloth; a low coffee table, standing crookedly on one broken leg. The floor at the eastern end showed traces of rainwater having found a way in, and the wall was streaked with remains of moisture. This must be why Mark wanted to have the roof fixed before tending to anything else. I tapped on the floorboards near the damp patches with my foot, and they shifted under my weight. One low window was set into the west wall. It wasn't covered with plywood, and the glass was intact, although absolutely filthy.

I climbed down the ladder. "Nothing," I said to Vicky. "We should check outside."

"Why?"

"I'll admit what we heard sounded like someone knocking on the door, but it might have been a tree branch hitting a window. The trees near the house need some serious cutting back."

We went down the stairs, the dogs running ahead of us.

"No need." Vicky attempted to laugh. "You're making me realize I'm being nervous over nothing. Too many horror movies in my youth, I guess. Remember those sleepovers we used to have with Tina and Anna? Oh, my gosh, I couldn't sleep for weeks after some of those movies we watched."

"You need to talk to Mark about this, Vicky," I said. "He needs to know if you're not comfortable here. You're both about to make a big commitment to this house and to each other. You have to be absolutely positive it's the right thing for you to do."

"Yeah." She reached out and wrapped me in a hug. "I'm glad you're my friend, Merry. You're always so practical. Sometimes I need that."

We'd only just separated and started walking back down the hallway when a low moan echoed throughout the house. Vicky gasped. I might have gasped myself as I grabbed her arm. Mattie barked and immediately went on alert. Even Sandbanks yelped, more in reaction to our behavior than anything he'd heard.

This was no branch scratching against a window or a floor-board settling for the night. Or even a horde of mice raiding the kitchen cupboards.

It came again, deep and low. Full of pain. Full of . . . horror?

Vicky screamed. Mattie threw back his head and howled. My skin crawled. I swiped up on my phone. "That came from outside. I'm calling the police. Something's out there."

At that moment, thoroughly modern, entirely practical, part-of-this-world headlights flooded the front hall, wheels crunched on gravel, and a car engine purred before being switched off.

Vicky ran for the door. Sandbanks, Mattie, and I followed, and we all tumbled outside to see Mark climbing the steps. "Hi," he said.

Vicky burst into tears and threw herself into his arms. He grabbed her and spoke to me over her shoulder. "What's going on. What's wrong? What on earth are you doing with those knives? Merry, are you guys okay?"

# Chapter Eight

We gathered in the kitchen. I put the kettle on to make Vicky and me hot sweet tea. I didn't know what I'd heard, but I'd heard something. Something I could not explain.

When Vicky finally peeled herself out of Mark's arms and stopped crying, she exchanged a look with me. I gave her a firm nod. It was time—long past time—she told Mark about her worries and her sleepless nights.

I made the tea, placed a steaming cup in front of Vicky, took one for myself, and sat down. We'd laid our weapons aside while Sandbanks settled on the rug in front of the stove and immediately dropped off to sleep. Mattie sat next to me, watching. But the tension was gone from his big body, and his posture was relaxed.

*Must be nice*, I thought, *to be able to get rid of that feeling of danger as soon as the immediate threat has passed.*

"We thought we heard something moments before your car pulled up," I said.

"No," Vicky said. "Not thought. *Did*. We did hear something. The dogs did too, and that's what freaked me out most of all."

Mark didn't laugh or try to reassure us. All he said was, "What sort of something?"

"Knocking at the door at first," Vicky said. "Twice. Two doors, front and back. We checked, but no one was there. Then we heard a sound like someone was . . . I don't know. In pain, or terror maybe."

"Or trying to scare us," I said. "After the knocking, we searched the house—all of it— thoroughly, but we didn't find anything that might be making those sounds. Then, moments before you arrived, we heard the . . . I don't know what to call it. A moan, a cry. This isn't the first time that's happened either. Vicky's been hearing things. Noises in the night."

Mark turned to Vicky. "You too?"

"You mean you have as well?" she said.

"Yeah." He rubbed his hands through his short hair. "I didn't want to worry you, so I didn't say anything."

"But you're always sound asleep when I've heard things. I've been so jealous of that."

"I figured you weren't sleeping well, but you denied it when I asked. I didn't push it, because I thought maybe you were having second thoughts. About this house. About me. We're on such different sleep and work schedules, I suppose our disturbance schedule's been off too." He spoke to me. "I sometimes don't get home until after midnight, particularly if we've had a big function like a wedding. Plenty of chefs are wired after a night's work and need to stay up for a while to wind down, and they hit a bar, have a couple of drinks. Never been that way for me. I drop the moment I get in. Vicky gets up around four to get to the bakery and start the bread, so she's usually asleep when I get to bed. These sounds you hear—have I been home when it happens?"

She thought. "No. Now I'm thinking about a pattern, I don't hear them when you're here. They start not long after I go to bed, and only when you're out. For the rest of the night, particularly after you get in, my imagination is working overtime."

"Same with me, in reverse," he said. "Once or twice, I've heard strange sounds in the early morning. After you've left. I've gotten up and checked out the house, but I never find anything. I don't believe in ghosts, but—"

"But," Vicky and I chorused.

Mark stood up. "If there is a ghost, it's unlikely to care much about our work schedules. A person, however, wanting to scare us so much we leave this house, would likely use the divide-and-conquer principal."

"You're thinking of Jim Cole?" I asked.

"I am."

"For what end? If you guys decide you don't want to live here, you're going to sell the house. Not hand it over to him and walk away."

"Anyone who's creeping around someone else's property at night, trying to scare people, isn't thinking straight, Merry."

"I suppose that's true. Might just be kids doing what we did when we were kids, and finding that having people living here has upped the stakes and the risk factor. You haven't seen evidence anyone's been inside the house, have you? The knocks could have come from the boards over the windows. The . . . whatever we heard tonight . . . did that sound close, do you think, Vicky?"

"Close enough. No, I don't think it was inside the house. It came from outside. Same with some of the noises I've heard in the night. Never anything I thought was in the room with me, or standing outside the door."

"Does Sandbanks ever do anything?" Mark asked.

Vicky gave the old dog an affectionate smile. "No. For him to react the ghost would have to walk across his nose."

I thought of the two women in the bakery the day Vicky told me she and Mark were going to buy this house. The grounds themselves were, the women said, cursed. The two elder daughters of Charles and Ethel Cole had died outside. Were they still here?

*Nonsense.*

"I'd say it's happening too often to be kids on a lark," Mark said. "Kids like to hang around and see the effect of their so-called-pranks. Laughing from behind bushes and peeking in windows. That sort of thing."

I agreed.

"Might be a recording," Mark said, "played on a schedule."

"Might be anything," I said. "If someone's been in or near your house, you need to step up your security. Did you have the locks changed when you took possession?"

"We did," Mark said. "The original keys have been at the lawyer's office all these years. Anyone could have taken a copy. Plenty of people probably did, as various cleaners and tradespeople had to be let in."

He put his hand on Vicky's shoulder. She reached up and touched it. "This is our home, and we're not going to be frightened out of it. By Jim Cole or bored kids or anyone else."

He rummaged in a kitchen drawer and took out a heavy flashlight, which he handed to Vicky. Then he pulled a knife out of the block on the counter and thrust it through his belt. "It won't come to using this, but I'll take it anyway. You guys make another sweep of the house. This time have a look for a way someone might be getting in. Loose boards on the windows, most likely, or an old latch not turned fully."

Vicky stood up. "What are you going to do?"

"I'm going to have a look outside. You said someone knocked on the door and ran away."

"You can't go alone."

"I'll be okay, Vic. You stay with Merry. Whoever knocked on the door would have run off when my car drove up."

"You can't be sure of that," I said.

"Sure enough." He hefted the flashlight. "It's dark out, so I likely won't find anything tonight, but I'm going to check under the windows and along the driveway. Look for prints or foliage disturbed. Something we can take to the cops, if it comes to that."

Vicky looked hesitant. Mark gave her shoulder a squeeze. "You and Merry check inside again. I'll do the outside. Take your phones. Scream if you find anything."

"Wouldn't have thought of that," she muttered. He gave her a grin and me a wink.

"Before I go . . . I have to ask. Are either of you qualified in knife fighting?"

"I own a Christmas gift shop," I said.

"I can wield a pastry blender to great effect," Vicky said.

"Maybe leave the knives behind. They can be turned against you."

"Are *you* qualified in knife fighting?" I asked.

He looked at the blade in his hand. "I spent some of my training working at a butcher's."

"Good enough," I said. I wasn't so sure separating was such a great idea. But Mark and Vicky intended to live here. They couldn't spend their lives looking over their shoulders, afraid to venture alone into the yard at night.

"Keep the dogs close," Mark said.

"That," I said, "is never a problem."

He slipped our knives back into the wooden block and then left the kitchen. Vicky and I followed, clutching our phones. Mattie came with us, but Sandbanks had gone back to sleep, and he didn't bother to get up again.

Mark let himself out the front door. Vicky and I looked at each other. The hesitation and the fear had gone from her face. "It seems so silly, doesn't it, the moment the strange noises stop? In the cold light of day, I've been able to tell myself I've been imagining things. Obviously Mark was thinking the same. Both of us keeping quiet about what we were sensing."

"A lesson, perhaps, for your married life," I said.

"Yeah. It's getting late. You can go on home. Mark's here now, and I'll be okay."

"Let's first do what he suggested and check the downstairs windows at least. I looked at them earlier, but I didn't try the latch on them all. Some of that metal is old and rusty; it might well have come loose and not be fastening property."

"Lead on," she said.

Once again we went from room to room. This big old house had a lot of windows. Other than rooms Vicky and Mark had reclaimed for their current use, the windows were old, dirty, and choked with dust. We pulled at the latches and rattled the frames, but nothing gave way or swung open. Mattie trotted beside us. His curious nose sniffed at everything, but he made no indication he'd located something out of place. Something like the scent of an unfamiliar human. Not that Mattie was exactly a bloodhound. He must smell so many different people in a day—people we pass on the street, those who come into the store or who are taking a shortcut through the alley behind Jingle Bell Lane—I don't know how or if he'd react to someone being in this house who shouldn't be.

"Let's do the same upstairs," I said. "Those trees near the house are so overgrown, it's possible someone can climb a branch and access a window that way."

As we headed for the stairs, Vicky said, "I'm hoping we can knock out a good part of the walls down here and put in bigger picture windows."

We were chatting lightly, comforted because Mark was outside and my dog wasn't on alert, but when Vicky's phone rang, we both yelped. I might have hit the top of my head on the ceiling.

"What!" she yelled into it. "The cops? What's happened? Are you okay? Be right there. No, I'm coming." She turned and ran down the hallway. "Call 911," she shouted to me.

"Vicky! Don't go out. Wait until the police get here." I fumbled at the emergency button on my own phone.

"It's okay." Vicky wrenched open the door. "Mark's okay. He found a body in the garden."

# Chapter Nine

I told the 911 operator what little I knew of what was happening. By *body*, I wasn't sure if Vicky meant someone was dead or just unconscious, so I told her we needed an ambulance as well as the police.

Mattie could run fast when he had a mind to, and he chased after Vicky without hesitation. A lamp burned over the front door, but outside of the dim circle of light it threw, all was dark.

Mark's shouts came from the south side of the house, and we headed that way. I focused the light from my phone at my feet as I ran, conscious of broken flagstones, fallen twigs and branches, holes dug by generations of squirrels and chipmunks.

Overgrown branches of large old trees stretched toward the house, scraping against the roof and the time-worn bricks. Saplings sprouted from what had once been flower beds and lawns. A light wind had come up, and the branches, some just beginning to show fresh new buds, rustled softly. Small animals fled at Mattie's approach.

In its glory days, the largest room at the south side of the house had been a summer room, a place for the ladies of the family to relax with a good book and a cup of tea or glass of sherry, a profusion of wide-leafed plants, big windows, and French doors opening onto the garden. The doors were hammered shut now, the windows covered in boards, the flower beds choked with weeds and thistles eagerly reaching up to welcome spring. The classical stone statue of a female figure draped in ropes, pouring water from a vase into the fountain at her bare feet, was green with algae, the stone chipped and cracked, the woman's nose broken off. No water cascaded from her vase, and the pool itself was full of decades' worth of slimy mulch, last season's decaying leaves, and broken branches.

On the far side of the statue, Mark crouched on the ground, next to something dark and shapeless. Vicky was behind him, tugging on Mattie's collar, trying to pull the curious dog away. Mark had thrown his knife aside, and it lay on the ground a foot or so away. To my intense relief, the knife appeared clean, unused. I left it where it was, knowing the police would be interested in having a look at it.

"Are you there, madam?" the 911 operator said in her calm, professional voice.

"Yes. Still here," I said.

"Police and medics have been dispatched. They will be there shortly. Please stay on the line."

I slapped my right thigh. "Mattie! Matterhorn! Come!"

"What?" said the voice on the phone.

"Sorry—calling my dog."

"If you can, madam, it would be best to put the dog in another room."

"We're outside. At the side of the house. Tell them the gates are open. Go to the right of the house when they arrive."

"I will."

Vicky dragged Mattie toward me, and I took hold of his collar. I looked deeply into his huge, liquid brown eyes. "Sit! Down. Stay there. Stay."

He sort of hovered into a half sit.

My friend turned to me, her face stricken. I stepped cautiously forward. Mark's flashlight illuminated the ground, but not the body. In the poor light of my phone, I could see a man lying on his back. His face was half turned away from me, his expression one of horror and shock emphasized by the deep shadows. At the back of his head, something dark and wet glimmered.

Mark stood up with a grunt. "Gone," he said. I glanced down. His hands were streaked with blood.

Sirens broke the night, and moments later flashing blue and red lights flooded the front of the house. Mattie broke his "sit" and bounded up, barking. He ran to greet the arrivals before I could stop him.

The phone in my hand was still connected and the operator was asking me what was going on. "They're here," I said. "Thanks." I hung up and chased after my dog.

Powerful lights rounded the house, followed by two police officers. Mattie ran up to them, barking greetings.

"Merry Wilkinson, is that you? I recognize your dog," said a man's voice from behind the wall of light.

"Yes. This way—he's over here."

"Get that dog out of here," a woman said.

I took a firm hold of Mattie's collar and, with a great deal of difficulty, dragged him up the stairs, across the porch, and into the house. When I opened the door, Sandbanks, finally roused from his nap by the commotion, tried to get out. I shoved Mattie, grabbed at Sandbanks, and struggled to get both dogs inside. Finally, I slammed the door shut as another siren turned into the driveway, additional red lights flooded the yard and the house, and an ambulance screeched to a halt. Two paramedics stepped out, and I jumped off the steps and pointed. "That way. Follow me."

Back by the statue and the empty fountain, Mark and Vicky were standing close together. Officer Williams crouched over the body while Officer Candice Campbell shone her flashlight onto my friends. The light focused on Mark's hands and the front of his shirt, dotted with bright red splashes.

"Outta the way—all of you," one of the medics said.

"Try not to touch those." Williams pointed to the knife and the flashlight on the ground.

"Shouldn't need to. Give us some light here."

The police stepped to one side, giving the medics room to work. Williams shone his Maglite onto the body on the ground. One of the medics opened her equipment bag while the other examined the unmoving patient.

"How'd you get that on your hands, sir?" Officer Campbell asked Mark.

Mark lifted his hands and stared at them in something close to shock. He said nothing.

"Sir?" she repeated.

"I"—Mark shook his head—"I found him. That man. Lying there. He was on his belly, his face down, not moving. I turned him over. I tried to help. I must have touched the injury. His head."

The medic said, "This isn't a knife wound, for sure. Looks like a blunt instrument. Baseball bat, rock maybe."

"Do you know this person?" Williams asked Mark.

Mark swallowed heavily and dared a quick glance. "I've never seen him before."

But I had. Vicky and I exchanged a look. Vicky took a deep breath and said, "I know who he is, but I've only met him once, and I've no idea what he's doing here, creeping around our property at this time of night. His name's Jim Cole."

Mark groaned, and the cop focused his eyes on him while he asked Vicky. "Why do you say 'creeping around'?"

"What else would you call being at the back of someone's house," Vicky said. "Without the residents knowing, at this time of night?"

"Other than creeping?" I added.

One of the paramedics knelt beside the body while the other talked on her phone in a low voice. It didn't look to me like they were in any sort of a hurry. What I'd seen from the quick glance I'd had at Jim Cole was enough to tell me he was dead.

"VSA," the first medic called, confirming my observation.

"I've called for a detective," Campbell said.

More police were arriving, bringing their big lights and crime scene tape.

"Is this your house, sir?" Officer Williams said to Mark.

Mark nodded. Vicky said, "Our house."

"I'd like you to wait inside. Officer Campbell will accompany you. Please do not talk among yourselves about what happened, and make no attempt to wash yourself or change your clothes. Sir."

"I didn't do anything," Mark said.

"That's to be determined." Williams nodded at Candy Campbell. "See to it."

I gave Candy a smile, but I'm pretty sure it looked as strained as it felt. Candy and I had known each other since childhood, although we'd never been friends. As far as I knew, she had nothing against Vicky, but high school rivalries spread to include entire circles. Come to think of it, Candy should have nothing against me either, and a lot of years had passed since we wanted the same position on the softball team, and the notice of the new and superhot guy in our class.

Vicky had ended up dating the newest and hottest guy in our class, although it hadn't lasted long. *"Total and complete idiot"* had been her assessment once she got to know him better.

Vicky was now engaged to the second hottest guy in Rudolph, New York—Alan Anderson being the first. Candy had dated Russ Durham for a while not long ago, but that didn't appear to have lasted long.

I smiled at Candy again. She did not return the smile.

\* \* \*

Mark, Vicky, and I were escorted under Candy Campbell's s no-nonsense stare, into the house. The dogs were overjoyed to see us return. Candy almost smiled when Mattie lifted his head and cocked one ear toward her, but she managed to refrain from showing her feelings.

"You have got to be kidding," she said as she looked around the foyer, at the water-stained ceiling, the dark chandelier, the cracked floor tiles. "I heard you'd bought this place, but I didn't think you'd actually want to move into the dump."

Mark had barely said a word since I'd found him with Jim Cole's body. He recovered to defend his house. "We intend to fix it up. It will be a true labor of love for us. Right, Vicky?"

"Totally," she said.

"Each to his own, I guess." Candy gave an exaggerated shudder for emphasis.

"You got a problem with that, *Candy?*" Vicky said.

Candy's face tightened, and I quickly said, "The back rooms are comfortable. Let's go there." Officer Candice Campbell simply hated her childhood nickname. Which, I thought, was fair enough, as Candy didn't exactly suit the hard-boiled, street-hardened cop image she tried so hard to project. Although, I had to admit, I sometimes called her Candy myself, deliberately trying to get a rise out of her.

It would be better, I thought, if she dropped that tough cop act and simply became what she was, a dedicated police officer in the small town where she'd grown up and where she might run into her old kindergarten teacher at a drunk and disorderly call. Never mind running into her imaginary high school rivals at what appeared to be a murder scene.

Mattie and Sandbanks led the way to the warm and welcoming kitchen. Mark pulled out a chair and dropped heavily into it. He tried not to look at his hands, on which the blood was already beginning to dry. Away from the lights, I could see there wasn't all that much—just a few spatters really—with more sprinkled across the bottom of the white chef's shirt with his name written across the breast pocket, which he'd worn to work.

Vicky grabbed a chair and pulled it close to Mark. "Don't touch his hands," Candy growled, and Vicky jerked her hand away.

"Be right back," I said. "I need to make a phone call."

"You're to stay here," Candy said.

"I'll be in the next room. I won't close the door. You can listen in if you want."

"I said—" she began, but I left the room anyway.

I should have called Alan hours ago, when this entire evening began to spiral out of control. Better late than never.

He answered almost immediately "Merry? What's up. It's late. Are you okay?"

"I'm fine, but something's happened, and I wanted to hear your voice."

"You're hearing it now. Do you need me to come? Are you at home?"

"No. I'm at Vicky and Mark's."

"What's wrong?"

I hadn't shut the door to the kitchen. I could see Candy standing on the far side of the room, her eyes focused on my best friend's fiancé.

"I can't give you the details right now. Mark might be in trouble."

"On my way," Alan said.

* * *

We didn't have to wait long in awkward silence before I heard the door open. I didn't have to hear the new arrival's voice in the hallway or the tread of her confident feet on the floorboards to know Detective Diane Simmonds was here. All I had to do was look at my dog.

Mattie leaped to attention. Every hair on his body stood up. He quivered in joy and excitement. His ears were high, his bright eyes wide with anticipation, his tongue drooped over his lips, emitting a stream of drool. His idol was here.

The detective came into the kitchen. Two people accompanied her, and another uniform took position in the doorway.

"Matterhorn," Simmonds said. "This is not a social call. Sit."

Mattie sat. Adoration poured out of his eyes, and bliss filled his face.

He never looked like that when I walked into a room.

Having had enough excitement for one day, Sandbanks snored lightly next to the stove.

Simmonds studied the humans, one after another. The detective was an attractive woman in her early forties. Tall and fit, with a mass of red curls and eyes an unusual emerald green, dressed in slim jeans and a black leather jacket over a blue striped shirt. Walking down the street in the company of her ten-year-old daughter, she might look like an average resident of Rudolph, but only if you didn't look closely. And then she would rarely be mistaken for anything but a cop. She held her thin frame straight and tense, and those emerald eyes were constantly watching everyone and everything. "Officer Campbell, you can go back outside. We'll need someone on the gate to discourage the curious and the ill-intended. Admit no one unless they're with us."

Candy threw me a stern look before leaving the room.

"I had a quick peek at the scene," Simmonds said. "I've been told some of what you had to say. First, Mr. Grosse, I'd like you to accompany these people to your washroom. They'll take samples off your hands, and they will want the clothes you're wearing as evidence."

"I didn't—"

"We can talk later. Do it now, please."

Mark stood up. He gave Vicky a long look and then walked past us and out the door into the TV room. One of the new arrivals followed, along with the uniformed officer.

"Vicky, Merry," Simmonds asked. "Did either of you touch the body?"

"Definitely not," I said.

"No," Vicky said.

"Did your dogs?"

"Sandbanks was in the house the entire time," Vicky said. "Mattie tried to get near, but we stopped him."

Simmonds pulled out a chair and sat down. "Okay. Can you tell me what happened here tonight? First of all, Officer Williams tells me you knew the dead man, Merry."

"I wouldn't say I *knew* him. I met him one time only, and then for no more than five minutes at the most. His name's Jim Cole. I don't know anything else about him, not even where he lives."

Vicky nodded. "Same. I was with Merry when we ran into him on the street. That's the only time I've ever seen him."

"Cole. People tell me this place is called Cole House. Same family?"

"He's a distant relative of the previous owner," Vicky said.

"Can you tell me about this encounter you had with him on the street?"

This time Vicky and I didn't need to look at each other to know what we were thinking. I'd have to tell Detective Simmonds Jim Cole had made threats toward us. Toward Vicky and Mark. Witnesses would come forward, possibly including my own mother, to say the encounter between him and us had been tense.

I thought about the way those uniformed officers who'd been first on the scene tonight had been eyeing Mark. Mark with blood on his hands, stains on his white shirt.

I assured myself he'd soon be in the clear. Jim Cole, creeping around in the dark for his own twisted purposes, must have tripped over a loose rock or a chunk of broken statuary. He'd fallen and hit his head. That was all.

But—if he hadn't fallen, if Mark hadn't killed Jim Cole—which he hadn't—then someone else had.

And that someone had slipped quietly away before the alarm could be raised.

"Mark and I bought this house from the estate of the late Emmeline Cole," Vicky said. "Jim Cole claims he should have inherited from her because they were cousins. That has nothing whatsoever to do with us. If he can prove his claim, and he wants possession of the house, then he can pay us what we paid for it, and have it. It's up to the lawyers to sort it all out."

"It would appear, at first glance, he wasn't content to leave it entirely up to the lawyers," Simmonds said. "Do you have any idea as to what he might have been doing here tonight?"

"I do not know. I didn't even know he was here until Mark found him. He didn't ring the doorbell or call ahead to say he was coming."

A spark of interest flared in Simmonds's eyes at Vicky's wording. "When Mark found him? Not you and Mark, or you and Merry and Mark?"

Vicky winced. "Mark went out by himself to have a look around after he got home from work."

"Why would he do that?"

The uniformed officer's radio cracked to life. Among all the static, I caught one word: *Anderson.*

"Some guy's here wanting to see Ms. Wilkinson," the cop said.

"Alan Anderson. I know him. Admit him to the property, but tell him to wait outside for a few minutes. Vicky, please answer the question."

"Okay." As succinctly as possible, leaving out all the fear and the drama, Vicky told the detective what happened tonight. She and I heard unexplained noises and searched inside the house but could find nothing that might have caused them. Mark arrived home and went outside to see if anything had been disturbed while Vicky and I once again did the same in the house.

Her voice dropped off as Mark came into the kitchen. His hands were scrubbed pink, and he'd changed into jeans and a T-shirt.

"Take a seat," Simmonds said. "Vicky was telling me what went down here tonight. You thought someone was on your property and that someone had been deliberately attempting to frighten her and Merry."

"I thought nothing," he said. "I just wanted to check the place out."

"You're not from around here, Detective," I said. "So you might not be aware this has always been a prime spot for local teenagers to break onto the property and party. You can tell by the state of the place, inside and out, it's been unoccupied for a long time. Kids like that. A place where they can be away from older people watching what they're getting up to, where they can try and scare younger kids. Pretend to be ghost hunting and such. We were worried that even though people are obviously living here again, some troublemakers were still at it."

Simmonds's piercing green eyes moved to me. Mattie had, ever so stealthily, wiggled himself across the floor, as slowly and steadily as his bulk would allow. He now sat at her side, alert and delighted.

If Simmonds decided to wrestle me to the ground, clap me in handcuffs, and drag me off to spend the rest of my life in prison, Mattie would assist in holding me down.

*Traitor.*

"How long were you outside before Vicky and Merry joined you?" she asked Mark.

"I can't say for sure. Couple of minutes."

It was at least ten minutes. More like fifteen or twenty. I said nothing and neither did Vicky.

"Walk me though what happened in those *couple of minutes* you were outside alone."

"I had a flashlight. I wanted to be sure no one was lurking. I took one of my chef's knives, just in case. I did not use it."

"A knife was found at the scene. Was that yours?"

"Yes." Mark nodded toward the wooden knife block on the far counter. "As you can see, one is missing. And only one."

"It's been bagged and taken away for analysis," Simmonds said. "Please continue."

"Like Merry said, kids think this is the local haunted house." Mark said. "They treated it—they used to treat it—like it's something at Disney World. I didn't see anyone tonight. I didn't hear anything. We're close to town but isolated here at the end of the street, at the end of a long driveway, the house surrounded by all these trees. I turned right when I came out of the house, going north, and I walked around the property. I made no attempt to be quiet about it. I took my time, checking under bushes, looking for sagging eaves troughs, branches sturdy enough to support a person growing too close to the windows, or a spot where someone might have snapped twigs or branches trying to get near the house."

"Did you see anything like that?"

"No. Not at the northern side or around the back. It hasn't rained for several days, so the ground is hard. Meaning nothing to see in the way of footprints. When I got to the southern side of the house, I spotted something on the ground near the fountain, and I hurried straight toward it, without searching anymore. I couldn't quite make it out in the dark, but it looked big. I hoped it wasn't a deer or a dog who'd come here after being injured. When I got closer and shone my light directly on it, I realized it was a person. My first thought was a drunk who'd collapsed under a tree. He was lying face down, and I leaned over him and gave him a nudge with my foot. Then I saw that the back of his head was bashed in. The blood. I turned him over, thinking I should give CPR or something. I realized right away it was too late." He lifted his clean hands. "That would be how I got the blood on me. Then I phoned Vicky and told her to call 911. That's it. That's all I can say."

"Mark was with the body when you and Merry reached him?" Simmonds asked Vicky.

She nodded.

The detective stood up. Mattie also got to his feet. "Thank you," she said. "That will be all for now. I need to get back outside and check out the scene in more detail. Before I go, one more question. How worried, Mark, were you about legal problems Jim Cole might cause you?"

He looked directly into her face. "Not at all worried. The late Miss Cole's lawyer assured me Jim didn't have a case, and even if he did have some nebulous rights of inheritance, we'd paid for this house and taken possession. All fair and square."

"He might not have graciously accepted that. You believed someone could be trying to break into your house. To deliberately frighten your fiancée. Did you take steps to stop him?"

Mark took a step forward. His body bristled with tension, and his fists were clenched at his sides. The uniformed cop who'd been leaning against the wall, not paying a lot of attention, straightened. Diane Simmonds simply raised one eyebrow. Mark took a breath, forcing himself to relax. "I did not. It all happened the way I told you. I was checking the property, *my* property, before turning in. I heard nothing, I saw nothing until I almost tripped over him. I tried to help, which is how I got his blood on me. I hope you're not going to use that against me."

"I'll be in touch," Simmonds said. "In the meantime, we need full access to this house and the property. You'll have to spend the night elsewhere."

Mark bristled. "We will not. I can't knock on a friend's door and ask for refuge at this time of night. The idea's ridiculous. Besides, nothing happened in the house. The man died outside."

"So it would appear," she said. "But initial appearances are not always correct. You yourselves told me you suspected someone might have been in the house tonight."

"I—"

"We'll find someplace to stay," Vicky said. "No problem. Right, honey?"

"Okay," Mark said.

"Matterhorn, you go with Merry," Detective Simmonds said. "You can meet Alan Anderson outside."

# Chapter Ten

Mark muttered and cursed as he and Vicky were escorted out of their own house without even being allowed to get their toothbrushes, pajamas, or a change of clothes. Sandbanks was roused from sleep, and he and I, along with Mattie, left the house with my friends.

Alan stood in the driveway, watching the activity. More cruisers had arrived, along with a couple of vans I knew to be forensic vehicles. The sirens had been switched off, but blue and red lights continued to illuminate the night, and more powerful lights were being carried around the side of the house.

Alan turned when he heard our footsteps on the stairs. His eyes briefly passed over Mark and Vicky and settled on me. I gave him a tight smile and a nod, to say everything was fine. For now. Mattie hurried to greet him, and Alan leaned over to give the big dog a hearty slap on the side. Dog duties over, he gathered me into a hug and kissed the top of my head.

"All okay?" he asked Mark when he'd released me.

"No," Mark grumbled.

"Okay for now," Vicky said. "We've been kicked out of our house, and we need a lift. We can't even take our cars."

"Happy to help. I parked on the street. Merry?"

"Mattie and I walked over. Do you want to come to my place?" I asked Vicky as we started walking down the long driveway. I had one bed and one couch. Hard to fit in four adults and three dogs, but for one night I figured we could try it. Unlikely any of us would be getting much sleep tonight—other than Mattie and Sandbanks. Dogs can always sleep as soon as the immediate danger has passed.

Must be nice.

"We'll go to the inn," Mark said. "They're probably not full midweek at this time of year."

Alan used his truck for transporting materials to make furniture and delivering the finished product to his customers. It was a big vehicle, which is what we needed tonight. Ranger, Alan's overly active Jack Russell, stood on the front passenger seat, scratching at the window in his enthusiasm to greet us.

We all clambered into the truck. Mark had to heft Sandbanks up and shove him into the back seat. I encouraged Mattie to follow while Ranger hopped between the front seats, and the three dogs greeted one another with great joy, falling all over themselves in their eagerness to sniff nether regions and catch up on one another's news.

Mark made a quick phone call while Vicky and I stuffed ourselves into the back seats of the truck, tails slapping our faces. We wiggled around so Mattie sat between us, Sandbanks was on Vicky's lap, and Ranger bounded from one side of the vehicle to the other, trying to see everything everywhere. And all at once. It was a battle to get seat belts fastened, but finally we succeeded.

Mark twisted around as Alan started the truck. "They've got a room for us at the inn. Looking on the bright side, I can sleep in tomorrow, as I don't have to drive to work."

"Anything I can help with?" Alan said. "Although I have absolutely no idea what's going on except there's a heck of a lot of activity happening at your place."

He pulled into the street. Lights were on in neighboring houses, occupants attracted by the colorful flashing lights and sirens. People stood at windows, looking out, and some had gathered on their front steps or lawn to enjoy the action.

"Not how I wanted to get to know the neighbors," Vicky said. "I was thinking more along the lines of inviting them over for tea and scones."

Mark answered Alan. "Some guy wandered onto our property, laid himself down, and died. The cops think I had something to do with it. Vic, from now on we keep that gate shut and locked at night."

Vicky and I exchanged a look over the heads of the dogs. Obviously, that was not what had happened, and closing the gate wouldn't stop a determined intruder such as Jim Cole. If Mark wanted to play tonight's events down, that might work for the rest of the night, but he'd have to face more police questioning in the morning. I thought about what I'd seen. Jim Cole had blood on the back of his head, and some of that blood had gotten onto Mark's hands and shirt. As would have happened to anyone who found an apparently unconscious person and tried to help them. I hadn't seen the body before Mark turned it over. Was it possible the man tripped and fell, and hit the back of his head on a rock or stone? Unlikely, if he landed face down, as Mark had said. In that case the injury would have been to the back of his head. Unless Jim Cole had sustained some degree of consciousness and managed to roll himself over before passing out. But wasn't it highly unlikely someone in danger would roll themselves onto their front?

Mattie attempted to jump to his feet. I got a mouthful of tail before settling him down again.

Alan asked Mark if he'd caught last night's hockey game, and Mark launched into a recitation of the disappointing mistakes and general faults of his favorite team. Vicky sat quietly, stroking Sandbanks's ears, gazing out the window as we drove out of town and hit the highway.

A few minutes later, Alan slowed and turned into the driveway of the Yuletide Inn. Lights shone above the welcoming entrance and from some of the rooms. The enormous planters on either side of the front doors were decorated for Easter with plaster bunnies and pink and blue eggs the size of footballs. White fairy lights were strung between trees and wound through hedges in the gardens on the other side of the driveway. The formal gardens at the inn were one of the highlights of Rudolph, and part of the reason the inn could charge as much for a night's stay as it did. The hotel restaurant, where Mark was the head chef, was another highlight of Rudolph and another reason for the rates.

"That reminds me," I said. "The hospital fundraising committee's spring garden event is on Saturday. My mother has invited us, Vicky. Meaning, it's a command performance, for me anyway. Are you able to come? Tour of the gardens under the guidance of the head gardener and then lunch."

"Must I?"

"I'm sure it won't be too bad."

"Not if I'm cooking for it," Mark said. "And I am. Cream of asparagus soup, choice of spring lamb with mint sauce or ratatouille for a vegetarian option. Accompanied by a salad of baby greens and hothouse heirloom cherry tomatoes. Followed by a fruit tart and vanilla cupcakes decorated to look like flowers."

"Can I come?" Alan said.

"I'll steal you a tart," I said.

Alan pulled up to the front steps. All was quiet. Inside the hotel, a young man stood behind the reception desk, but no one else was around. It was after midnight, and the kitchen and bar were closed for the night.

Mark lifted Sandbanks off Vicky's lap and placed him on the ground. Vicky climbed out of the truck, and I also got out after shoving Ranger off my lap and struggling to stop him jumping out of the truck.

I gave Vicky a hug. "You take care. Anything happens in the night, call us."

"Thanks." The smile she gave me was feeble, and I could see the worry in her eyes. The fallout from tonight's events was still to come, and both of us knew it might not be simple or easy.

* * *

Friday morning, I opened Mrs. Claus's Treasures at the regular time of nine thirty. Alan and Ranger had spent the night at my place. We hadn't heard from Vicky or from the police, which I decided was a good thing.

As we'd curled up on the couch, with mugs of hot chocolate and dogs snoozing at our feet, I told Alan in detail all that had happened. As is his way, he sipped his drink, said nothing until I finished, and took in every word.

"You think this Jim Cole was trying to frighten Vicky and Matt? And it was him at the house on those other occasions?" he asked.

"I can't think who else it would have been. He confronted Vicky on the street. He was found on the property when he had absolutely no reason to be there. No doubt about that."

"There's something you're not saying, Merry, and I think I know what it is. Mark went outside to search, and you and Vicky did the same inside. You're not telling me how much time passed while you were separated, so I'm guessing it was sufficient for him to, shall we say, confront Jim Cole."

"Mark didn't kill him," I said.

"I know that. You know that. Doesn't mean the police know that."

"What are you saying, Alan?"

"I'm saying Mark might find himself in some trouble," Alan had replied. "Which means Vicky will need you, Merry. Which means you'll need me. So I'll be here."

I looked around the store now, making sure everything was in place. The front window display was of pictures of vast fields of tulips behind green and lilac table settings. A small rack held spring- or Easter-themed books for young children, and a stuffed rabbit sat at a child-sized picnic table, reading a book. We were, of course, primarily a Christmas-themed store in a Christmas-themed town, so a stuffed Rudolph the Red Nose Reindeer kept the bunny company.

We had no customers before ten, when Jackie came in to start her shift. I'd slept in late, and then Alan and I had taken the dogs for a short walk before enjoying a comfortable breakfast of bagels and cream cheese. We had not talked about "the case", and I'd not heard from Vicky.

While waiting for customers to beat down my doors, I checked the online news and social media to see if there were any updates. The police issued a statement about a "suspicious death" at a Rudolph residence but said nothing about precisely where that death had occurred. Which didn't matter, as the neighbors had witnessed the screaming arrival of emergency vehicles, and they'd be eager to spread the word far and wide. A thought suddenly occurred to me. The tragic history of Cole House was sure to fan the flames of gossip. Two of Charles Cole's daughters had died on the grounds; and the fiancé of the third, in the house. And now, all these years later, the same happened to Charles's nephew.

I couldn't help the thought bubbling to the surface: *Is Cole House cursed?*

Of course not, I scolded myself. No such thing as curses or hauntings or other such rubbish. Besides, Vicky and Mark were not members of the Cole family. So they'd be safe. *Wouldn't they?*

"There's been a murder in Rudolph," Jackie said brightly. "On Lakeside Drive. Isn't that where Vicky and Mark bought that house? Kyle's heading over there now, to try to get some pictures of the activity for the paper." Kyle was Jackie's boyfriend. He'd originally tried to make a living as an artist but had soon given that up as he had no training, no talent, and no ambition. He then set his sights on becoming a professional photographer, at which he also had no training, no talent, and even less ambition. He snapped the occasional picture he sold to the *Rudolph Gazette* if Russ Durham wasn't available. In Kyle's eyes, that made him a newspaper photographer. In Jackie's eyes, it gave her bragging rights.

In Russ Durham's eyes, Kyle's photographs were better than nothing. Which is what they'd get if Russ wasn't available now that the paper no longer had a full-time staff photographer.

"What do you know about it?" Jackie said. "Did you talk to Vicky today? What does she have to say? Did she see anything last night?"

"I haven't spoken to Vicky this morning," I said in total honesty. "As it happens, I'm about to. I'm expecting a fairly quiet morning, so I'm going to pop over to the bakery. Want anything?"

"Sure. If you're paying, I'll have an extra-large, double-sugar, caramel macchiato with plenty of whipped cream on top and one of those giant breakfast bars. The ones with the chocolate chips."

I left the store, cursing people who could eat whatever they wanted and never put on weight.

At Victoria's Bake Shoppe the breakfast crowd had left, and the lunch bunch were still to arrive. Only two tables were occupied, and one lone customer waited at the counter for his take-out coffee.

"Morning," I said to Marjorie, waitress and barista as well as Vicky's aunt. "Is she in?"

Marjorie jerked her head toward the back as she handed the customer his drink. Before I could take more than one step, she rounded the counter and intercepted me. She kept her voice low. "What's happening Merry? I heard someone was found dead at Vicky's place last night."

"Yeah, that happened. We don't know anything yet. That is, *I* don't know anything. Is Vicky okay?"

"No, she is not. She pretends she is, but it's easy enough to tell she's upset about it. I suppose anyone would be at such a thing happening, but rumor is it's Jim Cole. Nephew of Charles and Ethel."

I nodded. No point in denying it. The Rudolph grapevine was a highly efficient organization.

"What was he doing there?" Marjorie asked.

"I don't know. No one seems to know."

"Strange family, that one. Comes from all those deaths happening in the house, I suppose. Although in the old days most people died at home. Children from diseases and accidents, the elderly in peace with their loved ones around them." She sighed. "But the tragedies of the Cole family weren't all that long ago. Charles and Ethel's daughters died in . . . let me think. Must be the fifties, sixties maybe? Before my time, but my mother remembers them. I do remember when Emmeline's fiancé died. Early 1980s that was. She'd brought him home to celebrate Christmas with her and then . . . Everyone was pretty upset about it. Plenty of people in town are remembering the tragic history of the Coles now that the house is going to be lived in again."

"Do any members of the Cole family still live around here?" I asked.

"Oh yes. Jim doesn't . . . didn't, but his daughter lives in Rudolph. I can't remember her name offhand. She's married, so it's not Cole any longer."

"Merry," came a voice from the kitchen, "if you're finished gossiping about me, I'm in here."

Marjorie and I exchanged guilty looks, and I went into the kitchen. Vicky's assistant, Janelle, was chopping a mound of vegetables, her knife flashing. Two giant soup pots bubbled on the stove, and the scent of something very delicious wafted out of the oven. Cupcakes were cooling on a rack on the counter prior to being iced, and a tray held gingerbread cookies cut to resemble rabbits. Vicky's gingerbread was a Rudolph tradition. Hearts for Valentine's Day, bunnies for Easter, Santa in his bathing suit in the summer, ghosts for Hallowe'en, turkeys and cornucopias at Thanksgiving, and most important of all, reindeer, decorated trees, and various -sized ginger people for Christmas.

"Everything okay?" I asked her.

"Not really. Can you manage here for a few minutes if I take a break, Janelle?"

"All under control."

"Give the soup a good stir every few minutes. When the oven timer beeps, check the cookies, and take them out if they're done."

"You got it," Janelle said.

Vicky took off her apron and pulled off her hairnet. The lock of pink hair drooped over her right eye. She grabbed a sweater and, without a word, left the kitchen via the rear door. I followed and we stepped into the alley. It was a nice spring day. Brilliantly sunny with a decided nip in the air and a strong, cool wind blowing. We stood together on the back step. A well-maintained brick walkway ran alongside the bakery, between it and the police station and town hall. Come May, beds of colorful annuals would be planted to give the path a touch of welcome cheer.

I wrapped my arms around myself against the chill wind and said nothing. Vicky looked across the parking lot toward the police station. "Mark's been hauled in for questioning," she said at last.

With relief I noticed she said *questioning*, not *arrested*. "That's natural enough, isn't it? He did find a body. The police will have uncovered further evidence during their search of the site and have more questions."

"I suppose so. I don't like it."

"Of course you don't. Did he say anything more last night after we dropped you off?"

"No. He didn't want to talk about it. He was pretty angry, but he tried to keep it to himself."

"That rarely works out well."

"Don't I know it. He was mad at Jim Cole for threatening us, for trying to scare us, for creeping around our house. And then later, he was mad at Jim Cole for dying and making it our problem. I hope he can control that anger in front of Diane Simmonds."

"Does he have a temper?" I asked. "Mark?"

"Not really. Probably less of a temper than a lot of chefs, which is why he gets on well with his staff. Buying the house has been stressful. Stressful for us both, but him in particular. Plenty of people told him he was nuts to buy Cole House."

I said nothing, and Vicky turned and grinned at me. "People like you."

"I never said—"

"I know you didn't. But you thought it, right?"

"Getting it into a reasonable sort of shape is going to be a heck of a big job."

"Mark loves old houses. Big rooms, fireplaces, high ceilings, ornate plasterwork. He's always wanted a grand old house on a big property with a lawn and lots of trees, room for a huge kitchen garden. Seems kind of odd for a kid from Manhattan who grew up in an apartment, but maybe that's it. He dreamt of having the space, the freedom to roam on his own land. The only way anyone can afford a house like that is to be rich or to buy one that's going cheap because it's falling down."

"And you're okay with that?" I asked. Her love for Mark clearly meant his dream had become her dream, but that sometimes has a way of not lasting, not once the reality of the situation settles in.

"Sure," she said with an excess of enthusiasm that rang slightly false to me. "My family's been in Rudolph as long as your dad's has. I'm excited about owning a part of Rudolph history. The house itself, I mean. Memories of the great place Rudolph had once been and is again, not the tragic story of one family. We'll fix it up, and then if we decide the house is too big for us and the yard too much to maintain, we'll be able to sell it for a good profit."

"Practical of you," I said.

"Yeah. But first, we have to get rid of this cloud hanging over our heads so we can get on with our lives. We might have to postpone the wedding."

"Don't be too hasty. The police might be able to wrap this one up quickly."

"I hope. That looks like him now. Yes, it's Mark."

Vicky pointed, and I followed the direction of her finger. Mark Grosse had come out of the police station. He stood at the top of the steps, facing back into the building. He waved his arms in the air, shouted something we didn't catch, and then turned and stomped down the steps. His body was stiff with tension and anger, his face as dark as a thundercloud.

I looked past him to see Detective Diane Simmonds standing in the doorway, watching him walk across the parking lot toward his car. Her face showed no expression, but I didn't care for the way she kept her eyes focused on Mark.

He looked toward us suddenly and saw us watching. His face cracked into a smile so forced it did nothing to make me feel any better. He lifted one hand in a delusory cheerful wave and used the other to press the button on his car fob. He got in and drove away. He did not look at Vicky as he passed us.

"I have the feeling that didn't go all that well," Vicky said.

"He didn't look happy," I agreed.

"He'll be heading back to the hotel. I'll give him time to get there and then give him a call."

"Simmonds is leaving the station," I said to Vicky. "I wonder where she's going. New evidence has come in maybe. Oops, she's not heading for a car. She's coming this way."

Indeed she was. She headed directly toward us. She must have been up most of the night, if not all night, but she looked fresh and bouncy this morning. Her green eyes were clear, her red curls neatly gathered at the back of her head. She'd changed into loose-fitting gray pants with a matching jacket over a light green blouse. Tiny gold hoops were in her ears.

"Good morning," she said.

"I hope you've come to tell us an arrest has been made in the murder of Jim Cole," I said.

"Unfortunately, I can't do that. I was about to give you a call, Vicky, when I saw you here. I need you to come in and have a chat about events of last night."

"I told you what happened," Vicky said.

"Yes, you did. Last night. Details are often remembered later, and things initially considered unimportant are reconsidered."

"When can I go back to my house?"

"Possibly this evening, although you'll have to stay away from that portion of the yard for a while still. I'll let you know. Shall we go?"

"I have work to do," Vicky said. "It'll be lunchtime soon, and my assistant can't manage on her own."

"You close at three, correct?"

"Yes, we do."

"Come and see me then. In the meantime, Merry, I'll get your statement."

"I have my own business to run," I said.

"You managed to find the time to come here, to have a chat with Vicky. Therefore, you can chat with me."

I glanced at Vicky. The corners of her mouth turned up, but she said nothing.

"Might as well get it over with," I said.

# Chapter Eleven

I had nothing new to tell Diane Simmonds, and she had little to tell me. We went to an interview room in the police station, and she asked someone to bring me a glass of water. I was pleased she took me to the nice interview room, the one with a comfortable couch, complete with cushions, a low coffee table to rest the water glass on, and a picture of the park at dusk on the wall. Not the not-nice interview room, which was all about intimidating suspected criminals.

She asked me to once again go over everything that happened last night, and to tell her more about when Vicky and I encountered Jim Cole on the street. She had questions about Mark I didn't care for. Such as how angry he'd been when he went outside to search the property and his state of mind when we found him next to Jim Cole's body.

"Annoyed, not really angry," I said. "And upset, as anyone would be."

"In our search we found clear signs of someone seeking ingress to the house," she said. "Scratching around the kitchen and back doors mostly. Some clumsy attempts had been made to pry plywood off the downstairs windows."

"Was that from last night?"

"Recent. Meaning at least since the winter, but impossible to determine precisely when it happened."

So Vicky and Mark hadn't been imagining things. Not that I'd thought they were. I didn't know about Mark, but Vicky most definitely didn't do "imagining."

"Have any other people in that neighborhood reported disturbances?" I asked.

"No. But I have to point out that Vicky and Mark didn't report any either. It's far too easy to dismiss sounds in the night, particularly in a heavily treed area. Deer and other animals cross those lots to access the lake in the evenings. We found something else that might prove to be of interest. Jim Cole's phone was in his pocket. On it were pictures of the house—Mark and Vicky's house. Taken at night, and showing the house and the property not in its best light."

"Meaning?"

"Pictures of graffiti on the boards over the back windows. The broken lamps at the front gate. Weeds and overgrown statues. The dead rose bushes. Close-ups of paint stripping off the window frames."

"Any pictures taken from inside the house?"

"Not that I saw. But I haven't looked at them all. Not yet."

"When were these pictures taken?"

"The phone's been sent to the techies for analysis. I want to know if he's been on the property other times than last night." She stood up and said, "Thank you, Merry. I'll show you out."

Detective Simmonds walked me to the lobby. She held the inner door open for me. As I passed through, heading for freedom, she said, "I'm asking you to keep yourself out of this,

Merry. Scratch that. I'm *ordering* you to keep yourself out of this."

"Isn't it too late?" I said. "I'm obviously involved, or you wouldn't have had me in for a pleasant chat."

"You know what I mean. No involving yourself in my investigation."

I said nothing. I've always liked Diane Simmonds. I believe she likes me. I've been introduced to her daughter and her mother. She and Charlotte, her daughter, have shopped for gifts in my store. My dog literally worships her. I've been of help to her in past cases, although she rarely admitted it. And even more rarely thanked me for it, even when I've put myself in danger. I liked her, but I was well aware she was a cop first and foremost. No vague concept of friendship would be allowed to come between her and her primary goal of bringing the killer of Jim Cole to justice. She knew how close Vicky and I are, and because of that, how close I am to Mark. She was warning me off doing what I could to help Mark.

And that had me worried.

I considered returning to the bakery to tell Vicky what had been said, but I decided not to. First, I had to sort out my thoughts. Obviously the police have a lot of different angles to pursue regarding cases like this, and Diane Simmonds has never been one to tell me anything she didn't think I needed to know. If she had a strong suspect other than Mark, she wouldn't be likely to tell me.

Simmonds had ordered me not to get involved. She didn't have the power to do any such thing. She might as well order the populace of Rudolph not to eat gingerbread over the holiday season, or not to gossip.

When I walked into Mrs. Claus's Treasures, Jackie was ringing up a set of holly-trimmed serving dishes for a customer, and two women were admiring the North Pole Village display. The latter had been handcrafted out of wood by Alan himself. A full Santa's village with a house for the big guy himself and Mrs. Claus, toy-making sheds, elves' accommodations, barns for the reindeer, a garage for Santa's sled—even trains and tracks to run between the buildings. The full set was large, and it was expensive, but it was specifically designed so pieces could be purchased individually and then added on over the years as further gifts or to hand the toy on to a younger child. They'd proven to be hugely popular.

"It seems early to be buying holiday gifts," one of the customers said to the other.

"If you don't get that now, you'll be sorry," her friend said, expressing a sentiment I like to hear. "You might not be able to find anything so nice later at other places."

"I'm glad you like those," I said. "They're handmade by an artisan who lives and works a few miles from here. He makes each piece specifically for this store and others in the area, and delivers each set personally."

"That's good to know. I always like to support local businesses whenever I can. I'll take the house and the barn, please. And some of the train tracks. My grandson will be four by Christmas, and he'll adore them."

I took two boxes off the shelf and put them on the sales counter while the women continued browsing. The friend bought several pieces of jewelry, and the toy buyer got a lovely spring-weight silk scarf in swirling shades of green and pink for herself.

"Good choice," Jackie said. "I adore these scarves. I brought one for my mom's birthday last summer, and she simply never takes it off."

That was true. Except for the "bought" part. Jackie had exclaimed so often about how much her mother would love the scarf, always adding too bad it was so expensive. Sigh. I ended up gifting it to her to keep her happy. Jackie was a good employee, and I needed to keep her happy.

"I'll be in the office if you need anything," I said to her once our customers had left.

"I never do," she replied.

Mattie was stretched out on the floor beneath my desk. His water bowl was empty and the carpet around it sodden. He lumbered to his feet when I came in and gave my shoes a good sniff, the equivalent of asking if I'd had a nice morning. I had not, but I didn't tell him so. Instead, I dropped into the chair behind my desk, pulled out my phone, and called Vicky.

"Is this your one allotted phone call?" she asked me.

"Fortunately not. I'm free and at the store. I'm just checking in."

"How'd it go?"

"She didn't tell me much, and I didn't have anything new to tell her. But . . ."

"I never like it when you say *but* that way. But what?"

"Most of her questions were about Mark. Like how angry was he when you told him someone had been prowling around outside."

"Did you say *prowling*?"

"I think I did. She tried to nail me down as to how much time passed since Mark went outside to check and when he called you to say he'd found Jim Cole. I refused to be nailed, largely because I genuinely can't say."

"That sentence ends with an unsaid *but*."

"But enough time did pass for Mark to . . . do something."

"Surely you don't believe he killed that man!" She kept her voice low, but the shout was implied.

"Calm down. Of course I don't. I fear Simmonds is considering it—that's all. So I'm giving you a heads-up." I didn't believe Mark had killed Jim. Not because I knew Mark all that well—I don't—or because I know for sure what he's capable of doing or not doing. But I was sure if he had struck Jim Cole, it hadn't been with the intent to kill him, and he would not have lied about what happened.

"Okay," Vicky said. "I just got off the phone with Mark. Did Simmonds tell you they found the likely murder weapon?"

"No, she didn't."

"Not one of our knives, thank heavens. She showed Mark a photograph of a rock. They found a rock, a common rock, under a tree within easy throwing distance of the body. Traces of blood and . . . other stuff, indicate it was likely the rock that hit Cole over the head. They're doing further analysis now. She also told Mark they might not be able to get fingerprints off it. Sometimes it's difficult to do on such rough surfaces."

That cinched Mark's innocence, in my mind. Mark was a big guy. He worked out regularly and was heavily muscled from swinging a cleaver and wrestling with heavy pots all day. He was in his thirties. Jim Cole had been short, overweight, and a great deal older. If Mark had wanted to scare off Jim with a physical attack, one good solid punch to the jaw would have had the man on the ground. He would not have snuck up behind Jim with a rock he just happened to pick up off the ground.

I reminded myself that whatever I thought about anyone's guilt or innocence was worth literally nothing to the police or the courts.

"She also told Mark they found signs of someone trying to break into the house."

"Yeah. She told me that too. If he'd been at your place other nights, someone might have known that. And either followed him there or lain in wait for him to show up."

"I'm scared," Vicky said.

"Simmonds is a good detective. You know that. She'll get at the truth."

"Maybe. Maybe not. Miscarriages of justice do happen, Merry. Suppose she never does find out who did it. Will suspicion hang over Mark for the rest of his life? People are talking about little else. The staff tell me a couple of customers have asked if Mark or I mistook Jim Cole for an intruder. Aunt Marjorie got a call from a friend saying she knows someone who said she'd never come in here again. I quote: 'That Vicky Casey never did have a lick of sense, and now she's going around stirring up ghosts best left to rest.'"

"Not good," I said. "Leave it with me."

"Leave what with you?"

"Investigating, of course. I'll find out what I can about Jim Cole. Maybe he had enemies lining up, waiting for the chance to catch him off guard. Maybe there's rumors of treasure hidden under your floorboards, and someone's after it."

"If there had been rumors of treasure in that house, Merry, everyone in Rudolph would know about it."

"Work with me here, Vicky. All I'm saying is I'll try."

"Thanks. That's good of you. If you come up with anything, let me know. Barring any unexpected developments, I'll come with you tomorrow."

"What's happening tomorrow?"

"The luncheon at the Yuletide. The hospital was so great to my dad when he had his heart attack, I want to do what I can to give back."

"Oh, right. That. Okay. I'll be in touch."

I hung up. I looked at Mattie. I sighed. "I'll do what I can do, okay? Wait here—I'll be right back."

I went to the front of the shop and told Jackie I was going out for a while, but I wouldn't be long.

"Investigating the Cole murder, are you?" she said. "Don't worry about a thing, Merry. I've got your back."

"I'm not investigating anything. I . . . have to go home for . . . something I forgot."

She gave me an exaggerated wink. "Right. Oh, when you do solve it, if you have a chance, can you call Kyle before calling the cops? If he can be there for the takedown and get a good shot of the action and the face of the killer, it would be a big boost to his portfolio."

"Yeah, sure. I can do that." An image flashed across my mind. Me holding a miscreant at knifepoint while I phoned Kyle Lambert, waited for him to find his camera and car keys, get his old truck started (if it did), drive far too fast to the scene of the citizen's arrest, fumble with his camera, set all the correct settings, and line up the shot, hopefully without forgetting to take the lens cap off.

I went to the office to get Mattie. As long as I was going out, he could use the walk. We were heading to the source of all gossip in Rudolph and environs: my house.

Like Shelob in her cave, my landlady, Mabel D'Angelo lurks at the center of the web of gossip that stretches throughout this part of Upstate New York. Mrs. D'Angelo lives for gossip. She isn't entirely reliable because if she doesn't know something, she doesn't like to admit it, so she makes things up. I hoped she wouldn't need to embellish the story of Cole House and the Cole family. If I wanted to know why Jim Cole died, a good starting place would be to learn what I could about his life.

I wasn't at all worried about not finding Mrs. D'Angelo in or unable to take the time to talk. Our house is the nicest kept on our stretch of the street. Not necessarily because the owner enjoys gardening, but because when she's outside, she can keep her eyes on the comings and goings. I found her on her knees next to a flower bed, carefully pulling burgeoning weeds away from the first fresh green shoots of hosta.

The moment she saw us coming down the sidewalk, she leaped to her feet with surprising agility, considering her age. "Merry Wilkinson! The very person I've been wanting to talk to. The entire town is abuzz about last night's happenings at Vicky Casey's new place. Time for tea? Good! I happen to have a pitcher in the fridge. It's a mite chilly for sitting outside today, but my porch blocks the wind. Come along, come along." Mattie and I were dragged in Mrs. D'Angelo's wake by the sheer force of her enthusiasm. "You sit right there. Don't move. I'll get the tea and be right back."

So far, I hadn't had to say a single word. I unhooked Mattie's leash before settling onto a porch chair. He knew we were home, and he wouldn't go far. He wandered off to check for squirrel activity under the trees. Mrs. D'Angelo was back in a flash. She'd perfected the art of getting the refreshments in record time before her victim, aka visitor, had time to recover and make their escape.

She dropped the tray onto the table. Her eyes gleamed with anticipation. She usually brought something for Mattie, and today was no exception. Having no luck finding squirrels to play with, he wandered onto the porch and politely accepted a dog biscuit. He gobbled up the treat and then settled himself at the top of the stairs, his chin between his paws, watching the activity on the street with almost as much concentration as Mrs. D'Angelo herself.

My landlady enjoyed spreading gossip as much as she did receiving it, so I didn't have any trouble getting her to talk. "Alfredia Cunningham—you know Alfredia of course." I didn't, but that never mattered. "Dear Alfredia—too bad about that incident with the priest, but never mind that now—lives on Lakeside Drive. She says the police presence near her house last night was massive. Good thing nothing else went amiss last night in Rudolph, or there would have been no one to take the call. The police got there at the same time as an ambulance. The ambulance didn't leave immediately, but more police continued to arrive, so Alfredia concluded someone was dead, and no need to rush them to the hospital. Then the detective herself showed up. Not long after that Alan Anderson arrived, but the officer guarding the gate wouldn't let him drive onto the premises, so he had to park his truck and walk in. And then, much to her surprise, you appeared, coming out of the property. With Vicky Casey herself and Mark Grosse and a pack of dogs, and you all got in Alan's truck and drove away." She beamed at me. Two dogs didn't constitute a pack, but I allowed her the literary license.

"All true," I said. "You realize, of course, I can't discuss confidential police matters."

"Of course, of course." She waved that trifle away. "My friend, whose daughter's a clerk at the police station—I will reveal no names—said it was none other than Jim Cole who'd been murdered."

It came as no surprise to me to discover that Mrs. D'Angelo's network of gossips had an inside source in the police station.

Unlikely it would come as a surprise to Detective Simmonds or the chief himself. "I don't think they've said if it was murder yet."

"They will. Soon enough. No one I've spoken to has any idea what Jim Cole would have been doing at that house last night." She smiled at me, expecting me to fill in the missing details.

Which I couldn't even if I wanted to. "That," I said, "is the mystery. Can you tell me anything about Cole House?"

"It's all such a tragedy. A once-impressive mansion reduced to little more than rubble. A once-great family suffering nothing but early death and heartbreak." She paused momentarily, emitting a heavy sigh to ensure I was aware of the importance of what she was about to relate. Vicky and Mark's house wasn't little more than rubble, and Emmeline Cole had lived into her seventies, which I wouldn't call an early death. I said nothing.

"Jim Cole hasn't visited that house in close to half a century, according to Alfredia, who would know. Over all the long years since Emmeline fled in the early hours one long-ago Christmas morning, never to return, he never once stopped by check up on the place. That was left to Emmeline's lawyer. The elder Mr. Casey, and then young Tom when his father retired."

She settled back in her chair. "As for the house itself, nothing but tragedy upon tragedy." The story she related was much the same as I'd heard from Dad. The deaths of Emmeline's two sisters. The death of Emmeline's fiancé. How the grieving Emmeline boarded up the house and moved away permanently, to live the life of a recluse, whereupon the house slowly fell into decay, becoming the stuff of legend at Rudolph High.

"Emmeline's father, Charles, had a brother didn't he?" I asked. "Jim's the son of this brother. Why didn't they move into the house if Emmeline didn't want it but didn't want to sell it?"

"Robert was the brother's name. He left Rudolph several years before Emmeline did. He and his family, of which Jim was his only child. Offhand, I can't recall where they went. People come and go all the time these days, don't they? There was substantially more going than coming in the years before the town's renewed prosperity. I'm delighted that some of the descendants of the old families are returning. Tired of the big cities, most likely, where everyone thinks they're entitled to get involved in other people's business."

Mrs. D'Angelo scowled in disapproval at the very idea. I choked on a mouthful of tea.

"Are you all right, dear?"

"Fine. Perfectly fine. Tea went down the wrong way."

"If you're sure. No one knows why Robert didn't come back and take over the house. Perhaps he or his wife didn't want to live in Rudolph. Maybe Emmeline didn't want them to have it. The house belonged to her remember, even after she ceased to live there. Ties in that family in those years were not strong. Henry Cole married twice. Robert was considerably younger than the children by his first wife. Robert's own son, Jim, was a good generation younger than his first cousin, Emmeline. They had little in common."

So far I'd learned nothing new. Perhaps Mrs. D'Angelo wasn't going to be a font of knowledge after all. "What did Jim do for a living?"

Her eyes gleamed, and my heart soared.

"Very little." She leaned across the table toward me. "Robert didn't inherit the house on his father's death, naturally the family home went to Charles, the elder son. But Henry was a wealthy man and Robert inherited a substantial sum."

"There were two daughters also, weren't there? Are they still around?"

"Henry did have two girls by his first wife. They, far as I know, married and moved away. I can try and find out more about them, if you're interested?"

"I am."

"Consider it done. Anyway, back to the point, Robert inherited money as well as interests in his father's businesses. Charles got the house and control of the business. Robert cut his ties almost immediately with the family company. Sold all of his shares. The company lost money steadily almost from that point on. Meaning, in later years Robert was considerably better off than Charles. Robert used his proceeds to invest widely and wisely, whereas Charles was left with a too-big house and a struggling company. Charles died sometime in the 1960s. The first daughter predeceased him, and he left his wife, Ethel, and two surviving daughters without much more than the property. Ethel was content to remain in the house for the remainder of her years. She was from Muddle Harbor, so what would you expect?"

I wasn't entirely sure what Muddle Harbor had to do with not selling the family home in Rudolph, but never mind that now. "Jim Cole?"

"Oh yes. Robert was considerably well off, as I might have mentioned, so his only child, young Jim, didn't have to do much of anything in the way of earning a living. I believe he has a law degree but he never practiced. That is to say he never practiced as a lawyer. He practices law a great deal."

"Huh?"

"Jim spends much of his time instigating frivolous lawsuits. Now, I must confess Merry, some of this news came to me only recently. Karen Ogdensburg lives next door to Cindy Farrar and Cindy filled her in. Cindy and her father never had a relationship when she was a child, but she's trying to build one now, but it's not easy for her considering Jim's proclivities. Was trying to build one, I suppose I should say. Poor girl. Nothing but tragedy in that family."

My brain hurt. I didn't know Karen or Cindy or what they had to do with anything, and I was having trouble sorting out Mrs. D'Angelo's maze of pronouns to figure out who had fallen out with whom. Cindy, I guessed, was Jim's daughter. Marjorie had mentioned she lived in Rudolph. I decided to worry about the details later. Given a chance, Mrs. D'Angelo would go on a wild tangent that might take me just about anywhere. "Proclivities?"

"He liked to sue people."

"Sue them? About what?"

"Anything, Merry, anything and everything. The neighbor for cutting the adjoining hedge back too far. The city for knocking over his mailbox with the snowplow. The city offered to install a new mailbox, but he insisted on taking them to court because he, apparently, hurt his back trying to fix the aforementioned mailbox. Most recently she's upset because he's trying to have her friend's dog put down because she showed her teeth to him."

Mattie's head swiveled. He stared at Mrs. D'Angelo, and let out one disapproving bark.

"Karen's dog?" I asked.

"Of course not, Merry. Do try to keep up, dear. Cindy's friend's dog. Cindy's father wanted to take Cindy's friend to court claiming the animal was vicious and needed to be destroyed."

Mattie growled.

I leaned over and gave him a reassuring pat. "Cindy's father? Just so I'm sure, you mean Jim?"

"Of course I mean Jim. Who else are we talking about?"

"So Cindy is Jim's daughter. What's Cindy's last name?"

"Farrar, as I just told you. Cindy is married to Kevin Farrar, that would be Joe and Marie's youngest son. She works for the insurance broker in town and they have a house on Windrush Lane."

"Cindy's the insurance broker? Or is it Marie?"

"Marie's not in insurance. What put that idea in your head? She works at the hardware store. Alan is sure to know her."

I tried to focus on the most important detail. Jim Cole had a hobby of starting frivolous, mean-spirited, lawsuits. He spent the money he'd inherited going after the sort of people who didn't have a lot of resources to fight back. He was prepared to take his 'hobby' to such lengths he'd fallen out with his own daughter over a threat to her friend. Any suit he might have attempted to bring against Vicky and Mark had no merit, we knew that from the beginning. But merit didn't matter to Jim. He saw an opening to have some fun, not caring about the cost or about inconveniencing and even hurting innocent people.

Jim Cole had very likely made himself a great many enemies over the years.

"Are Jim and Cindy's mother still married?" I asked.

"Divorced. It was the talk of the town about twenty or so years ago. As you know Robert and his family left Rudolph when Jim was a young boy. They settled in the Syracuse area, nowhere near here, but Cole House itself is still a powerful presence in Rudolph and people are naturally interested in the family."

"Naturally."

"I believe it was Jean Lewis who has relatives in Syracuse and thus kept us up to date on the Cole family goings on. The divorce was extremely bitter. Jim dragged it out for ages, determined to drain his wife's finances until she had to stop fighting. The lawyers on both sides made an absolute fortune. It was all extremely hard on Cindy, who was still a young girl at the time. They moved away after. To no one's surprise. The former Mrs. Cole would not have wanted to risk running into Jim on the streets." Mrs. D'Angelo sniffed in disapproval. "According to Jean, not one person in Syracuse was on Jim's side. Nasty, nasty man, he was." She lowered her voice and leaned closer toward me. "No one's sorry he's gone."

# Chapter Twelve

I f Santa Claus himself had a hand in organizing the weather, it couldn't have turned out better for the hospital committee's garden tour and luncheon.

Temperatures soared overnight to the mid-seventies, the wind dropped, and a bright yellow sun rose into a clear blue sky. It was early for summer clothes, but I decided to be a rebel and break with tradition. I selected a short-sleeved, knee-length green dress splashed with huge pink and red flowers, and paired it with bare legs and white sandals. After a winter spent in jeans and leggings, my legs were a rather shocking shade of fluorescent white, but I decided I'd do. My summer tan had to start somewhere.

As I was going to be out most of the day, I left a disappointed Mattie at home when I headed for work. The lovely weather would bring out the tourists in hordes, and I needed to get the day at the store started before Jackie and Melissa took over at noon.

"You won't forget our deal, will you, Merry?" Jackie said as I waited by the shop door for Vicky to pull up out front.

"What deal?"

"You're going to notify Kyle before you act on any leads."

"Oh, right, that deal."

"You're investigating the murder?" Melissa said. "Is that safe? My mom says you and Vicky Casey are always getting yourself involved in things that are none of your business."

"She does, does she?"

Melissa failed to notice the frown in my voice. "Yup. She wasn't too sure if it was entirely safe for me to work here, but I told her no one had actually been murdered here in the store."

"That's not true," Jackie said. "Remember when that guy was killed right here while we were down at Santa's boat parade?"

"Oh yeah," Melissa said. "And the time someone attacked Merry in the store. I guess Mom forgot about that."

I cleared my throat. "Perhaps best not to remind her. Spreading gossip about your employer and her business is not a good way to get a promising job reference."

"Huh?"

"What she means is"—Jackie gave Melissa a broad wink—"what happens in Mrs. Claus's stays in Mrs. Claus's."

Melissa looked baffled for a moment, and then she winked in return. "Got it! You must have some stories, Jackie."

"Stories that cannot be repeated," my assistant manager said, "because of the aforementioned rule."

I decided not to point out to Jackie that the only reason someone had wandered into the empty shop, through an open door in the middle of the day, was because Jackie'd slipped away from work to meet Kyle at the parade, thinking I'd never find out, as I was down by the waterfront in my role as Mrs. Claus.

I had found out. Jackie managed to weasel out of that one, and she remained employed.

Vicky's cute little Miata pulled up, and I told my staff to call me if they ran into any problems.

"We won't," Jackie said.

\* \* \*

Most of the other garden tour attendees thought the same as I had. Ladies were in a riot of summer dresses or bright colorful blouses worn with white pants. The few men wore golf shirts and khaki trousers or lightweight suits. Vicky herself had paired her pink lock of hair, the color recently refreshed, with a blouse of a similar shade, worn over a short jean skirt that showed off her long legs to perfection.

She'd called me last night to let me know she and Mark had been given permission to return to their house. I assumed that meant Mark had not been arrested, and I was pleased to hear it. Vicky had been interviewed after work by Detective Simmonds, but the detective had nothing new to report. I told her what I'd learned about Jim Cole. "Basically," I concluded, "he worked hard at making enemies. He's been away from Rudolph since he was a kid, but his daughter lives here now. That might have renewed his interest in the family house he seems not to have thought about for decades."

"Did you tell Simmonds this?"

"No. She'll find out easily enough. Attempted lawsuits are a matter of public record."

"Yes, but the public record doesn't usually detail people's emotions. Feelings can run high. That bit about Jim's daughter and the friend's dog is interesting. People can get mighty emotional over their pets. As you and I know."

"You're right. I'll give Simmonds a call in the morning. I once suggested she put Mrs. D'Angelo on the payroll. She thought I was joking."

Vicky had laughed.

"You okay with taking this much time off work?" I asked her now. "Town might be busy today."

"I'm good, and we're well stocked. I went in extra early this morning to get the baking and lunch prep started. I told Detective Simmonds yesterday my assistant can't manage lunch without me—that was a lie. Janelle's doing such a good job, I might start thinking about retiring."

"Are you serious?"

"No. Although if my book is a huge bestseller and I have to go on book tour and all that, it would be nice to know I can leave the bakery in capable hands."

"Speaking of the book, is your proposal ready for me to show to my publishing contacts?" I'd told Vicky what she needed to have ready before she and I started submitting: details of Vicky's experience, why she was the best person to write this particular book, where it fit in the market, and what was different about it. A list of suggested recipes and/or chapter breakdowns. Sample recipes complete with photographs.

"Afraid not—sorry. I want to get this book done, Merry. I'm excited about it. But finding the time is becoming a real challenge."

"Sleep," I said, "is vastly overrated. Speaking of sleep, any mysterious disturbances at your place last night?"

"Other than the usual gaggle of Rudolph gossips hanging over the gate, asking if they can be of help, and by the way, what really did happen here that night—no."

My mother broke away from a circle of friends when she saw Vicky's car pull into the parking lot of the Yuletide Inn. She greeted us both with a kiss. "I'm so pleased you could come. You can send me an e-transfer for the tickets." She walked us over to her friends. "Do you know everyone? Ladies, you all know my daughter, Merry, and Vicky Casey."

Everyone greeted us with smiles and hugs.

Mom looked stunning in a calf-length pale green dress with a jagged hem. The bodice was adorned with white embroidery, and it was topped with a green jacket with three-quarter-length sleeves. Her long dark hair was wrapped behind her head, tucked beneath a fascinator in the same shade of green.

"Here comes Grace now. She looks lovely." Mom bustled away, and Russ Durham joined us. A large black Nikon camera hung around his neck.

Vicky said, "I do not have a statement for the press."

"I was going to say hi you both look nice. Can I take your picture for the paper?"

"You don't want a picture of us," I said. "You want Mom and Grace."

"I can do both."

"I'd rather not," Vicky said, and clearly she meant it.

He edged away from the group of women, and we followed as the circle closed in behind us.

"I get it," he said. "We're here for the gardens, right?"

"And lunch," Vicky said. "Don't forget lunch."

"I never forget lunch. I even paid for my own ticket. While we're waiting for this show to begin, Vicky, you know I have to ask about what happened the other night at your place."

"Ask away." She dropped the smile. "Doesn't mean I have to answer."

"Diane Simmonds is being tight-lipped about the whole thing. People suggested I look into the history of what they're still calling Cole House, and I did so. It's mighty interesting."

"Leave us alone, Russell," Vicky snapped.

He lifted his hands. "You and Mark are my friends, and I value that friendship, but I have my job to do."

"Next you'll be telling me the public have a right to know."

"They do," he said.

If there's one thing my mom knows, it's the importance of timing. She slipped into our little circle, her arm tucked into that of Grace Olsen.

"Russell, darling," Mom said, "so lovely to see you, and you've brought your camera. How nice. The gardens are obviously not at their best yet, but everyone's dressed so nicely, and the day is gorgeous. Why don't I introduce you to the hospital committee, and you can take some pictures? We need all the publicity you can get for us." She released Grace and very firmly took hold of Russ's arm. Propelled by the sheer force of her personality, not to mention the grip she had on him, he went with her.

Poor Russ. It can't be easy these days, when local newspapers are struggling to survive and so many losing the fight. Once upon a time, the *Rudolph Gazette* filled an entire two-story building in the center of the town's main street. It would have employed a social page reporter with his or her own photographer, as well as a crime beat reporter. Other reporters would cover sports, business, and town politics—not to mention all the administrative staff needed to support them. Now, the paper had only Russ Durham, trying to do it all with the help of Kyle Lambert.

"Nice to see you again, Vicky and Merry," Grace Olsen said once Mom and Russ had moved off. Like my mother, Grace knew how to dress for any occasion. She was all in white—a loose, flowing white dress topped with a wide-brimmed white hat. The only touch of color was a deep red bow at the side of the hat. Her lipstick had been chosen to match the bow.

Greetings over, Grace clapped her hands and raised her voice. "Ladies and gentlemen. Good afternoon, and welcome to the Yuletide Inn. I'm so excited about having you here and giving me the honor of hosting the hospital fundraising committee." Grace and her husband, Jack, were the owners of the inn.

Grace then introduced us to her head gardener, Frank Lowville, a short but beefy, red-faced man in dirt-stained overalls and muddy work boots. Frank was shy and spoke in a low voice, but once the tour began and he talked about the work he so clearly loved, he gained strength and confidence.

The advertised topic was preparing your spring garden for summer beauty. Not something I have the least bit of interest in. Before long, Vicky and I fell back. At this time of year there wasn't much to see but neatly raked lawns, turned-over flower beds, small green shoots poking their heads up out of the ground, and the first of the buds appearing on the trees and the holly bushes. The attendees appeared to be hanging onto Frank's every word as he told them when to cut the lawn for the first time, when to rake up winter debris, and when to mulch the beds; what bushes to prune and when; how to determine if tiny shoots were weeds or much desired plants; how to apply fertilizer and what type to use where.

"You should pay attention to this," I said to Vicky.

"Why?"

"You have a big garden to look after now."

"All we need is to get the grass cut and the overgrowth trimmed back."

"Eventually you'll want to do something nice with it. Did you see the auction list?"

"I got it, but I didn't read it."

"Frank's offering a home consultation. You should bid on it."

"I might do that," Vicky said. "The money goes to the hospital expansion, right?"

"Yup. My mom's donating tickets for a night at an opera at the Met next season. With her and Dad taking them to dinner before the show and sitting with the lucky winners in the theater. I should say Dad donated it. Mom's not happy about potentially having to spend an entire evening with a couple she doesn't care for. Dad reminded her it's for the good of the hospital, and the honor of her hospitality will push the bidding up substantially."

"I'm sure that went some way toward mollifying her."

"It did. My dad knows, after all these years, how to talk Mom into doing something she doesn't particularly want to do."

Finally the garden tour ended. Grace thanked Frank effusively, and he blushed and stammered his thanks. "Now," Grace said, "I believe it's time for lunch."

"Not a minute too soon," a man shouted from the back of the crowd. Everyone laughed politely as his wife dug her elbow into his ribs.

A private banquet room had been put aside for our use. Fresh flowers and an attractive arrangement of tiny chocolate Easter eggs graced every table. The tables were set with white linens, polished silver, and crystal glassware. We were seated with Mom and Grace; Sue-Anne Morrow, mayor of Rudolph; Roberta Conroy, chair of the hospital fundraising committee; and a couple of women representing the hospital. I accepted a glass of champagne to begin the luncheon, and Vicky declined because she was driving.

"I'm surprised Cindy Farrar came," Roberta said, unfurling her napkin.

My ears pricked up. Vicky threw me a look. Her lips moved. "Isn't that—?"

I nodded.

"She bought two tickets when they first went on sale," one of the women said. "They're not refundable, so she likely thought she might as well use them."

"It's not as though she and her father were close," replied Sue-Anne. "Rather the opposite I thought. Odious man. I trust you'll not repeat that, ladies."

"Mum's the word," Roberta said.

"Which one's she?" I asked, and Roberta indicated a table at the back of the room, near the kitchen. "The woman in the blue dress." Cindy was close to Vicky's and my age, thin face, pert nose, chin-length blond hair. "The man next to her is her husband, Kevin."

"Did you know him?" Grace asked.

"Jim Cole?" Sue-Anne said. "Never met the fellow in person, thank heavens. He lived in Syracuse, and the mayor of that town and I are quite good friends. Jim was constantly complaining about every little thing and threatening to sue over something that could be easily rectified if he'd just calm down about it. He did sue the town a couple of times, until finally the court got so tired of his complaints he was threatened with a nuisance charge."

"Wouldn't that cost a lot of money?" a woman asked. "Lawyers don't come cheap."

"The money didn't matter to Jim," Sue-Anne said. "As my friend explained it to me, some men have boats and some men have fancy cars. Jim Cole had lawyers on tap. It was nothing but a game to him. Although"—she glanced toward Cindy Farrar's table—"he wasn't quite so generous with his own family, and that caused some problems." She smiled at the women listening to her. "More town secrets, not to be repeated."

Roberta turned to Vicky with a wide smile. "We were so thrilled to hear people will be living in Cole House once again. It's nothing but a disgrace the way it's been allowed to decay all these years. None other than my own grandmother was a house-keeper in that house. That would be in the 1930s, when the second Mrs. Charles Cole was in residence. My grandmother positively hated her, and she quit as soon as my grandfather landed a job at the shipyard."

"We heard Jim Cole died at that very house the other night." A large-haired, large-bosomed woman leaned toward Vicky, her eyes bright with curiosity. "Do you have any idea what—"

"I do not," Vicky snapped. "I wasn't there." The woman's eyes widened, and she pulled back.

Fortunately, at that moment waitstaff began serving the soup, and the conversation moved on. The food was marvelous, but nothing other than I expected considering Mark Grosse had made it. At first I made polite conversation with my tablemates, aware that Vicky was uncharacteristically silent, clearly not wanting to get into a discussion of her house and the death of Jim Cole. I understood that. Natural curiosly could sometimes turn to virulent interest. I turned my attention to my friend, and we spent the rest of the delicious meal discussing Vicky's deco-rating plans for the house, in low voices.

Finally the dessert dishes were cleared away, staff began serv-ing coffee and tea, and Roberta began the afternoon's program. She introduced Sue-Anne, who thanked us all for coming and launched into an overly long, excessively boring speech about the importance of the hospital to the town. I glanced over to see Vicky's hands beneath the table and her fingers flying. She saw me watching and gave me a guilty grin. "Just checking the bakery. All under control."

At last Sue-Anne sat down, to polite applause, and Roberta took the mic again. "Ladies and gentlemen, you have been warned. It's time to get those checkbooks out."

"No one uses checks anymore," a man yelled. "It's all about e-transfer."

Roberta did not like to be interrupted. Her face stiffened. "I don't care how you pay, Julian, as long as you pay. And pay a lot."

Everyone laughed. Julian beamed, delighted at being the center of attention.

"We have a great many interesting and marvelous things for you to bid on. Some people were not able to join us today, so their opening bids have already been accepted, and Norma is on the phone keeping them informed." Norma, earbuds in her ears and phone in hand, waved. "Be warned—those bids are high. Now, before I open the auction, I'm aware that some of you have to be on your way soon, so I'd like to thank a few people." She began reciting names. The women stood up and bobbed when their names were called. "Grace Olsen for providing the lovely premises and the delicious luncheon. Grace has asked our chef, Mark Grosse, to come out and take a bow."

Obviously waiting in the wings, Mark came into the room, strikingly handsome in his chef's whites, smiling and waving. I glanced at Vicky, proud and happy.

A woman at our table sighed. "A man who can cook and who looks like that to boot. If I were but thirty years younger."

"I think you mean fifty years, dear," the woman next to her said.

Vicky grabbed my wrist. At first I thought she was going to share a laugh with me about the woman admiring her fiancé.

But I soon realized the grip was too strong for that, and her smile had died.

The man sitting next to Cindy Farrar had risen to his feet. He stepped away from his table, into the center aisle. He was in his mid-thirties, with thinning brown hair cut close to his head and a neatly trimmed goatee. Large round glasses perched on his prominent nose. Average height, verging on scrawny.

Conversation slowly died. Mark saw the man, hesitated, and his wave died.

"You've got a nerve, buddy," the man shouted when he had everyone's attention. "Standing up there in front of all of us as though you've done nothing."

Grace lifted her left hand and beckoned to a hovering waiter.

"Do I know you?" Mark asked the man.

"No, you don't know me. You knew my father-in-law, Jim Cole. My name's Kevin Farrar."

Cindy slipped up to Kevin. She touched his arm, but he shook her off. "You know Jim of course. Jim Cole—the man you killed."

Mark's face was tight, his eyes narrow. "Like I said, *buddy*, I don't know you. I don't want to know you. But I suggest you keep your mouth shut."

"Or what?"

Vicky jumped to her feet. Before I could stop her, she darted between the tables to stand next to Mark. If looks could kill, Kevin Farrar would be writhing on the floor.

Russ Durham had been given a table at the back of the room. He'd also stood up, camera in hand, hesitation on his face.

"Call Security," Grace whispered to the summoned waiter. He ran for the doors.

"Or," Mark said, "I'll shut it for you."

"The way you shut Jim's?" Kevin spoke to the crowd. "I hope you all got that. It was a clear threat."

A uniformed security guard came into the banquet room at a rapid pace, hand on the radio at his shoulder. He looked at Mark in his chef's uniform, Vicky standing firmly next to him. He looked at Kevin, bristling with indignation, and the woman beside him, wringing her hands in embarrassment.

Grace stood up in a river of smooth white. "I'd like you to leave, Mr. Farrar." She didn't raise her voice, but the command was clear. "If you have accusations to make, the police will be happy to hear them." She nodded to the security guard, who took a step toward Kevin.

"Please, honey," Cindy Farrar said, "don't do this. Let it go."

"If you wish to bid on any items, Mrs. Farrar," Grace said, "you may do so by telephone."

The security guard stepped in front of Kevin. Kevin took his wife's hand in his. "Okay. We're leaving. You," he said to Mark, "haven't heard the last of me."

"Isn't it late for you to be making threats?" Vicky said. "After you ate Mark's food? I didn't notice you sending any of it back."

"It's okay, babe," Mark said to Vicky.

Kevin marched out of the room, dragging Cindy behind him. She threw an apologetic look toward Grace as she went. "I am so very sorry," she said to no one in particular. "It's been a very stressful time for my husband. I don't . . . I mean, I'm sorry."

"I'm glad you folks enjoyed your lunch," Mark said once the door had shut behind the couple. "Feel free to bid on the dinner for four at the restaurant here. I promise not to poison the food." He walked away, returning to his kitchen. Vicky hurried after him.

All was quiet for about a half a second. Then conversation erupted everywhere.

"That," my mother said, "was highly unfortunate."

"Kevin Farrar never has known when to keep his mouth shut," a woman said. "He was in my third-grade class. He was always getting himself into trouble. None of the other children liked him."

"Do you think there's anything to what he had to say?" Sue-Anne asked. "Everyone knows Jim Cole died at Chef Mark's house. The police are treating the death as suspicious."

"There is absolutely nothing to it," I said. "I'll thank you, of all people, Sue-Anne, not to go around repeating that slander."

"I'm just asking."

"Well, don't."

"I believe the auction is about to begin," my mother said calmly.

A noticeably nervous Roberta had resumed her place at the front of the room. She tapped the microphone to get our attention.

Grace's phone buzzed with a text. She checked it and then leaned between Mom and me to whisper, "The gentleman in question has left the premises."

"Glad to hear it," I said.

"His wife didn't go with him." Grace pointed to where Cindy was slipping back into her chair. Her face was flushed, and the other people at her table greeted her in soft, questioning voices.

Vicky did not return to her seat, and I bid on the garden consultation for her. I'd call it an early Christmas present.

* * *

133

I sent a text to Vicky, telling her if she wanted to leave, I'd get a ride back with Mom. She replied: *We're fine here. Helping with dinner prep.*

Judging by the look on Roberta's and my mother's faces, the auction was a roaring success. I wasn't able to get the garden consultation for Vicky. The bidding went far, far higher than I could afford. My mother herself took the stage to lead the bidding for the opera outing, and it was heavily bid on. One by one, disappointed bidders dropped out before it eventually went for an eye-popping amount. When the highest bidder finally emerged triumphant, Mom gave her a radiant smile and dipped into a half curtsy that had the audience engaging in another round of applause.

The whole thing wrapped up at four o'clock, and attendees departed in a babble of excitement.

"Thank you so much, Aline," Roberta said. "For all your help in organizing this afternoon, as well as your very generous gift."

"An evening at the Met is no hardship for Noel and me," my mother said.

I texted Vicky to say I was ready to leave.

"If your father dares to do something like that again, I'll divorce him," my mother said to me as we left the banquet hall.

"You didn't seem too unhappy with the winner," I said.

"Let me remind you, dear, I am an actress as well as a singer. Fortunately the tickets will have a date on them. If I'm lucky, Mr. Sommerset will come down with a dreadful illness the night before, and his devoted wife will thus be forced to reluctantly bow out of the expedition."

As arranged, Vicky was waiting for us in the lobby, standing next to the center table decorated with a collection of toy bunnies and fluffy yellow chicks and a huge flower arrangement.

"Everything okay?" I asked her.

"I'm okay. Mark's pretending to be okay. He's not. Grace came into the kitchen a while ago, asking for a quiet talk in his office."

"And?"

Vicky's face was troubled. "And she told him to keep a low profile until this business blows over."

"That was unwise of her," Mom said. "Mark did nothing at all out of order."

"He told her that. Grace said she wasn't accusing him of anything, but she didn't appreciate his remarks about not poisoning the food. She added that rumors of that sort won't do the inn any good. Mark was about to tell her what she could do with her inn as well as her rumors, but fortunately for his employment prospects, he thought better of it. We went for a walk in the gardens after, and he was pretty upset. I was my usual cheerful, encouraging self in front of him, but I'm worried."

"The police do not listen to rumors. Diane Simmonds most of all. That Kevin Farrar is an attention hound," said Aline Steiner Wilkinson, a woman who knew something about being a diva. "He deliberately waited until lunch was over and the program about to begin before making his overly dramatic statement. And, I might add, making a total fool of himself in the process."

"Do you know him, Mom?"

"I do not. And I do not intend to ever make his acquaintance. Now, I must be off. Your father invited the Wongs for dinner tonight, and by now the house will be in full dinner preparation uproar."

We left the hotel together. A few people were enjoying another stroll through the gardens, but the visitors' parking lot was mostly empty. As we reached the bottom of the stairs, Cindy Farrar stepped out from behind a row of holly bushes. "Ms. Steiner."

Mom jerked back. She was accustomed to being approached by strangers wanting to meet her, and she usually handled it with grace and aplomb. She might later complain, and usually did, loudly and often, about the annoyance of being accosted in public, but when it came to concealing her delight, her acting skills failed.

Today, she was noticeably not pleased and made no attempt to pretend to be so. "This is not a good time, Mrs. Farrar. My daughter and I have to be on our way."

"I wanted to say I'm sorry about my husband's behavior. Please accept my apologies."

"You do not need to apologize to me."

"My husband disrupted the lunch."

"Then he may apologize. First to Chef Mark, then to Grace Olsen and Roberta Conroy."

Cindy glanced at Vicky. "I am sorry," she said.

"Don't apologize for something you didn't do. Like Aline said, your husband can apologize, although I doubt he's going to."

"Sorry," Cindy said again. "I realize this isn't a good time, not after what happened, but I've been wanting to meet you for ages, Ms. Steiner. I'm a big fan of yours. My mom used to save up all year so she could take me to the Met at least once a year to hear you perform. She adores you, and she has all your records.

I came here today, hoping to bid on the opera tickets as a present for my mother. But the bidding went way too high for me." She gave an embarrassed laugh.

"Most unfortunate." Mom took one step. Then she stopped abruptly and turned to face Cindy, a big smile fresh on her face. "There will be other opportunities, I'm sure. Are you new to town, Cindy? May I call you Cindy?"

Vicky and I exchanged questioning looks.

"Gosh yes. My husband grew up in Rudolph, but I didn't, even though my dad's family's from here. I was born in Syracuse, but my parents divorced when I was young, and my mom and I moved to Brooklyn. Kevin—that's my husband—went to New York City for college and stayed. When we met, we realized we had something in common: Rudolph. Isn't that fun? We moved here about a year ago. Kevin started up a business of his own, and he can run the company as well from here as in the city, and he convinced me to move here. I didn't need much convincing. Like I said, my dad's family has strong ties here, and Kevin never stops singing the praises of Rudolph. Plus we're close to his parents, which will be nice when we have kids." Cindy was babbling on, but Mom simply smiled at her. I didn't know if she always talked in such an unrelenting stream, or if she was so nervous meeting the woman she admired, she couldn't stop herself.

"Are you enjoying living here?" Mom asked. She slipped her arm through Cindy's and began walking. Vicky and I followed. We were not, I couldn't help but notice, heading for our cars, but for the gardens.

"I love it. We're hoping to have kids one day, once we're settled and Kevin's business is on an even keel, and I can't think of a place I'd rather raise my family."

"That's what we Rudolphites like to hear," Mom said. "I teach vocal lessons; did you know that? Perhaps when your children are old enough, they'd like to join one of my classes. Or have a private tutorial."

"Oh my gosh! That would be unbelievable. Thank you so much."

I had absolutely no idea where this was heading. My mom taught voice to both children and adults. She had no criteria at all. Anyone could take her classes. Anyone willing to pay her substantial fees.

We strolled slowly between the long rows of American holly, its evergreen leaves a bright and welcome contrast to the early spring bareness of the rest of the trees and shrubs. Frank and one of his assistants were standing in the rose garden as he pointed something out to a small cluster of luncheon attendees.

"My condolences on your recent loss," Mom said. "Your father must have enjoyed having you living close."

"Not so you'd notice," Cindy muttered.

"I'm sorry, dear—what was that?"

"My dad, Jim. We didn't get on all that well. Truth be told, Ms. Steiner—"

"Please, do call me Aline."

"Thank you. That's such an honor."

"You were saying, dear?"

"My dad and I never did get on very well. I'm like brokenhearted about his sudden death, but he could be difficult. He and my mom fought about money all the time. He could have afforded way more in child support than he wanted to pay, and Mom had to fight him for every last cent. Her health's never been good, and I believe all the conflict over money drained her of what strength she had in her. She's doing better now, though. I'm hoping she can come for a visit over the summer."

I was beginning to feel like a lady's maid, walking a respectful distance behind my employer as she and her friend strolled the gardens. Vicky nudged me and presented me with a puckered face. "What is going on?" she mouthed.

I shrugged. Although I was beginning to get an idea.

"Shocking what families can do to one another," Mom said. "Surely that was all in the past?"

"The child support ended when I graduated high school. Mom still needs financial help, but she simply didn't have it in her to try to get him to keep contributing even a tiny amount. He married again about ten years after my parents split. He's divorced from her now too. They didn't have any children, but the new wife was another reason for him to try to hold off giving Mom what the courts had ordered him to. He gave me some money to help with college, though—more than I expected. When Kevin first suggested moving here, to Rudolph, where I'd be closer to Dad, I thought it would be a chance to rebuild a relationship with him. I mean, he and my mom had issues, but he was still my father, right? Perhaps I was being naive, like Mom told me I was. I tried to get on with him—I really did—but if anything, he got crankier and meaner as he got older. My next-door neighbor has this dog. I mean, yeah, the dog barks a lot, particularly whenever anyone walks past their yard or when we come into ours, but the yard's fenced, so he's not dangerous. My dad threatened to have the dog put down, saying he was a menace. He had my neighbor served with papers and everything. I mean, we're new here, and sometimes it can be tough getting to know people in a small town. I was hoping we could be friends with the neighbors, but now they're really angry at us."

"That is too bad," Mom cooed in a soft, sympathetic voice. "Some men have dominance issues. But it wasn't all bad, I'm sure. Your husband—what is his name again, dear?"

"Kevin."

"Oh yes, Kevin. He and your father were obviously close. I know you feel the need to apologize for his earlier behavior, but I do understand. In our grief we sometimes lose control of our common sense. Perfectly natural."

Cindy snorted. "Grief. Hardly. Kevin and my father couldn't stand each other. I mean, things were okay at first. Dad came around a couple of times for dinner. Kevin didn't care much about the dog business. He thought Dad had a point. But then Kev asked Dad to invest in his business. Dad immediately began laying down conditions, such as wanting to have a veto over major decisions. When Kev realized that Dad not only wanted to be actively involved, but he was offering a loan at interest rates not far off what we'd get at the bank, rather than outright investing, he was furious."

"It can be difficult doing business with family members. Perhaps your father was simply not wanting to cause complications."

"Maybe. But I thought it was more like the same way he was with Mom. My dad inherited a lot of money, and he enjoyed holding it over people. He liked making them beg. Kevin didn't want to beg."

Vicky nudged me. She opened her eyes wide, and her mouth formed an "O."

I nodded in return.

"What's the name of your husband's business, dear?" Mom asked sweetly. "I might be interested in finding out more. Noel and I have a great deal of influence in this part of the state, you know."

"Crypto-Masters."

Mom put her free hand behind her back and snapped her fingers at me. I blinked, then realized she expected me to make a note of the name. I pulled out my phone and typed it into Google but didn't start the search yet.

My mother, I finally realized to my considerable shock, was investigating.

"What an odd name," Mom said. "Something to do with computers, dear?"

"I don't know many of the details, other than it invests in cryptocurrency. I have to confess, Aline," Cindy continued, "I'm starting to get worried. Kevin keeps telling me it's tough getting a business off the ground, and I'm trying to understand—really I am. But it's been a long time, and nothing much seems to be happening. He's still spending more than he's earning. I don't see how we can start a family if we're dependent on my income alone."

"Things are so difficult for young people these days." Mom positively oozed sympathy.

"Kevin wanted me to talk to my dad's cousin, Emmeline. I told him that would be a waste of time. Emmeline owned some property in Rudolph, but other than that she had scarcely enough income to care for herself. That's what Dad told me, anyway."

"Did you visit Emmeline regularly?"

"Never met her. I heard she was a total recluse, and she and my dad never had anything to do with each other. In her will, she left everything she had to a charity for homeless women. I didn't expect to get anything, but Dad wanted the Rudolph house. He was absolutely furious to hear he was completely cut out. Didn't get so much as a memento of the family." Cindy chuckled, pleased at the idea of her father being disappointed about something. "He wouldn't have wanted any memento, but that was never the point."

"Aline! Aline Wilkinson. I'm so glad you're still here." An elderly couple approached us, all smiles. "The summer Christmas concerts are still a while away, but shouldn't the children's rehearsals be starting soon? Our grandchildren are eager to participate again this year."

"I'd better be going," Cindy said. "Kevin will be wondering where I am. It was *sooooo* nice meeting you properly, Aline. How about lunch one day next week?"

"Lunch?"

"We can go to a restaurant in town. I'd love to finish our chat."

"I'll have to check my calendar. I have a very busy schedule. You understand."

"Totally. Why don't you give me your number, and I'll call tomorrow to set something up?"

Mom turned to the new arrivals. "I'm so glad you caught me. I intend to send out notices next week. I have some ideas for our program, and I can't wait to hear the parents' thoughts. And the grandparents' as well, of course."

As if my mother ever changed her concert program on the whim of anyone's parents.

Not yet realizing she'd been dismissed, Cindy said, "Sounds important. I'll leave you to it then. Bye!"

She walked away, a decided spring to her step.

Mom bid her friends good afternoon and said to us, "Come along, girls. Don't dawdle." When we were out of earshot, she said, "I trust you got all that. I do not want to have to engage in empty chitchat with that woman again."

"Not empty," I said.

"Nor chitchat," Vicky said. "Did you do that on purpose, Aline?"

"You mean question the fool of a girl in the guise of being a concerned friend? Of course I did. You two seem to need some help in this matter."

"I'm not investigating," I said.

"If you are not, you should be. In full view of a roomful of Rudolph's most influential citizens, including the mayor, not to mention Mark's employer, that odious Kevin Farrar accused Mark of killing someone. Following that incident, Grace felt compelled to tell Mark to keep himself out of sight. I chastised her for her failure to support the man largely responsible for the success of her restaurant and banqueting facilities, and she, not so politely, told me she'd do what she had to do to maintain the reputation of the inn."

"I've been wondering about that," Vicky said. "From what Cindy told us, Kevin Farrar didn't get on with his father-in-law. Why would he be so upset at the man's death to cause a public scene and have himself thrown out of the hotel?"

"Because," I said, "Kevin Farrar himself could be considered a logical suspect in the murder. Cindy too, despite all her 'gee whiz' thrill at meeting the great Aline Steiner. They didn't like Jim Cole. He made Cindy's childhood a misery and damaged her mother's health; he embarrassed her in front of her neighbors. He dangled the promise of money, attached to considerable conditions, over Kevin. Did Kevin and/or Cindy decide to eliminate the embarrassment and get the money in a more direct way? Such as through Jim's will?"

"I don't suppose you know what's in Jim Cole's will?" Mom asked.

"No, I don't."

"I can ask my dad to find out," Vicky said. "He's still the lawyer for Emmeline's estate, and Jim was threatening to sue the estate, so he'll know Jim's lawyer." She laughed. "Homeless women rather than unappreciative relatives. Good for Emmeline."

"It might be worth knowing, but it doesn't really matter," I said. "If Kevin and Cindy had an expectation of inheriting, that's good enough. Cindy is, as far as we know, Jim's only child."

"I'm thinking of giving up voice teaching," Mom said as we approached her car.

That came as a shock to me. "You are? Whatever for? What would you do instead?"

"I can hang up a shingle. 'A. Steiner Wilkinson. Private Investigator.'"

# Chapter Thirteen

"That took a lot longer than I expected," Vicky said. "I'd intended to ditch you and let you catch a ride with your mom and get back to the bakery before closing. After what happened with Kevin Farrar, Mark needed some calming down. Which, for Mark, means grinding spices and chopping vegetables, so I stayed to give him a hand. And then . . . I didn't think your mom had it in her. That was some mighty skillful questioning."

"Detective Simmonds told me not to do any investigating. It's not my fault if people repeat pertinent points in my hearing, now is it?"

"Not at all. It would be a failure of your civic duty not to report what you heard."

"Is Mark okay?"

"He will be. He's angrier at Grace for not standing up for him than he is at Kevin Farrar. The bartender came into the kitchen and told him Kevin had had a couple of drinks while the garden tour was going on. Grace's security people shouldn't have allowed him to drive home."

"A shot of courage maybe?" I asked. "If Kevin intended to accuse Mark, to throw suspicion off himself or for some other reason, did he need to fortify himself first? No need to drive past your place to drop me off. I can walk."

"Are you sure?"

"It's a block and a half, Vicky. Yes, I'm sure. I'll give Simmonds a call and tell her what we learned, and then I want to see what I can find out about Kevin and Cindy Farrar, particularly as regards this business of Kevin's."

"The game is afoot," Vicky said as she pulled her sporty little car into the alley behind the bakery.

I went into the bakery with Vicky, thinking that because I'd be getting back to the store later than expected, some treats for Jackie and Melissa would go a long way toward mollifying them. Jackie, anyway. I didn't yet know about Melissa, but Jackie could always be bribed.

*   *   *

Detective Simmonds wasn't as wildly excited about my new information as I'd hoped. Then again, maybe she was keeping her enthusiasm under control.

When I got back to Mrs. Claus's, bearing a bakery box of today's leftovers, I called Simmonds to tell her what Cindy Farrar had told us. Told my mother, rather, in my hearing.

The detective said she was in the area and would drop in rather than talk on the phone. About a minute and a half later, she came into the store, carrying a takeout cup from Cranberry Coffee Bar next door. Reluctantly, Jackie held out the box I'd just presented her with, and after some deliberation Simmonds accepted a chocolate pecan tart.

"Let's take a walk," the detective said to me. "Matterhorn could use the stretch if you've been out all afternoon."

"I left him at home today. Mrs. D'Angelo will let him out for a romp a couple of times."

"We can still walk."

"Sorry," I said to Jackie and Melissa. "Be right back."

"Does she ever do any actual work here?" Melissa asked Jackie as the door swung shut behind us.

We strolled along Jingle Bell Lane while Simmonds sipped her coffee and munched on her tart, and I related where I'd spent the day and what I'd overheard.

"Some of this I knew," she said when I'd finished. "But I was not aware of the degree of animosity Kevin and Cindy had toward Jim Cole. When I spoke to her, I already knew about the incident with the dog. She laughed it off, saying her father was a kidder and it would come to nothing. I wasn't so sure, considering Jim Cole's record of suing people over very little, but I couldn't see a standoff over a barking dog being a reason for patricide. She told me she and her father had a distant relationship when she was growing up, but said nothing about the animosity between her parents. As for her husband, I have checked, and Kevin Farrar's in a financially perilous situation. Neither of them told me he'd asked Jim for money."

"Is that suspicious?" I asked.

"Not usually. People rarely come right out and tell me they didn't like the deceased or had long-standing disagreements with them. I would have found out about the legal troubles between her parents soon enough, but not the matter of a loan for Kevin's business. Not if they didn't want to tell me."

We walked on. "When Kevin Farrar accused Mark of killing Jim Cole, he didn't say why he believed Mark would have done such a thing. I believe the reason he made the accusation was to distract attention from himself."

I peeked at Simmonds, checking her expression for a clue to what she was thinking. "Is Kevin Farrar considered a suspect?"

"Nice try, Merry, but you know I'm not going to tell you that. I will tell you Mark's name came up when we initially questioned Cindy and Kevin. Kevin told us what we already knew: that a great many people didn't like Jim. He had a way of making enemies."

"Mark's no longer a suspect," I said. "Good."

"Don't make assumptions," Simmonds said. "I thank you for the information, and I'll ask you to keep me informed if you again happen to overhear something I might be interested in knowing. No one, however, has been ruled out of my investigation."

"Oh."

Up ahead, Candy Campbell, in uniform, was standing on a street corner, talking to a woman. Candy caught sight of us approaching and pointed. The woman headed our way at a rapid clip. She was in her late fifties, with dyed blond hair, face caked with an excessive amount of makeup. She wore a red blouse with the top buttons undone, shredded white jeans, and ankle boots with three-inch heels. Both ears had multiple piercings, and numerous bracelets danged at her wrists.

"Detective Simmonds?" she asked.

"Yes. May I help you?"

"My name's Trish Dawson, and I was on my way to the police station. I stopped that nice young officer to ask for directions, and I told her I need to speak to the detective in charge of the Jim Cole murder." She smiled. A touch of red lipstick was stuck to her teeth, and she smelled very strongly of tobacco. "And here you are. What a coincidence."

Simmonds glanced past her to where Candy Campbell was watching us. Judging by the detective's expression, Candy would be in for a good talking-to. She must have realized so, and she turned her head and slunk away.

"I don't conduct interviews on the street," Simmonds said to Trish Dawson. "If you want to speak to me, please present yourself at the front desk at the station."

"No need. Now that I have you here, we can chat so much easier." She noticed me at last and said, "Hello. Are you a detective also?"

"Do you have information for me about the Jim Cole case?" Simmonds asked before I could get into an explanation of who I was.

We stood in the center of the sidewalk while cars passed and pedestrians moved around us. I should excuse myself and get back to work. I didn't know this woman, and I didn't recall seeing her around before. She probably didn't have anything useful to tell the police, just wanted to make herself seem important by wasting the detective's time. But in case she did know something, I stayed where I was, glad at the chance to hear it too.

"I was hoping you could tell me what's going on." Trish pulled a tissue out of her cavernous tote bag and dabbed at her eyes. "I've been away, visiting friends in Florida, and I only just heard the news. I came here as soon as I could. I'm Jim's wife."

Simmonds's expression didn't change. "According to official records, Mr. Cole was not married at the time of his death."

Trish laughed lightly. "I should say his ex-wife. We're divorced, officially, but we're still very good friends." She touched the tissue to her face again. "I should say we *were* good friends. Like I said, I only got here today. I tried calling his daughter, Cynthia something, but she hung up on me. Sad, isn't it, when adult children continue to carry resentment over their parents' disagreements for so many years?"

149

Cindy had said something to my mom about her dad remarrying and then divorcing. She'd been totally dismissive of the matter, and Mom hadn't asked further. Perhaps she should have.

"Do you have information pertaining to Mr. Cole's death?" Simmonds asked.

"Not directly. Like I said, I was in Florida until yesterday. I came as soon as I heard."

"How did you hear?"

"A friend in Syracuse—that's where Jim and I lived when we were married—heard about it and called me."

I'm not exactly an expert on human emotions, but I am well aware we all experience grief in different ways. I searched Trish's face for signs of such grief and didn't see any. Her eyes were moist, but not red and puffy, and her makeup didn't seem to be covering any residue of weeping.

"When did you last see Mr. Cole?" Simmonds asked.

We stood in the middle of the sidewalk, three rocks blocking the river of pedestrians, forcing them to flow around us. A few people gave us curious glances, but most simply carried on with their business.

"I spend much of my time in Florida these days." Trish pretended to think. "Winters in the north don't agree with me. Must be, oh, about a year ago."

"Yet you claim you remained close after your divorce."

"We talked on the phone all the time."

"I am treating Mr. Cole's death as suspicious."

"Yeah, I heard he was killed by some guy who'd moved into his house and refused to leave. Jim was going to have to sue him to get him out."

"His house?" I said, before remembering I was trying to pretend I wasn't here.

"Jim's family owns this really big mansion in Rudolph. It's been in his family, like, forever. Jim's aunt died recently. Or was it a cousin? I'm not entirely sure, but she left the house to him. This guy she didn't even know moved in before the will was even read, and he's been claiming she left it to him. As if Jim's aunt would let her grandfather's house leave the family." She turned to me. "Do you know the house? Is it nice?"

"I know it. Grand old home. Big piece of property near the lake."

Greed glimmered in Trish's eyes. *So that,* I thought, *is why she's here.* Hoping she'd have a claim to Jim's estate.

"Do you know of any reason someone might have wanted Mr. Cole dead?" Simmonds asked. She hadn't so much as glanced my way since we'd met Trish. She could have told Trish to come to the police station. She could have told me to get lost. But she hadn't done either of those things. The good detective might feel compelled to tell me to keep out of a police investigation, but she was well aware that I'd been of help in the past. I'm a lifelong Rudolphite; Simmonds is not. Gossip flows in and out of Mrs. Claus's and Victoria's Bake Shoppe all day long; gossip stops at the door of the interview room at the police station. People tell me things they don't tell the police, either because they don't want to waste police time (no one ever minds wasting my time), they don't think it's important enough, or they don't want to "get involved." Simmonds was allowing me to listen in, I thought, with the hopes that I'd start digging up the dirt on Jim Cole and his ex-wife.

Considering I'd never met the man, and Trish had never been to Rudolph before, I didn't know how I was going to accomplish that.

"Dear Jim could occasionally be difficult to get along with," the ex-Mrs. Cole said in answer to Simmonds's question. "He was a man of firm principals, and he believed in standing firm behind those principals. Some people didn't like that."

I thought of Cindy's neighbor's dog. No principals involved there—just a desire to be mean.

"It hurts me to admit it, but he occasionally made enemies. He didn't get on at all well with his daughter, no matter how hard he tried. His first wife, the girl's mother, turned her against him. It broke his heart, the poor man." Trish's eyes opened wide as though a thought had suddenly occurred to her. "I've just remembered something. The girl, Cynthia, recently moved to this very town, and he was eager to try to build the relationship he was never allowed to have with her when she was young. I hope her childhood bitterness didn't get the better of her."

Was that ever a subtle way of turning suspicion onto Cindy. Not. I didn't think Trish did subtle.

"Let's talk further at my office," Simmonds said. "We can walk there. Ms. Wilkinson, thank you for your time."

"Sure," I said. "Anytime. Always happy to help."

"Have you spoken to Louise Ferguson yet?" Trish asked.

"I don't recognize that name," Simmonds said.

"You'll want to. I wouldn't put it past her to have done it. The jealous . . . you know what I mean. She couldn't accept that Jim realized he'd made a mistake, and he and I were making plans to get back together."

"This Louise is?" Simmons prompted.

"A temporary girlfriend. She didn't last. Not once he finally realized what a gold digger she was. Jim was not short of funds, Detective." Trish sniffed in disapproval. "It brings the worst out in some women."

# Chapter Fourteen

My suspect list, not that I have a suspect list, was growing—and growing quickly.

Diane Simmonds and Trish Dawson went to the police station, Trish spewing poison all the way. As they walked off I heard her describing this "girlfriend" to the detective: short, too thin to be healthy, surgically enhanced bosom, probably had some work done on her face too—for all the good it did.

Jim Cole had a great deal of money, and he enjoyed spending it pitting people against one another and against him in court. He must have made plenty of enemies over the years.

Which should mean Mark was in the clear. But Simmonds had strongly hinted such was not the case.

Jim Cole might have enough enemies to put on a Santa Claus parade, but he had been killed at Mark and Vicky's house, and found by Mark after Mark had been alone searching for him.

Had one of those enemies followed Jim to Cole House, found him snooping around, killed him, and run away?

That's what I believed. How to prove it was another matter entirely.

"It's five thirty, Merry," Jackie said when I came into Mrs. Claus's. "I told Melissa she could leave at five, but you owe me half an hour overtime."

"Sorry," I said.

"You can't expect me to pick up the slack all the time. I might have had plans, you know."

"I know. I am sorry, Jackie, but if the police want to talk to me, I can't tell them this isn't a good time."

She sighed mightily. "I suppose not. We all have to do our civic duty, don't we?"

"That's the spirit," I said.

She went into the back for her bag and then bade me a cheery good night.

My phone had buzzed with an incoming text while I'd been with Detective Simmonds and Trish Dawson. I took it out now to check the message.

Alan: *Plenty done today. Free for dinner?*
Me: &
Alan: *Pick U up at 7?*
Me: &
Me: *Do not get into conversation with Mrs. D'A.*
Alan: *How do I avoid that?*
Me: 👧

\* \* \*

I took a back route home, tiptoeing across our rear neighbor's yard and slipping through the loose fence boards between the properties. A dash across the lawn got me to the door to the apartments, and I ran upstairs as fast as I could. I made it without being stopped and burst into my apartment with a gasp of relief.

Mrs. D'Angelo was sure to have heard about the events at the auction, and I did not want to be waylaid. She'd also likely know I'd been talking to Detective Simmonds on the street about an hour ago, and would want to hear all the details regarding that.

Alan and Ranger arrived promptly at seven. While the dogs greeted one another, he said, "Mrs. D. was on the sidewalk when I pulled up, but she was talking to someone, so I was able to park the truck and make a run for it."

"We'll have to leave by the back way," I said.

"You have a back way?"

"A secret entrance in case it's needed."

"You lead a surprisingly interesting life for a small-town girl, Merry Wilkinson."

"Don't I wish I didn't."

We told the dogs to guard the house, slipped through the fence, and walked into town.

Over dinner at A Touch of Holly, I filled Alan in on the day's developments. He agreed with my reasoning about Jim Cole and his numerous enemies, but as far as he was concerned, that was all the more reason for me to keep out of it.

"You've put yourself in danger before when trying to help the police, Merry."

"All I'm doing in this case is listening. I don't even have to ask any questions. People tell other people stuff in my hearing. I can't help that, can I?"

"I guess not."

"I'm beginning to wonder if I'm so unobtrusive, people don't even see me."

He grinned. "*Unobtrusive* isn't the word I'd use. People trust you, Merry. They instinctively know you're a good person, so they are not on guard around you."

"I doubt that very much, but thank you."

* * *

On Sunday the store doesn't open until noon, so Alan and I enjoyed a long walk with the dogs, followed by a leisurely breakfast of bagels with smoked salmon and cream cheese. Eventually Alan and Ranger left, and Mattie and I got ready for work. As I did most mornings, before leaving I had a quick glance at the store email account to see if I needed to attend to anything right away.

I'd received a notice from the Rudolph police. I opened it quickly and saw, with a feeling of relief, that the message had been sent to all the businesses on Jingle Bell Lane, not just me.

The relief didn't last long. The purpose of the email was to inform us there had been an attempted break-in on the street last night, at Victoria's Bake Shoppe. It went on to say no damage had been done, apparently nothing had been stolen, and no one harmed. We were reminded to check our own security arrangements and notify the police if we saw anything out of order.

I called Vicky.

When she answered, I could hear the buzz of her busy bakery in the background. Someone called for the sugar, and someone else asked if the blueberry muffins would soon be ready.

"Not a good time," Vicky said to me.

"I'll be quick. I heard the news. About last night. All okay?"

"Hold on a sec. Janelle, see to those muffins. I'll be right back."

The background noise died as Vicky moved into a quiet corner. "No harm done. I got an alert from the security company around midnight. The alarm on the back door went off. By the time they arrived and the police had been called, whoever it was had gone. Nothing damaged, nothing seems to have been stolen. I've always figured we're pretty safe here. I can see the entrance to the police station out my window."

"Someone looking to make trouble, maybe?"

"Maybe. They scarpered when the alarm went off and they realized the police would be here as soon as they finished their coffee and dusted donut crumbs off their pants."

"You need to get the lock changed."

"Already done, although our perpetrator doesn't seem to have gotten it open. I did not need to be woken up and have to come into town in the middle of the night, but it couldn't be helped. I gotta run, Merry. The Sunday brunch crowd is out in full force today, and we can barely keep up."

"One quick thing—you don't suppose this has anything to do with what happened at your house, do you?"

"You mean Jim Cole and the strange noises? No. These things happen, even in Rudolph. Troublemakers. Petty thieves. Chancers looking for a phone or an iPad left unattended. That's why we need alarms and a security company, right? And inconvenient midnight phone calls."

"Right. I'll check my own alarms when I get to the store."

"Hold on! I'm on the phone," Vicky called out to someone in the bakery. "Sorry, Merry—like I said, gotta run." She disconnected the call.

If Vicky wasn't worried about an attempted break-in, I told myself I needn't worry either.

My determination to let it go didn't last long. Not worrying is not in my nature. According to the police's email, no other business had been attacked (if it could be called an attack) last night. Only Vicky's bakery. It was possible the miscreants were a bunch of hungry teenagers on the hunt for after-party treats. Possible, but I wouldn't have expected them to slip silently away into the night. If they were locals, they would have known how close the bakery is to the police station. Then again, teenage boys don't always think straight when they're famished.

Last night, Alan and I managed to get in and out of my apartment without being stopped by Mrs. D'Angelo. This morning my luck held. She was nowhere to be seen when I left home shortly before noon. I even took a moment to admire the tulip bed in the center of the lawn. The stalks were reaching toward the sun, leaves spreading, buds still closed tightly enough that the color wasn't visible, but soon they'd make a brilliant, cheerful display.

Melissa wasn't working today, and Jackie was scheduled to come in at one for a half day. The shop was satisfyingly busy almost from the moment I unlocked the doors.

Shortly before three, the tide of customers dropped off. I gave my back a good stretch and said, "I haven't had lunch yet. I'm going to go out and get something. Do you want anything?"

"Where you going?" Jackie asked.

"Probably the bakery. They close at three, so I might get a discount on remainders."

"Ham and Swiss on rye, if they have it. Otherwise, whatever. But only if it's half price. Unless you're paying?" Jackie looked at me from under her lashes. "Are you?"

"If I must," I said.

"Then I'll have a piece of gingerbread to go with it. And an iced tea. Extra-large."

Grumbling, but reminding myself of some of the horror stories I heard about staff from other business owners, I headed out the door.

At five to three, only a few people were in line for takeout. The bread bins behind the counter were empty, and a thin scattering of premade sandwiches and desserts remained in the display cases. A new employee, whose name I didn't know, ferried used dishes into the kitchen. One table was still occupied. I recognized the young woman who'd been in here the other day, looking for a job. Her iPad was open in front of her, next to a plate containing a half-eaten fruit tart, an empty cupcake wrapper, and a torn muffin. As I watched, she peeled the tart pastry apart with her fingers and studied it. She wiped her fingers on a napkin and typed on her iPad.

"Is Vicky in?" I asked Marjorie, who was serving customers from behind the counter.

"Vicky! Merry's here!"

Vicky came out of the back, wiping her hands on her apron. She started when she saw the young woman with the iPad and rolled her eyes to the ceiling. "Good afternoon, Brittany. I didn't realize you were here. Again. Everything okay?"

Brittany lifted one hand while she kept typing with the other.

"Is it all to your satisfaction?"

She didn't look up. "Yup. Thanks."

"I find a touch of arsenic in the pastry dough gives it a nice crunch."

That got Brittany's attention. She looked up. "Arsenic? What's that?"

"She's kidding," Marjorie said. "Pay her no attention." She gave Vicky a warning look, and Vicky shrugged.

"We're closing in a few minutes," Marjorie said.

"Okay. I'm done here anyway." Brittany closed her iPad and began collecting her things.

"How was today?" I said to Vicky.

She half turned so her back was to Brittany. "An excellent day. We have a lot of orders for ready-made meals for Easter dinner next week—ham and scalloped potatoes and the like—so that'll keep us busy. That plus pies and cakes for people who don't want to make their own company desserts. Right, Aunt Marjorie?"

Marjorie handed a customer his drink and said, "Right, because busier is what we need around here."

"Never complain about being busy," the customer said.

"If you can't manage with the staff you have," Brittany said, "I'm still interested in working here. I can help you with the baking. I make a mean red velvet cake. Everyone says it's the best they've ever had."

"I'll keep that in mind," Vicky said. "Thanks for your interest."

The last customer held the door open for Brittany, and when it had shut behind them, Vicky let out a long sigh.

"What was that about?" I asked. "Arsenic?"

"That Brittany's starting to become a pest," Vicky said. "Every time I turn around, she's there. At least this time she didn't try to barge into the kitchen."

"Only because I intercepted her," Marjorie said. "You'd better get used to it, Vicky. When your cookbook becomes a best-seller, which it will, baking groupies will be falling all over themselves for your attention."

"Is there such a thing as baking groupies?" I asked.

"Oh yeah," Marjorie said. "With the success of programs like the *Great British Baking Show*. That Paul Hollywood's a genuine star now. It helps"—she sighed happily—"that he has the most amazing blue eyes."

"I also have blue eyes." Vicky batted her lashes. "Maybe I can become the Upstate New York version of Paul Hollywood. Perhaps I should change my name to Victoria Broadway. Brittany isn't any sort of a groupie. Meaning she's not interested in me. She's interested in my baking, and she's trying to deconstruct my recipes."

"Is that a problem?" I asked.

She shrugged. "Not really. At least she pays for the food she buys, even if she doesn't eat most of it." She nodded toward the table where Brittany had been sitting. "Most of my baking's pretty basic. Old favorites I've given a bit of a twist to. Like my gingerbread, with the super special secret ingredient known only to me. The full recipe of which is kept in my bank vault under lock and key."

"Is it?"

"Of course not. It's in the folder marked 'Super Special Secret Recipes,' open on the counter, and on my computer. And, eventually it will be not only in my cookbook, but I'm hoping for it to be the cover photograph. What I'm saying is, Brittany's not going to learn much, if anything, by deconstructing my pastry. She'd be better off trying things on her own. Without even tasting it, I can tell you her red velvet cake is likely straight out of a 1960s cookbook. There's a lot more to baking than following the recipe exactly and measuring ingredients. Talent and heart have a big part to play. When I interviewed her, she said she's intending to write a cookbook. Nothing wrong with that, and nothing wrong with trying to learn how others do it, as long as she doesn't interfere with my business and unless she tries to recreate my recipes for her book. Enough of her. What brings you here?"

"Lunch. What else?"

The new assistant came out of the back. "What would you like me to do now, Vicky?"

"Soon as the last table's free, you can begin the end-of-the-day routine, Taylor."

"Sorry, sorry. Didn't mean to overstay our welcome. We're leaving now." Four women I regularly see around town hurried to gather purses and shopping bags.

"I didn't mean—" Vicky began.

"As you can see, we're done. Just having a nice long chat."

"We're trying to avoid going home and thinking about what to make for dinner."

"We have several pies in the freezer," Marjorie said. "Fully cooked and needing only to be heated. Your choice of turkey, chicken, or curried vegetable."

"That would be nice for a change. I'll try the chicken."

Marjorie rang up the charge while Taylor fetched the pie.

The customers left happy, one of them clutching the box containing a frozen chicken pie.

"For a start," Marjorie said to Taylor, "stack the chairs on the tables, and start washing the floor."

Taylor went into the back for cleaning equipment, and I asked Vicky, "How are things at the house? Any more noises at night and the like?"

"I've heard nothing more, and neither has Mark. Thank goodness for that."

"So it definitely was Jim Cole creeping around."

"Probably, but not necessarily. Someone else could have been causing trouble, and they were frightened off by what happened."

"If that's the case, we can definitely eliminate any ghosts or spirits. They're unlikely to be scared away by a death on the premises and police activity."

Vicky jerked her head, indicating for me to follow, and led the way to a back corner. She kept her voice down. "That's one positive thing. As for the other . . . Simmonds called Mark again last night. She had questions about Kevin Farrar's accusation."

"Can't say I'm surprised she heard about that."

"Mark told her what he thought of Kevin's accusation. In fairness, she told him she'd spoken to Kevin, and he admitted he didn't have anything but, in his words, 'a gut feeling' about Mark. Anyway, enough of that. What can we get you?"

"A couple of sandwiches, please. And gingerbread if you have any left."

"Marjorie, any of today's gingerbread left for Jackie O'Reilly?"

"All out," Marjorie said.

"How'd you know it's for Jackie?" I asked.

"You spoil that girl," Vicky said. "If I didn't have my own place to worry about, I'd come and work for you. The things she gets away with."

"What sort of things?"

Vicky just laughed and went into the kitchen. Behind me, the chimes over the door tinkled.

"We're closing in a few minutes," Marjorie said, "but I can get you something for take-out."

"Thanks. A coffee'd be good. Black, no sugar."

I went to the counter to get my order. The woman who'd come in was shorter than my five foot four despite the fact that she was wearing pumps with substantial heels. She was in her mid-thirties, at a guess. Her jeans were so formfitting I wondered if she would be able to sit down, and a cropped, tight pink T-shirt with a big red heart drawn in sparkles strained over her chest, which, considering how thin she was otherwise, unlikely had anything to do with genetics.

Marjorie poured the coffee into a take-out cup and snapped on a lid. The woman handed her a five-dollar bill, and Marjorie made change.

I picked up my own brown bag and the cup containing Jackie's drink and turned to leave. The door opened again, the chimes sounded again, and Trish Dawson marched in. I could tell by the look on her face she was not here for coffee and a cookie.

The younger woman turned around. A sly grin appeared on her face. "Well, well. Look who's here. Are you following me?"

"I can't come in for a cup of coffee?" Trish said.

"Not if I got here first."

This, I realized, must be Louise Ferguson, Jim's either ex- or his last girlfriend.

"I had a nice long talk with the detective in charge of Jim's case," Trish said. "I told her all about you. She'll have questions for you."

"Then she can come and find me. I'm not hiding."

Trish turned to me. "You can tell your boss she's here. We'll wait."

"My boss? I don't— Oh, you mean Detective Simmonds. I'm not with the police."

"You couldn't even get that right." Louise laughed. "Take some advice from me, Trish honey. Don't make even more of a fool of yourself than you already have."

"I'm not taking any advice from the likes of you."

"It hurts, doesn't it, knowing you need advice from someone as young as me. Give it up, Trish. Go back to Florida, where you belong. With all the other *retirees*."

"I'm not leaving without what I came for," Trish said.

"What you came for? You mean Jim's money? Sorry, babe, but he forgot you a long time ago." Louise picked up her coffee and took a step toward the door. "I'm at the Caroler's Motel," she threw over her shoulder to me. "If the police want to talk to me, I can tell them all about how *she* tried to manipulate Jim into giving her a payout when he dumped her for me."

"Manipulate!" Trish's hand flew out, and she sent Louise's cup flying. I hopped out of the way as hot coffee sprayed in all directions.

"Hey!" Marjorie yelled. "Vicky, we need you out here."

Vicky ran out of the kitchen, very formidable indeed with her five-foot-ten height, gripping a wooden rolling pin and bristling with indignation. "What's going on? If you two want to have a disagreement, take it into the street."

Taylor stood behind Vicky, holding a broom and looking unsure of what she was supposed to do.

The two women ignored Vicky. Which is never easy.

"If anyone manipulated Jim, it was you," Trish yelled. "Playing your silly, childish games. Getting him at his weakest. Convincing him to leave me. He came to his senses soon enough, didn't he? He phoned me only last week—did you know that? He begged me to forgive him, to come back to him."

"As if," Louise sneered. "Lies, all you have are lies."

"Is that why you killed him?" Trish yelled. Her eyes were wild with rage, and her face had turned a frightening shade of red. Her fists were clenched, and a vein pulsed at the side of her neck. "Because you couldn't accept that he wanted me after all.

A mature woman, not a simpering, brainless gold digger like you."

I glanced at Vicky. She'd tucked the rolling pin under her arm, taken her phone out, and was snapping pictures of the women's faces. "I'm ordering you both to leave the premises. Now. Or I'm calling the police."

Louise threw herself at Trish. She pulled her right hand back and slapped the older woman across the face. The blow landed with such force the echo of it bounced around the room. Vicky, Marjorie, Taylor, and I gasped. Trish was knocked backward, landing against the shelf displaying items for sale. She recovered faster than I might have expected. She grabbed a jar of strawberry jam and swung it at her enemy's head.

It connected, the jar shattered, jam flew everywhere. Louise snatched a cake stand off the counter, one last lonely slice of carrot cake left, and threw it, platter, lid, cake and all at Trish. Trish dodged the projectile, and it hit the wall behind her, shattering into a shower of thick pieces of glass and once-delectable cake.

Marjorie and Vicky were both yelling into their phones. Vicky threw her phone onto the nearest table and wrenched the broom out of Taylor's hands. I dropped my sandwich bag and take-out cup of iced tea, and took the rolling pin from Vicky. Thus armed, my allies standing steadfast next to me, I braced myself and faced the combatants.

I had absolutely no idea what to do. Could I wield the short but heavy rolling pin like a battle-ax? Bash one or both of the women over the head? I waited for Vicky to act first.

Trish had lost her clip, and her hair hung around her face, showing a line of solid gray roots. Her lipstick was smeared, and black mascara dribbled down her cheeks. Louise didn't look a heck of a lot better.

They watched each other, chests heaving, faces choked with hatred, circling like two long-past-it prize fighters stepping into the ring for one last bout.

Vicky hefted the broom and waded into the ring. I gripped my rolling pin and lifted it high. Vicky put herself between the two women, using the broom as a weapon and a shield. "Stop this! The police have been called."

"You saw what happened," Trish said, "She attacked me! I'm defending myself."

"Is that what you call it?" Louise snarled. She grabbed the end of the broom and tried to wrench it out of Vicky's hands. Vicky held firm. I darted forward and gave Louise a good shove in her more-than-adequate chest. She lost her balance, fell back, and landed solidly on her flat rear end with a whoosh of shock. I heard the distinct sounds of thread and fabric tearing as the seams at the seat of her jeans gave up the battle to keep everything together.

Unfortunately, while our attention was on Louise, Trish had taken the opportunity to resume the attack. She snatched at jars of preserves and began throwing them in a steady volley. Louise crouched, her arms held protectively over her head. Glass broke, and jams and jellies spattered the floor. Fine china cups and teapots followed.

I threw aside the rolling pin, took one leap, and crashed my entire body into Trish's side. She was knocked flat, taking me along with her. I lay on top of her, feeling her deep breath and her rage, along with a rainstorm of china and glass. She bucked and squirmed, yelling at me to get off her. I was aware of Vicky using her broom to force Louise into a corner.

Marjorie had run to the door, where she stood jumping up and down, yelling, "Help, help! They're killing each other!"

And then the police were in the room, and strong arms were pulling me to my feet. "Stop that!" Candy Campbell yelled at me.

"I'm not doing anything!" I yelled back. "Arrest her! Arrest *them*! They're out of their minds—the both of them."

Vicky threw her broom aside.

"Vicky and Merry were only defending the place," Marjorie said. Fine china crunched beneath her feet as she crossed the floor. The tiles were sticky with blue and red jelly and stepped-on remains of one slice of carrot cake. Shards of glass sparkled like diamonds in a night sky made of jam. My bag of sandwiches had the outline of a footprint stomped into it, and the empty cup lay in a puddle on the floor.

"That was really something," Taylor said.

Louise and Trish continued to throw death stares at each other, watched over by two police officers.

"She started it," Trish said.

"I truly do not care who started it," Candy said. "Vicky, what do you want us to do?"

"Arrest them. Charge them. Send them down the river for the rest of their miserable lives. I expect them to pay for all this."

"I'm a grieving widow," Trish said.

"Ha!" Louise said. "More like a vengeful ex-wife who lost her meal ticket."

Trish took a step forward. Candy jerked her back. "Let's go."

Detective Diane Simmonds stepped into the bakery. Behind her, I could see a substantial crowd gathered on the sidewalk, trying to see what was going on. "What have we here? Ms. Dawson." She looked at Louise. "Ms. Ferguson, I presume."

Louise nodded. She half turned to the detective. Thin straps of a pink thong peeked out from the substantial tear in the rear of her jeans, doing absolutely nothing for any dignity she might be struggling to retain.

Simmonds spent a long time looking around the bakery. Vicky, feet apart, still clutching her broom. Me, cradling my side, where I'd hit the floor when I brought Trish down. Marjorie and Taylor, wide-eyed. All the damage. "Here for the funeral of your husband and partner are you?" she said at last.

"You can be sure I'm not catering that," Vicky muttered.

"*Ex*-husband and *ex*-partner, from what I hear," Simmonds said.

"We were having a temporary break from each other," Louise said.

"Is that what you call it? These two ladies and I will have a chat down at the station," Simmonds said. "Officer Campbell, after you've escorted us, come back and get statements from the witnesses."

After the police and the miscreants had left, to the accompaniment of an excited babble of voices from the sidewalk, Vicky, Marjorie, Taylor, and I dropped into chairs.

"That was . . . weird," Taylor said.

"You did pretty good there, Vicky," Marjorie said. "Merry too. Did you play football in school?"

I groaned.

"An experience never to be repeated, I hope," Vicky said. "We're a bakery and café, not a bar."

"Those two have some serious issues to deal with," Marjorie said. "I don't know about the younger one, but as for the older one, her behavior is nothing more than I'd expect from a girl from Muddle Harbor."

"You mean Trish? She's from Muddle Harbor?"

"Patty Dawson, she was. Pride of MH High. *Not.* I started to say hello when she came in, but it was clear she intended to ignore me, so I didn't. I remember her from the girls' softball team we played against a few times." Marjorie chuckled. "We won every single game. No surprise considering most of their players were on the level of Patty." She got to her feet. "The only reason our team got as far as the regional playoffs is because of our victories against MH High. As soon as we encountered decent ball players . . ." She swiped her index finger across her throat. "Toast."

# Chapter Fifteen

"Sorry," I said to Jackie when I returned to Mrs. Claus's late and empty-handed. "Your lunch got stepped on."

"I don't even need to ask what that means. Marg Thatcher ran in here a few minutes ago, saying the police had been called to Vicky's place because a riot had broken out and a gang of middle-aged women was arrested."

"Not exactly a riot and not quite a gang, but that's more or less right."

"What happened?"

"Two women brought their personal disagreements into the bakery with them. They refused to leave when politely asked to do so. In all the chaos, someone stepped on our sandwich bag. The tea got spilled too. Sorry."

"I'm sorry I missed it," she said. "We had customers until a short while ago. They all ran out to see what the commotion was."

"Take a break if you like. Get something for us both for lunch from Cranberries. I'll have anything at all."

"You okay, Merry?" Jackie studied my face. I gave her a grin, pleased at her show of concern, but also surprised. Jackie could be amazingly self-absorbed at times.

"I'm fine. It didn't have anything to do with me. I was nothing but an innocent bystander."

"'If you think the rest of the gang's going to be out to get revenge on you and Vicky, maybe we should close the store for a couple days. I'd expect to be paid, of course, because that's not my fault."

"Nice try, but I am not closing the store. Mainly because there is no gang, as I just told you."

"Whatever," Jackie said.

Customers began returning. Once it was all over and the miscreants taken away, I'd slipped out the back of the bakery to avoid the crowd of the curious, so not many people knew I'd been involved in the action.

"I have to say, Muriel, I thought this was a safe town," a woman said to another as they came into the store.

"Is any place truly safe these days?" Muriel asked, probably rhetorically. "Has any place ever been truly safe at any time? Teenagers will be teenagers, particularly when they're on vacation."

"So true." They began selecting table linens. I wasn't sure how a battle between two women of an age to know better had morphed into teenagers on vacation, but that was a good thing. Rudolph did not need to get the reputation of a place where fights broke out in the middle of town, in the middle of the day. The town hall was located close to the bakery. No doubt town staff had quickly set to work trying to downplay the incident and calm the waters.

Now that I was thinking of towns with reputations . . . So Trish Dawson was from Muddle Harbor. I'd have thought nothing of it except it reminded me I'd heard Muddle Harbor mentioned recently. Wasn't Charles Cole's wife, Edith, from that town? Muddites, as we called them, had been known to try to cause trouble for Rudolph in the past. I remembered the time they'd tried to promote themselves as America's Easter Town, and the Chocolette fiasco that had followed.

A customer broke into my thoughts. "I adore this children's village, but it's rather expensive. Is it possible to buy a few individual pieces rather than the full set?"

"Absolutely. It's designed to be added to over the years. Let me see what we have." I turned my attention away from murder and fistfights, and concentrated on my customers and my store for the rest of the day.

\* \* \*

Jackie had left, and I was about to lock the door, when someone I didn't expect to see came in. Brittany, who'd been taking notes in the bakery earlier. At first, I assumed she was disappointed she'd missed all the action and was here to ask me about the fight, but she didn't even mention it.

"You go to Victoria's Bake Shoppe a lot, don't you?" She took a small notebook and a pen out of her bag.

"Yes, I do."

She flipped the notebook open and held the pen over a blank page. "I thought so. I've seen you there. Would it be fair to say you and Vicky are friends?"

"It would. Where's this going, Brittany? I'm closing the store now."

"Won't take long. As her friend, I wouldn't expect you to criticize her cooking, but I'm hoping you can give me a fair appraisal. No one needs to know we've had this conversation."

"What conversation might that be?"

"What treat or dessert made at Victoria's Bake Shoppe do you like the best?"

I didn't see any reason not to answer, so I did. "Mince tarts."

She wrote that down and added a big tick next to it. "A holiday favorite. Made only in the period between Thanksgiving and New Year's to keep interest high. What do you like the least?"

"I like everything Vicky makes."

"If you had to say something, what would it be?"

I thought. "Generally I don't like Danishes with jam filling. Too sweet. And the jam dribbles down your front."

She wrote *Danish* and put a scratch through it. "Anything else?"

"I like her pies. If I had to choose, my favorite is blueberry when it's blueberry season. Also the chocolate raspberry pie. Vicky tries to use local ingredients when they're available, and nothing beats seasonal berries."

A star next to blueberry pie and a tick beside chocolate raspberry. "Local fruit can be expensive, though, right? And it's not always available. The imported stuff is often cheaper. What does it matter if it's going to be cooked?"

"It matters a lot, cooked or not. Cheaper isn't usually tastier. You know she doesn't add arsenic, right? That would be bad. She was kidding about that."

"I tried looking that word up, but I don't think I got the spelling right. How do you spell arsenic?"

I did so.

"Yeah, that's what I found. It's a slow-acting poison."

"Right. Thus she does not use it in her baking. Or in anything else. If that's all . . . it's past closing time, and I'm leaving for the day."

"That helps—thanks." She folded her notebook and put it away.

'Are you writing an article for your local paper?" I asked.

"No. I'm writing a cookbook all about baking for the holidays. I'm getting ideas of what to put in it."

* * *

I wasn't able to make my escape before I was interrupted yet again, this time by Detective Diane Simmonds. I'd twisted the lock on the door and was tidying the book rack when an excited woof came from the back, and a moment later I heard a firm rap on the door to the street.

"Detective, come on in. What's up? Dare I hope you're coming to tell me one of his wives and/or lovers has confessed to the murder of Jim Cole."

"No, and if they had, you would not be the first person I'd tell." She came into the store, and I locked the door behind her. She looked around. "You have some Easter things, I see. I've never known anyone who decorated their home for Easter."

"Some people take advantage of any excuse to bring out the fancy dishes. Can we go into the back before Mattie knocks the door down?"

"Of course."

Mattie outdid himself in his enthusiasm when Detective Simmonds came in. She simply said, "Good afternoon, Matterhorn. Shall we go for a walk?"

He bolted for the door.

When I first met her, Diane Simmonds told me she'd grown up in Los Angeles, where her parents trained animals for movies and TV. She'd grown up around animals and had helped her parents as soon as she was able. I'd never asked why she became a police officer and moved to Chicago. She left that city for a new job in Rudolph during the fallout of a bad divorce to a fellow cop.

"Let's talk in the alley so he can have a stretch," Simmonds said to me.

I fastened the leash to Mattie's collar, and we left by the rear door. We walked slowly, the dog trotting contentedly between us.

"If this were a simple case of a couple of women getting overly argumentative and breaking a few things, I'd send a uniform to get your statement," the detective said. "Seeing as how both women were involved with Jim Cole, I decided to ask you myself what happened this afternoon."

I related the story before concluding, "They each implied the other had reason to kill him, the reason being they were jealous that he preferred the other woman to her. But neither of them said anything that makes me believe they knew anything specific about his death. Did they to you?" I dared ask.

"No. They came over all contrite and ever so sorry about what happened. What the other woman had forced her to do— the poor innocent thing. They each informed me that Jim was about to come back to her, and they're both devastated about his death. Can't say I saw a lot of devastation in their manner. They asked me if I knew when the will would be read, before they remembered to ask about the release of the body."

"Greed has a way of focusing the mind."

"That it does."

Mattie trotted happily between us, only occasionally catching a whiff of something in a trash bin that required investigating.

"They were both released a short while ago and ordered to stay away from each other and from Vicky's place. Hopefully they'll abide by that. I can see you're dying to ask, so I'll put you out of your misery. I'd previously checked on their alibis, and both are shaky for the time of Cole's death. Trish tried to tell me she left Florida as soon as she got word, but it was easy enough to get her to admit she was already in New York State. On her way, according to her, to the joyous reunion with Cole. She spent the night he died at a motel near Syracuse. The motel confirms she checked in, but no one can precisely account for her whereabouts at any time. Easy enough drive from there to Rudolph and back.

"Jim lived in Syracuse. That she had to stay in a motel means the marital home is not hers any longer," I said.

"Precisely. They are divorced. Trish says the divorce was amicable. The home was his originally, and as they didn't have any children, she didn't ask for financial support. She used her own money to move to Florida. I haven't yet seen their divorce records or final agreement, but you can be sure I'm trying to get my hands on them."

"She knew Jim was visiting Rudolph. Did he tell her that?"

"She says he did. They were going to attempt to reconcile, so they kept in touch. Again, I can't be sure. As for Louise, she was at a party in Syracuse, where she lives."

I interrupted, "Did she get her pants fixed?"

The edges of Diane Simmonds's mouth turned up. "One of the uniforms gave her his jacket for the walk to the station, and then a civilian clerk found a baggy old sweater in the back of a closet. The moths seem to have been at it, but it was enough to provide Louise with some degree of modesty."

"Her alibi? How strong is it?"

"Not exactly iron clad. A big house party, countless people coming and going all night. She was there, but so far, no one can say when she arrived or when she left. One woman remembers her weeping that her boyfriend had dumped her before she got much out of him. The Syracuse police asked the witness what she thought that meant, and she said Louise was expecting a payout. Jim Cole was an old guy—her words—and not exactly George Clooney. Again her words."

"Any other suspects?" I asked.

She threw up her hands. "The list is beyond exhaustive. I've got officers all over this part of the state looking into Cole's history, and I can barely keep up with the reports flooding in. He seemed to relish making enemies. He tried to sue a woman in her nineties for blocking the sidewalk outside her residence with her walker, causing him to trip. That one came to nothing, I was pleased to hear. We're trying to match the most likely candidates with opportunity. Meaning people who were in Rudolph or unaccounted for that night. My own officers have canvassed Lakeside Drive extensively, asking if anyone or anything seemed out of place, but we're having no luck. It's a quiet neighborhood of big yards, most of them heavily treed. Near the public path running along the lake. The incident didn't happen all that late, and it was a pleasant night in early spring. People were out walking dogs or taking a lakeside stroll."

"So you're getting nowhere."

She turned and looked at me. I gulped, wishing I could swallow the words. "I said, it was proving complicated. That's all. They'll have tripped up somewhere, and when I find that, then I'll have them."

"Mark?"

"Speaking of getting nowhere, we're almost at the end of the alley. Let's turn around."

Mattie was sniffing at a rock. Usually I have to call and beg and plead and tug on the leash to get him to leave something interesting. Simmonds clicked her tongue and said, "Come Matterhorn," and he bounced cheerfully after us. It really was unsettling.

"I understand your concern for your friend, Merry," she said. "Mark Grosse is by no means in the clear. But—"

"I—"

"Hear me out. It was night. Jim Cole was on Mark Grosse's fully fenced and gated property, uninvited. Mark had reason to believe the man had been attempting to frighten or even harm himself and his fiancée. If Mark had fought with Jim, he would have solid grounds to claim self-defense. That he did not do so makes me, personally, believe he was not responsible."

"Glad to hear it."

"My personal opinion will carry little weight in a court of law. Evidence is what matters."

I dared to ask a question that had been on my mind. "What about the murder weapon? Did you find it?" I knew from Vicky what it likely was, but I was hoping Simmonds would provide me with additional information.

"We did. A rock. A common or garden rock, one like many on that unmaintained property. Meaning no special skill or equipment was needed to commit the murder."

As long as she was chatting so comfortably, I tried another question. "What did the autopsy reveal?"

"The results are of course confidential, Merry, but it will come out in court. If it comes to that, and I'm confident it will. Jim Cole was sixty years old and considerably overweight. He drank heavily and smoked equally heavily. He was in very poor health, and according to an aside from the pathologist, he likely wasn't long for this world. But none of that contributed to his death. He was struck on the back of the head by a heavy, solid object, almost certainly the rock found nearby, and died instantly."

"Might he have tripped, fallen, and hit his head?"

"No. The rock was not found under or near him, but a good ten feet away. It didn't get there by itself, and it's too heavy to be carried by an animal. Not that sufficient time has passed for that to be a possibility. Someone threw it."

She suppressed a sigh. Detective Simmonds might have said she was confident of an arrest. Her demeanor suggested she wasn't so sure. "Jim Cole's enemies list goes back years. Makes me wonder sometimes why I even bother."

# Chapter Sixteen

I tried to work on my accounts for a while after my walk with Diane Simmonds, but I couldn't concentrate on the rows and columns of numbers and eventually I gave up.

The detective had been surprisingly forthright about the difficulties she was facing in this case. If all the might of the police couldn't come up with a more-than-possible suspect, what luck would I have?

My thoughts meandered down another path. Maybe it wasn't revenge on Jim himself the killer had been after, but possession of Cole House. Did this person believe Jim had been in the way of their getting it?

Ethel Cole, wife of Charles and mother of Emmeline, was originally from Muddle Harbor. Did one of Ethel's relatives want to claim Cole House following Emmeline's death? It seemed a heck of a stretch, even to me. Ethel and Charles died a long time ago.

Jim Cole's father, Robert, had been Charles's brother. As far as I knew, Jim had no immediate living Muddle Harbor relatives, but family relationships could twist and turn all over themselves. Case in point: Trish Dawson, the second (now ex-) wife of Jim, was herself from Muddle Harbor.

Dusk was falling as Mattie and I walked home after work. I tried to sort out those relationships in my head. It was all a jumble; I needed to write it down if I was to understand it. Vicky had once tried to explain to me how she was related to Ryan, who sometimes made her morning deliveries. After describing one branch of her family in which two brothers had married two sisters, and another where a third wife had been a second cousin of the first wife, she threw in some first cousins twice removed, leaving me thoroughly confused.

I could try to draw a Cole family tree. Or I could, once again, go to the source of all gossip: Mrs. D'Angelo.

In that I was to be severely disappointed. I found her tidying the tulip bed, and I'd barely said, "Hello," before I was dragged onto the front porch for iced tea and cookies. After pumping me for everything I knew about yesterday's "shocking incident at the hospital luncheon," she told me everything she knew about the "riot" at the bakery earlier today. Apparently unaware I'd been there, Mrs. D'Angelo told me it was a couple of "mob dolls" from New York City. I nodded politely and accepted another cookie.

Finally, Mrs. D'Angelo paused for breath, and I slipped my question in. "Now that Vicky and Mark are living in Cole House, I'm interested in its history. Ethel, Charles's wife, was from Muddle Harbor, wasn't she?"

"I believe so."

"Are any members of Ethel's family still living there?"

A veil descended over Mrs. D'Angelo's face. Empty eyes stared at me.

"Are you okay?" I asked.

"Yes, yes. I'm perfectly fine. I'm sorry about the cookies. Donalda called me with an update about the Smith situation, and I momentarily forgot about the cookies and left them in the oven for too long." I had no idea who Donalda was or what the "Smith situation" might be, but at the moment I wasn't particularly interested. The cookies were baked perfectly. Good enough that Vicky could put them on her menu. Which reminded me about the rather odd Brittany and what appeared to be her intention to write a cookbook based on the food served at someone else's place.

Back to why I'd come. "Esther Cole," I asked. "What was her maiden name?"

"I . . . I don't know."

"You don't know?" I almost said, *How can you not know?*

"People from Muddle Harbor are not like us, Merry. They're distant. Unfriendly. Hostile to strangers. Close-mouthed about their own."

"Oh. I get it." And I did. Mrs. D'Angelo, who I believed could be an informant for the FBI if she were willing to stick to the truth, had no contacts in that town.

Judging by the look on her face as she apologized once again for the cookies and poured me more tea, even though my glass was three-quarters full, she considered that to be a personal failure. And so she covered it up with an unfortunate us-versus-them attitude, which wasn't all that unusual between residents of the two towns.

"Back to Rudolph, then," I said. "Did you find out anything about the whereabouts of any descendants of Henry Cole's two daughters?

Her face brightened. We were once again on comfortable ground. "The Cole family, as you know, Merry, was very prominent around these parts at one time. The richest family in the entire area for many years, and one of the largest employers. Henry had three children by his first wife: Charles and two sisters. And then one son, Robert, father of Jim, by his second wife. Now, we're clearly talking a long time ago. More than a hundred years have passed since those children were children. It took some digging"—she beamed proudly at me—"but I managed to find out what you wanted to know. Both girls were educated privately. Meaning at home, as sometimes still happened at the turn of the last century. The eldest married a man from Rochester, and she moved with him to that city, where they appeared not to have distinguished themselves in any way. They had no children, and both of them died at a respectable age. The second girl became a nun."

"A nun?"

"A Catholic nun—to the dismay of her proper Presbyterian parents, I believe. She lived in a convent in Kansas until her death at the age of ninety-five."

"There are convents in Kansas?"

"There were when she lived there. I don't know about now."

* * *

I called Vicky as soon as I got in. "I can't believe I'm saying this, but we need to make a trip to Muddle Harbor."

"I can't believe you're saying that either. What brought this on?"

"There are Muddle Harbor threads running through this whole thing. Marjorie told us Trish Dawson, ex-wife of Jim Cole, was from there. As was Ethel Cole."

"Who's Ethel Cole?"

"Charles's wife."

"Which brings us to the question of who Charles is."

"Charles's father, Henry, built Cole house, and Charles inherited it. Charles and Ethel were the parents of Emmeline. You remember who Emmeline was, don't you?"

"Yeah, that name I know. Okay. We know Jim Cole wanted to overturn Emmeline's will and inherit her estate, which consists mostly of the house. *My* house. You're wondering if other relatives might be hiding in the woodwork and considering doing the same now that he, as the closest potential heir, is conveniently out of the picture."

"I am. Most specifically Trish herself. If Trish turns out to be not only Jim's ex-wife but also a distant relative of Emmeline, she might think she has a case for the inheritance."

"Except she hasn't made a claim. No one has. My dad's the lawyer for Emmeline's estate, remember? He's keeping us up to date on that, and no one other than Jim has come forward. According to Emmeline's will, the house was to be sold on her death, which it was. The proceeds from the sale of the house have been transferred to Emmeline's estate. From there it will be distributed to the charities she designated."

"Doesn't mean they're not biding their time, gathering the evidence."

"Seems a stretch, Merry. No one can take the house from us, no matter what they say."

"The money from the sale of the house and whatever else Emmeline's estate consisted of is another matter. Apparently Charles left money in trust for the maintenance of the house. Do you know what's going to happen to that?"

"According to Dad, that's rather nebulous. The fate of the trust, in the event that the last of his descendants died and the house passed out of the family, was never mentioned in Charles's will. I suspect he believed the Coles would always be a prominent and fruitful family."

"Did you hear from Simmonds again, about the fight at the bakery?"

"Candy came in for my original statement, and Diane dropped in after with some questions. She didn't tell me anything in return except that Trish and Louise screamed insults at each other as they were being led away to separate interview rooms. Both of them said Jim Cole was the love of their life." She chuckled. "They seem not to have heard the news."

"What news might that be?"

"Jim Cole, rather than being as wealthy as everyone believed, was barely able to afford a ham sandwich at my place."

"What?"

"Yup. Dad was checking into Jim Cole's situation even before he died. Jim inherited a pack of money on his father's death and proceeded to make a lot of seriously bad investments. He tried to recoup some of his losses by, of all things, gambling. Which worked out about as well as you'd expect. He went to law school when he was young and his parents were still alive, but he never practiced or had much of a job of any sort. He squandered what little he had left after the bad investments—what he should have been holding onto for his old age—in his frivolous lawsuits. The guy was broke and soon to be completely underwater. The last couple of years, he's been caught in a juggling act, pretending to be well-off while he borrowed from one account to pay another, and trying to keep the circle going. That never ends well."

"Does the true state of affairs matter? If he was pretending to have money, it could still be a reason for someone to bump him off. Someone who didn't know they were going to end up with nothing."

"Right, and that brings us to Kevin Farrar. What do you have to report?"

"Report?"

"Yes, report. You were going to check into him. We decided it's possible Kevin accused Mark so publicly as a way of distracting attention from himself. A poor attempt, as he put himself directly under our microscope, but that's his problem. What did you find out?"

I winced. Mattie lifted his head from the rug and gave me a disappointed look. "Sorry. Alan and I went out for dinner last night, and with all that's been going on, I guess I forgot."

"Concentrate, Merry. Concentrate. Okay. You do that tonight, and tomorrow we'll hit Muddle Harbor for what passes for breakfast. I feel my arteries clogging as we speak."

"Why would they clog? You never eat anything there."

"In sympathy with your arteries. I'll pick you up at the usual time. Seven o'clock."

"Okay. Before you go, are you sending out invitations? I haven't gotten anything yet."

"Invitations to what?"

"To your wedding. Details of when and at what church and what time's dinner."

Vicky sucked in a breath. "Oh, that."

"Don't tell me you forgot! You forgot your own wedding! It's next week!"

"I've had things on my mind."

"As I believe someone just said, concentrate, Vicky, concentrate."

"I'd better call my mom. She's probably wondering why I haven't confirmed a date to get her dress yet."

"Never before, in the entire history of the world, has a bride forgotten her own wedding," I said to Mattie after I hung up.

\* \* \*

I settled myself at the kitchen table and opened my laptop. I didn't need to be some sort of tech guru or hacker to find out what I needed to know about Crypto-Masters, Kevin Farrar's business. The information was readily available on the company's website. The premise of the company was that investors would pay a substantial fee to join, and they would then be able to use the software provided to trade cryptocurrencies between accounts, getting a higher rate of return with every transaction. Kevin might not have been a blood relative of Jim, but it seemed as though he had just about as much business sense.

Meaning none.

The front page of the website was nicely done and very slick, which must have cost a bundle, and the photographs were top-notch, also costing a bundle. The description of the company's goals was full of words like *innovative* and *creative*. Potential clients were described as *daring* and *unafraid*. I doubted Cindy had looked past the company image if she was hoping she'd soon be able to quit her own job to start a family.

As I clicked through the website, the pages were increasingly less glossy and professionally designed. The "About Us" page should have been called "About Me," as Kevin was the only staff member mentioned. The list of recommendations from satisfied clients was equally sparse, and when I clicked on the links, most of them gave me an error.

I'm well aware that it can take time to build a successful business. Companies have to grow; seed money has to be raised; contacts nurtured; good employees hired. I considered it highly unlikely Kevin had any more of the needed time. From what little I knew about cryptocurrency, it had already passed as the next big thing. I then did a wider search on Kevin and his wife, Cindy, and found nothing unexpected. They'd lived in New York City until little over a year ago, when they moved to Rudolph. Cindy worked for an insurance broker, as I'd been told. She was involved in several community groups, as suited someone new to town, trying to make friends. She was a member of a bridge club, served on the hospital fundraising committee, and put in one day a week at the hospital's secondhand shop. I found a photo of her dressed in a green and red sweater and skirt, smiling broadly as she served hot apple cider at last year's children's holiday party. My dad was in the background, in his full Santa Claus uniform, Alan next to him in his role of head toymaker.

Kevin himself didn't seem to have any outside interests. He had a business degree from NYU, and he'd been employed by a major investment bank in New York City. He'd quit or been let go (details were murky), and he and Cindy moved to Rudolph, where he started Crypto-Masters. As I am not a hacker, I had no way of telling how he was financially able to manage leaving his job. A bank loan, most likely. If so, the bank would expect to be repaid at some point. Maybe he'd taken the money out of the couple's savings. In that case, Cindy would not be happy to realize the business was not working out as planned.

I closed my computer. Kevin needed money. He believed his father-in-law had money. Jim Cole couldn't have bankrolled his son-in-law if he wanted to, but instead of saying so, he'd put up a pretext of expecting to be closely involved in the business. I considered it likely he'd known Kevin would never agree.

The question was, had Kevin taken steps to get the money without having Jim interfering in the company, which in turn would mean Jim would have discovered exactly how badly Kevin was doing?

All speculation. I sat back with a sigh. I was spinning my wheels and getting nowhere. Plenty of people had reason to want Jim Cole dead, and I knew next to none of them.

He really must have been an awful man. Even dead, he brought out the worst in people.

It would be nice if Trish or Louise had spat out a confession in front of Detective Simmonds. Trish called Louise a gold digger. Louise was a considerable number of years younger than Jim; therefore, it was easy to conclude she'd been with him because she thought he was wealthy. What might she have done if she discovered such was not the case?

What might Trish have done if she thought Jim was going to leave Louise and come back to her, when she found out he had no intention of doing so?

"Enough," I said to Mattie. "We have to get up early tomorrow, so let's have our walk and get to bed."

# Chapter Seventeen

Vicky picked Mattie and me up at seven as arranged. Rubbing sleep out of my eyes and trying to pat down my hair, I'd grumbled about the time, and she cheerfully reminded me she'd put in three hours of work already. "Besides, it's a bright and sunny Monday morning. We need to catch the Muddites before they disperse for what they laughably call a day's work."

The state maintains the highway between Rudolph and Muddle Harbor, which is just as well as otherwise it would be nothing but a muddy, overgrown track these days. Old rivalries sometimes die hard, if ever they do die, and traffic rarely moves along this stretch of road. From my, admittedly biased, point of view, the estrangement between our towns was entirely on the people of Muddle Harbor. They could have tried to ride Rudolph's coat tails to success by offering overflow accommodation and satellite activities, but they stubbornly refused to admit we were doing better than them. They occasionally came up with a brilliant idea that would grant them instant prosperity, but without people like my dad to actually put in the work of making those ideas come to fruition, their town continued to decline.

"What's your plan?" Vicky said.

"You're assuming I have a plan."

"Don't look at me. This wasn't my idea."

"All I want is to gather information. My in-depth investigative reporting tells me no descendants of Henry Cole himself are still living, other than Cindy Farrar, daughter of Jim. So that seals off one line of enquiry."

"By in-depth investigative reporting, you mean Mrs. D'Angelo told you."

"Yes, but I first asked the right question. It's sad, when you come to think of it. Henry Cole had four children. All these generations later he has but one living descendent. Cindy would be his great granddaughter."

"Speaking of Cindy, what did you eventually find out about her and her husband?"

"Plenty. On his part anyway." I related what I'd learned and concluded by saying, "Kevin Farrar had good reason to want Jim dead. Not only to possibly inherit, but he must have been worried Jim would find out the real situation at Crypto-Masters. Jim was an out and out mean man, and to be that mean, he had to enjoy digging up the dirt on people."

"How about Cindy? For the inheritance?"

"I might be wrong, but I can't see it. They might have been estranged most of her life, but Jim was still her father and that's a powerful bond."

"Do we know anything about the current whereabouts of Cindy's mother? She had reason to hate Jim Cole."

I winced. "I never thought to check into her. I also didn't ask Simmonds if Kevin and Cindy have alibis."

"Some detective you are, Merry Wilkinson."

Vicky had brought the bakery van this morning, rather than her two-seater car. Mattie stuck his wet nose between the seats, reminding me he was there. I gave his ears a rub. "As I keep saying, I don't want to be a detective. I just seem to get involved in things I'd rather not."

"Thus the trip to Muddle Harbor. Tell me again why we're doing this when I could be hard at work at my own place. Which, by the way, took some considerable time to clean after yesterday's foofaraw. You can be sure I've itemized every jar of preserves and piece of china that got broken. Not to mention the overtime for my staff to clean up."

"Our sandwiches and Jackie's tea. I never did get lunch."

"It's on the list."

"Back to the matter at hand. We've accounted for all the descendants of Henry and Charles who might think they have a claim on Emmeline's estate, that being only Jim and through him Cindy and Kevin. If any relatives of Charles's wife, Ethel, still live in Muddle Harbor, I'd like to know more about them."

"Under what pretext are you going to get this information?"

"*You* are, Vicky. You've bought Ethel's house, and you want to know more about its history and the history of the family who lived there. You have to admit, it is a fascinating story. Although a tragic one. Poor Ethel."

"I suppose I can do that."

"I'd like to know if anyone had any contact with Emmeline after she moved away. If so, that person, or their descendants, might have had some expectation of getting something when she died."

"Something like my house?"

"Or even just a minor bequest. We can then try, cleverly and subtly, to work Trish Dawson into the conversation. Maybe she's bragging around town about how she's about to be rich rich rich."

Vicky touched the brakes as the speed limit decreased when we crossed into the town of Muddle Harbor. The rising sun disappeared behind a thick bank of clouds, and the temperature dropped a good ten degrees. Main Street was largely deserted, many of the shops boarded up, dusty displays in the few struggling to stay in business, tattered curtains in the windows of the apartments above.

Mattie let out a low whine and retreated to the back seat.

"I'm surprised no one's ever suggested setting a movie here," Vicky said. "A Stephen King eight-part horror series or a postapocalyptic saga. They wouldn't even have to do much work—just film everyday Muddites going about their business."

As usual, the only sign of activity along the main street was at the Muddle Harbor Café. Lights glimmered in the windows, and a row of cars was parked outside. Vicky slipped her car between a couple of rust-covered pickups.

Lights were on inside the restaurant, the windows were clean, and every bulb in the sign worked. I almost salivated. I love a good old-fashioned American diner breakfast, and the Muddle Harbor Café did a great one. Vicky would pretend to be totally dismissive of the high-fat, high-cholesterol, low-vegetable offerings. And then she'd try to steal a piece of bacon off my plate.

I told Mattie to stay, and he promptly curled himself into a ball and closed his eyes.

We opened the door of the café to be enveloped by the marvelous scents of hot buttered toast, fried grease, and fresh coffee.

Nothing had changed since the last time Vicky and I had been here. I've been to places in Manhattan that have spent a lot of money trying to recreate 1950s soda fountain decor. The

Muddle Harbor Café hadn't needed to spend a cent: they'd never tried to keep up with the times. Black-and-white-checked tiles on the floor and the walls, red vinyl–topped stools in front of the long counter, booth seating around the room. The pictures of smiling young people holding soda bottles and advertising for long since departed products that hung on the walls were not modern art; they were the real thing. There were even a couple of posters of tough-looking men on horseback, smoking cigarettes.

The café might be out of date, but it was spotlessly clean and even welcoming.

A group of young mothers, babies in arms or toddlers snoozing in strollers, exchanged news over their coffee. A cluster of old men crowded into a booth, complaining about the weather, their wives and children, and the price they were getting for their crops, as they and their fathers before them had no doubt done every Monday morning for the past hundred years. An elderly couple had newspapers propped in front of them, and spooned up eggs and bacon without looking at each other or speaking. In contrast, a teenage couple, clearly on their way to school, were tucked into the back of a booth, holding hands across the table as they stared deeply into each other's eyes. They even had tall glasses of milkshakes in front of them. They didn't talk either, but unlike the long-married couple, they were saying plenty.

A collection of businessmen were seated around the big center table. I knew Randy Baumgartner, mayor of Muddle Harbor, and Jack Benedict, real estate agent and brother of Janice, owner and head waitress of the café. Two men I didn't know had open binders in front of them. One wore an out-of-place suit and tie, the other was equally out of place in a golf shirt and ironed pants. Dirty plates and empty coffee cups had been pushed aside. Randy and Jack were in sports team T-shirts.

Janice looked up from pouring a round of fresh coffee as Vicky and I came in. She was short and heavyset, round cheeks and wiggling jowls, brown hair streaked with gray pulled sharply off her face and folded into a clip at the back of her head. She wore a gray and white waitress uniform with a frilly pink apron, black stockings, and thick-soled brown shoes. The day had barely started, and she already looked as though her feet hurt, but her eyes crinkled in amusement as she saw us. "At last. They're here. That's twenty bucks you owe me, Jack."

Grumbling, Jack pulled out his wallet and peeled off a bill. He slapped it into Janice's hand.

"What's that for?" Vicky asked.

"Folks are saying there's been yet another murder in Rudolph," Janice said. "I figured you two would show up sooner or later with your suspicions and your questions. Jack said you'd be here yesterday. I bet on today. Randy, pay up. I think you were in for ten."

Randy also handed her some money.

"Seats free at the counter," Janice said, although she needn't have bothered. No one was sitting at the counter. She poured coffee into one waiting cup as she bellowed toward the serving hatch leading to the kitchen. "Two poached eggs, soft, with bacon *and* sausage. Side of mushrooms and onions. Hash browns done to the point of being burned. Wheat toast."

That was for me. Janice was a darn good diner waitress: I didn't even have to order. I slid onto a stool. Vicky perched awkwardly on hers.

"Couple of extra rashers of bacon to-go for the dog?" Janice asked me.

"Yes, thanks."

Vicky clicked her tongue in disapproval.

"What'll you have, hon?" Janice asked my friend. "Dry bread and water good enough for ya? 'Cept my bread isn't made with hand-ground flour made from wheat descended from Egyptian pharaohs."

"Neither's mine," Vicky said. "Just good old prairie-grown wheat and rye. With, sometimes, a handful of barely or oats added for extra nutrition."

I threw Vicky a glare. She shrugged.

"Okay," I said. "We're here. As expected. I come to your place because I enjoy your food, Janice. I hope you know that."

She shrugged, slightly mollified.

"Vicky has some questions, don't you Vicky?"

"What?"

"Questions. About the house. Vicky and her fiancé bought Cole House in Rudolph. Do you know where that is?"

"Of course we know where that is," Mayor Baumgartner yelled. "Place is ten miles down the road."

"I mean the house, not the town."

"I heard it was for sale," Jack Benedict said. "Got sold before I could so much as arrange a showing for my clients."

"Did you have much interest in it?" I asked.

"Not immediately," he admitted. "But there would have been some. Eventually. I think."

"The mother of the previous owner was from Muddle Harbor, wasn't she?" I asked.

"As if you didn't know," Janice said.

"Poached eggs, soft, bacon and sausage. Hash browns and side of mushrooms and onions, up," came a voice from behind the serving hatch. Janice put the laden plate in front of me. I reached eagerly for the ketchup.

"You can run home," Vicky whispered. "You'll have to work some of that off."

"Sorry, I didn't catch that. I was too busy chewing. Sure you don't want some?"

"Dry bread coming up." Janice slapped a plate containing one piece of soft, pure white bread in front of Vicky. "Minimum order is ten bucks."

"Ten dollars!"

"Comes with butter and jam." Janice put down a saucer containing individual little packets. Vicky poked at them with the edge of a knife.

"Bacon to go!" the cook called.

"Okay, you're here now." Janice put a foil-wrapped package next to me. "We might as well talk. Ethel Edwards married Charles Cole in 1935, and she moved to his father's house in Rudolph. Back then folks didn't know better than to move to Rudolph."

"Most amusing." Vicky squeezed a piece of her bread between her fingers. It remained squished when she took her fingers away.

"Does she have relatives still living here?" I asked.

"Jack!" Janice called. "Know of any Edwardes still around?"

"Other than our grandma? No." He laughed heartily.

"What's all this about?" one of the men at his table asked.

"Nothin'. Just nosy neighbors. Now, let's get back to it. You're interested in bringin' your hotels to our town. We're interested in hearin' what you have to say—right, Randy?"

"You got it, Jack," Randy said.

Plenty of businessmen passed through the Muddle Harbor Café. Information was exchanged, notes made, hands shaken. Very little ever happened after that.

"Your grandmother?" I prompted Janice.

"Our grandma, Iris, was Ethel's younger sister."

"That's . . . interesting."

"Ethel was never happy in that big, drafty house. Once she moved to Rudolph, she had a lot of tragedy in her life. You heard about her two daughters?"

"Yes. So sad."

"Iris and Ethel grew up close, but Iris, our grandma, had her own family eventually, so she couldn't do much to help her sister when tragedy struck." Janice leaned one hip against the counter, prepared to settle in for a nice long chat. I continued eating. Vicky hesitantly spread jam on her bread. "It was a bad marriage from the get-go, Ethel's was. Or so the story goes. Not much anyone could do about a bad marriage in those days. Not even a loving younger sister. Eventually, they just stopped visiting, and then stopped writing letters. Nothing but a card at Christmas-time toward the end."

'Did anyone else in the family try to keep in touch over the years?"

"Iris and Ethel were the only kids in their family. Their mom died when they were young. Their father was happy to marry Ethel off to a rich man as soon as he could. She was a great beauty, or so folks said. Iris married a farmer from Muddle Harbor, but she ended up the better off of the two. She was a good grandmother. Wasn't she, Jack?"

"What?"

"Iris was a good grandma."

"Oh yeah. Those parties we had on the farm. I remember eating my weight in corn picked straight out of the field. Slathered with butter she churned herself. Her tomatoes, best in the state everyone said."

I was pleased someone in that family had had a good life. "What about later? Did you know Ethel's daughter, Emmeline?"

"No. Charles died long before Ethel, but by then the sisters had nothing in common. I don't recall ever visiting. Do you, Jack?"

"What?"

"Ever meet Emmeline, Grandma Iris's niece?"

"No."

"Excuse me," the man in the suit and tie said, "we're here to do business. Time's money."

"Not in Muddle Harbor," a man called from across the room.

I popped the last piece of sausage into my mouth. That had been sooooo good. Vicky was eying my bacon. I pretended not to notice. I'd learned what I'd come here for. Emmeline had no relatives in Muddle Harbor who might think they had rights to her property.

"Do you know a woman named Patricia Dawson?" Vicky asked.

"I know the Dawsons," Janice said. "I think they had a girl name of Patty, played softball, far as I remember. Haven't heard of her in years. Jack, do you remember what happened to the Dawson girl?"

"Little Flora? No. What's happened?"

"Not Flora. Patty, from school. Girl around our age."

"Are we doing business here or not?" the man in the suit asked. "If not, I have other places I could be."

"Haven't heard of Patty in years," Jack said.

"Didn't she want to be a movie star or something?" Randy said. "Left town and never came back, far as I remember."

"Guess we're done here." The golf-shirted man slammed his iPad shut.

"Hold on a sec," suit-and-tie-man said. "I'm thinking your offer's not quite good enough yet, gentlemen. We need some further concessions on the rights to that creek running behind the property." He raised his voice, clearly intending Vicky and me to overhear. "I hear there are some good investment opportunities over in Rudolph."

"Let's not be too hasty," Jack said. "Not everything in Rudolph is on the up-and-up, if you get my meaning."

"You can have that last rasher of bacon if you want," I said to Vicky. "I'm stuffed."

"For research purposes only." Vicky snatched it up as if afraid I'd change my mind.

I'd had a delicious breakfast, although I would later come to regret eating so much of it, and I'd learned what I needed to know. It was highly unlikely anyone in Muddle Harbor was expecting an inheritance from Emmeline Cole, and if Janice Benedict hadn't seen Trish (aka Patty) Dawson in years, I could be confident Trish Dawson hadn't been in Muddle Harbor in years.

I crumpled up my napkin and placed it next to my plate, empty but for a smear of ketchup and egg yolk. Before I could climb off my stool, the kitchen doors swung open, and Brittany Pettigrew emerged, carrying a tray with two pies on it. She wore a gray dress with a white collar and a black belt, and sneakers. The dress was similar to Janice's, presumably the standard waitress uniform, but Brittany had rolled her skirt up several times before tucking it into the belt, and she wasn't wearing the frilly pink apron. Her heavy hair was pinned at the back of her head; a few loose tendrils caressed her cheeks. She stopped short when she saw us. Her eyes widened in surprise, and then she broke into a huge grin. "Gosh, hi. Vicky, I didn't know you were here. Welcome."

"Yup, here I am," Vicky said around a mouthful of bacon. "Hi, Merry."

"Brittany, hello. I didn't realize you worked here." I'd forgotten that Vicky had told me that.

"I sure do. I'm the pastry chef."

Janice rolled her eyes.

Brittany indicated the tray she was holding. "I tried making blueberry this morning, like you said."

"Like I said?" I asked.

"Sure. You told me blueberry's your favorite pie. It's not blueberry season yet, but I got these at the supermarket. They were on sale. Would you like a piece? I'd love to know what you think."

"Sorry. I just had the most gigantic breakfast."

"Vicky, would you like—"

"No," Vicky said. "No, thank you. Too early for pie for me."

"Can someone get rid of these plates," the suit-and-tie man called. "They're in the way. I'll have another coffee while you're at it."

Janice nodded to Brittany.

"What?" Brittany said.

"Get the man a coffee, and then clear the tables."

"But I made pie. I'm going to do a cake next. I have this great new recipe—"

"I said, clear the tables."

Brittany dropped the tray on the counter, gave Janice a look that could curdle the cream in my coffee, and went to do as she was told. Janice put the pies onto serving dishes and placed glass domes on top. They looked good, I thought. The pastry was nicely browned, the edges carefully fluted, although the blueberry filling was likely too runny. Some of it was leaking through a crack in the crust.

Brittany came back with a tray loaded with dirty dishes, and marched into the kitchen. The floorboards shook under the force of her indignation. Janice gave Vicky a knowing look and said, "I hear you hire family at your place sometimes. How's that work out?"

"Usually, it works out fine. On occasion, not so good. I hear what you're saying."

"She's my sister's girl." Janice lowered her voice. "Too darn pretty for her own good, I always said. Her daddy spoils her rotten, and her mother pretends not to notice. Makes her think she can get whatever she wants out of life without so much as trying. I figured a season here would put some work ethic into her, but so far that's not working out like I might have hoped. She figures she's too good to be washing dishes and waiting tables. She wants to be a *chef.* Like she sees on those TV cooking shows."

"She came to my place, looking for a job, not long ago," Vicky said. "She told me she worked here. Made it sound as though she's been such a success here, she wanted something . . . different." I thought Vicky showed enormous restraint by not saying "better."

Janice's face scrunched up. "I didn't know that. You didn't hire her, obviously."

"I thought the same as you: she isn't prepared to put in the work. No restaurant, from family diner or hometown bakery to a Michelin-starred joint in Manhattan or Las Vegas, is a place for slacking off. And the only person allowed to have any sort of ego is the head chef. At my place, that's me," said the most un-ego-driven person I know.

"Being the prettiest and most popular girl in a small-town high school never did anyone any good," Janice said. "They grow up thinking they're something special. Hard when they find out they're not so special in the bigger world." She lowered her voice. "Didn't do her any good when her long-time boyfriend, captain of the football team, got a scholarship to Cornell. Brittany didn't have the marks to get into the sort of college she thought good enough for her. Then, first month he was away, he told Brittany not to bother visiting him. Have a nice day, ladies." She started walking away and then hesitated and turned back. "I might pay a call on Rudolph some time. I hear the soup's good at your place."

"You'd be welcome," Vicky said, meaning it.

Janice went through the swinging doors into the kitchen.

Behind us, the two businessmen were telling Randy and Jack they might consider building their hotel in Muddle Harbor if something could be done about loosening those waterfront regulations.

I swung around on my stool, but before I could hop down, I heard angry voices coming from the kitchen.

"What are you doing?" Janice said. "I need those pots and pans washed."

"I'm not a dishwasher, Aunt Janice."

"You're a dishwasher if I say you're a dishwasher. You're a busboy, if I say you are, and if Norm asks you to make the toast for him, you're the toast maker."

"Hey! Leave me out of this," a man said.

"I didn't come here to make toast," Brittany replied. "Any fool can make toast. You said I could practice being a pastry chef."

"You'll learn to wash dishes first, my girl."

"I made that blueberry pie, didn't I? At home on my own time. You didn't even say thank you."

Janice let out a long breath. "Thank you for the pie, Brittany. It looks good, I will admit. But this is not a pastry shop. Other things need doing around here. Such as the making of toast."

"I quit!"

"That's entirely up to you."

The kitchen doors swung open one more time, and Janice came out. She saw us watching, along with the rest of the occupants of the diner. "Employee difficulties," she said calmly.

# Chapter Eighteen

"If Brittany is Janice's sister's daughter, then Brittany is a relation of Emmeline Cole," I said. "We know for an absolute certainty Brittany has been in Rudolph recently. And we know that because we saw her. I think we might be onto something."

"I'm having trouble seeing it, Merry. The family relationship wasn't exactly close, and according to Janice, who quite likely knows everything that goes on in that town, Emmeline's mother—never mind Emmeline herself—never so much as dropped in for a visit with her family in Muddle Harbor. Why would Brittany think she'd be in line to inherit? If her own aunt and uncle, and presumably her mother also, don't?"

"It doesn't have to make sense to us, Vicky. Just to her. You heard what Janice said about Brittany. She thinks she's entitled to whatever she wants. Duck! Here she comes."

"I'm not ducking, and she's not looking at us anyway."

We were sitting in Vicky's van, still parked outside the Muddle Harbor Café. I'd just given the last slice of bacon to an overjoyed Mattie when Brittany came around the corner, presumably having left the café by the back entrance. She looked positively furious as she stormed past us. She'd put a waist-length red leather jacket over her café uniform and pulled high-heeled ankle boots onto her feet. Her long black hair swung loose behind her. We watched her walk away until she turned the next corner and disappeared. Mattie nuzzled my hand, searching for more edible delights.

"She didn't do it," Vicky said. "Brittany wants to be a celebrity pastry chef. She has dreams of starring in a reality TV show. Owning a run-down mansion in Rudolph, New York, doesn't fit into those dreams."

"She might think she could sell the house and use the money to start her baking empire," I said.

"I can't see her thinking that far ahead," Vicky said.

We drove out of Muddle Harbor. The sun came out as we crossed the town line.

* * *

"Did you call your mom last night?" I asked.

"Yes, I did. She gave up waiting for me to arrange something and went shopping by herself to get a mother-of-the-bride dress. She says she got something really nice. Merry . . ." Vicky's voice trailed off.

"What?"

"Do you think I'm being too hasty?"

"Hasty? You've known Mark for a couple of years now. That's not hasty, but if you think it is . . . then it probably is."

"I was thinking it over last night. I forgot that my wedding's next week. How crazy is that? It's like my subconscious is pushing it out of the way."

"If you want my opinion . . ."

"You know I do."

"If your subconscious had doubts, it would keep those doubts front and center at all times. What I'd ask isn't if you want to be with Mark, because I think you do and I know for sure he wants to be with you, but are you really okay with having such a small, casual wedding?"

She turned and smiled at me.

"Watch the road," I said.

Fortunately there wasn't a car to be seen on the road between Rudolph and Muddle Harbor, and Vicky swerved back into her lane. "I am totally okay with the wedding we've planned. Even if I wanted a big splashy affair, which I don't, when on earth would I get around to organizing it? We have the house. I have the book. We both have busy jobs, and the full summer tourist season will be here before we know it, and then the holiday season itself."

"How's the book coming?"

"Not as well as I'd hoped. You told me what you need for the proposal, and I have started on that, but . . ."

"But?"

"First, house buying and moving got in the way, and then all this about Jim Cole dying on our property hasn't helped focus my mind. I'm thinking of asking Kyle Lambert to do the photographs."

"No."

"No?"

"Absolutely and completely not. Are you doing a cookbook to be displayed at the hospital charity shop, for your mom to show to her friends, or one you want published by a real New York publisher for not only your mother but people all over the country to buy and use? If the latter, you need a professional photographer, even for the sample recipes. The publisher will arrange the final photography for the book itself."

"That costs a lot."

"So it does. I hope Mark's not suggesting you cut corners to save money."

"Gosh no. Mark's as keen on the book as I am."

"Good. You're right that so much has been happening lately, but I wouldn't want you to lose momentum on this. It has *bestseller* written all over it. I told you I'd make some calls when you were ready. I'll start on that this afternoon."

"But the proposal's not finished yet."

"Doesn't matter. The concept is what you're selling right now. The concept and your reputation as a baker will get your foot in the door. But once I've done that, you have to get that proposal done soon. Doors don't stay open in the publishing business for long."

\* \* \*

Jim Cole's daughter, Cindy, came into Mrs. Claus's Treasures in mid-afternoon. She greeted me effusively and gushed over the goods we had for sale. She may have gushed, but she didn't show any indication of buying. She admired the jewelry and the table settings and asked Jackie questions about where the locally made items came from.

I waited patiently for Cindy to get to the point. Which, eventually, she did. She finally chose a Christmas tree ornament on sale for $4.99 and brought it to the counter for me to ring up. "It was so nice meeting you and your mother at the luncheon on Saturday, Merry."

"It was a lovely afternoon." I hesitated before adding, "Apart from that one incident." Might as well get it out in the open.

"I am truly sorry about that," Cindy said. "I was totally humiliated, and you can be sure I gave that husband of mine a good talking-to when I got home."

"How did he take that?" I asked.

"About as well as you'd expect." Embarrassed giggle. "Kevin apologized for creating a scene, but—it's been difficult you know. My dad being murdered, no one arrested. The police constantly poking around, asking about Dad, asking questions about us. I can't help but feel as though I'm under suspicion for something I didn't do. We were even asked to provide alibis!"

"Did you have one?" I kept my tone casual. Nonchalant. Just a couple of acquaintances chatting.

"My dad died late at night. Kevin and I had work the next morning. We were home all evening. Our alibis are each other. The detective didn't seem to think that was good enough. Well, too bad for her. Like I said, it's been a difficult time. On Saturday at the lunch, the pressure got the better of Kevin, and he lashed out. That's all."

"No excuses, please. Mark Grosse had nothing to do with your father's death other than being the one who found him and called for help."

"I know that. I told Kevin that. But"—she shrugged—"we were trying so hard to build a relationship with my dad. It wasn't easy, but he was my dad, right? Speaking of parents, I'd love to get that lunch date with your mother settled. We started to arrange it on Saturday, but she got called away before she could give me her number. Do you have it?"

"My mother's phone number? It's not a secret. Her voice studio has a landline and the listing is on 411."

Cindy had the grace to look embarrassed. "I called that number, and I got voicemail. I left a message, but she hasn't called me back. I tried a couple of times but . . . I thought maybe she's not checking it if she's between classes. I was hoping you'd have her personal number."

"I can't give that out," I said. "I hope you understand."

"Oh yes, I totally get it. She wouldn't want random fans calling her up at all hours of the day or night. It'll be okay for me. You heard us talking about that lunch, right?"

"Sorry," I said. "She'll return your call when she gets a chance." Which, I suspected, would be never.

My mother was no longer a star, with an agent and a personal assistant and a publicity team. She taught voice to uninterested children and adults who'd always wanted to sing for fun. She still had some fame in our town because she had been a star, and she could and did play that up when it suited her. These days, she answered the phone in her studio herself. If she wasn't returning Cindy's calls, it would be because she didn't want to. I popped Cindy's ornament into a small brown shopping bag. I was about to hand it to her, when I had a thought.

"You mentioned you and Kevin moved to Rudolph when he started his own business. That must be so interesting. What sort of business is it? Something I might be interested in knowing about? I have the store." I waved my right arm to indicate the premises. "And some small savings from when I worked in Manhattan." That was a lie. I'd cashed in everything I had to start up Mrs. Claus's. So far, it was working out, but retail is a risky business. Like the town of Rudolph as a whole, I'd barely survived the pandemic, although we were now roaring back, stronger than ever. People were eager to get out and travel again. And to shop.

"It wouldn't be right for you, Merry, but your parents would be good candidates for what Kevin can offer." I could almost see the lightbulb appearing above her head as an idea burst into Cindy's mind. "Your mom's got to be more than financially comfortable after the enormous success of her career. Your father's semiretired, people say. My husband owns an invest-ment company. He deals with high-net-worth clients and prom-ises excellent returns." She leaned over the counter. I leaned toward her. "By high net worth, he means a very exclusive clien-tele. Returns are proportionate to risk, and he's prepared to take that risk."

By "he" I knew Cindy meant his clients would be taking all the risk. Not that Kevin had many clients.

I studied her face. Everyone thinks they're a good judge of character, but I've learned the hard way I'm not. Cindy might be thoroughly involved in Kevin's schemes, but I didn't think so. She looked totally delighted at the idea of helping the great Aline Steiner manage her finances. I could almost see her calculating how to invite my parents to her house for dinner to talk it over. If she knew the business was not only failing but had already failed, she wouldn't be so eager to get Mom involved.

"Your husband's doing well, then?" I said. "That's good to know. Are you involved in the running of his business?"

"Oh no. Not me. I simply don't have a head for finance and investments and all that. When I was growing up, my mother had to watch every single penny. She taught me never to go into debt and never, ever risk as much as a cent. Since I finished col-lege and left home, she's been able to put a bit of money aside for the occasional treat or a vacation, but she still won't consider taking her savings out of her bank account. The interest rates she gets are simply shocking. I suggested Kevin help manage her money, but he said he doesn't want to mix family and finances."

Wise of Kevin, I thought. The first Mrs. Cole didn't sound like she was anyone's fool.

Cindy, however, might be. I briefly considered telling her she might want to have a closer look at what her husband was up to, but my attention was distracted by a face peering in the window. Trish Dawson. I wondered how long she'd been standing there watching me. Or was she watching Cindy?

She realized I'd seen her, gave me a little wave, and pulled away from the window.

A moment later, I was handing Cindy her shopping bag when the bells tinkled, and Trish came in. She headed directly for us, hand outstretched. "Cindy. How absolutely wonderful to run into you like this. I was hoping we'd get a chance to meet at last."

Cindy blinked. "Uh. Hi. I'm sorry. Do I . . .?

"Patricia Dawson Cole. Everyone calls me Trish. I recognize you from the wedding picture your father, my darling Jim, so prominently displayed in our living room. Such a gorgeous bride you were. I'm so sorry we weren't at your wedding, but . . . things happen, don't they? Can't do everything. It's so awful that we've never met. And to finally meet like this, under these horrible circumstances." She lowered her eyes and dipped her head.

"Trish? You're my father's second wife?"

Trish's head lifted and a big smile appeared. "That's me! The very one. Jim and I were having our little difficulties, and we were going through a temporary separation when you came back into his life. He told me all about it, of course. How absolutely delighted he was that you and he could be a family again. After the way your mother kept you separated when you were growing up."

"My mother did nothing of the sort." Cindy's voice, previously wary, turned instantly to pure ice. "If my father wanted to be a dad to me, he could have been. I never sent him any wedding pictures. I sent him an invitation, though. He said he was busy. He gave us cash as a gift. And not much of it."

That set Trish aback, but she quickly recovered. "All water under the bridge, dear girl. I don't have any children of my own, and now a grown stepdaughter has come into my life. I'm so delighted." She enveloped Cindy in a hug. Cindy's back straightened, and her arms flapped in the air.

Trish's expression was not one of joyful reunion. More like calculating, I thought. She caught me looking at her and gave me a stiff smile before finally releasing Cindy.

Cindy stepped back, taking herself out of the way of any more demonstrations of unnecessary familiarity.

"I'll be in town," Trish said, "until the police release your father's body. You and I need to discuss his last wishes and make final arrangements."

"We do, do we?" Cindy said.

"Yes. I asked the detective in charge of the case when that might be, but she wouldn't say. I'm staying at the Caroler's Motel. No place for family, is it, particularly if we're going to be waiting for a long time? Do you and your husband have room at your house, dear? I'm dying to meet him."

"No," Cindy said. "We do not." She was making no attempt to be friendly. In this, I was on Cindy's side. Trish was coming on rather strong, and I suspected she had an ulterior motive for all this gushing stepmotherly friendliness.

The store was busy, and Jackie was helping customers. She'd caught the tension in the air, even if Trish hadn't, and was keeping one eye on us while showing an elderly couple the toy display. I'd like to think Jackie was preparing herself to intervene if such became necessary, but it was more likely she was hoping to catch some good gossip she could spread later.

If Trish had never met Cindy, and she'd never seen a picture of her either, she must have been asking around. Maybe she found Cindy's address and waited outside the house to follow her into town.

"The detective couldn't say or wouldn't say? I don't mean to be rude," Cindy said rudely, "but you are not my father's next of kin. I am. All decisions pertaining to his last wishes will be up to me and me alone. You're divorced, right?"

Trish had the grace to look slightly abashed. "That's true, on the surface."

"The surface," Cindy said, "is all I care about. All the law cares about, I dare say."

"What can I say, my darling girl? Your father and I made a terrible mistake, but we were determined to put things right and get back together where we belonged."

"Be that as it may," Cindy said, "my dad didn't have a will. That means he died intestate. And that means, because he was not married at the time of his death, that I, as his only child, will inherit everything he had. No one else."

Anger flashed across Trish's face. So that was what was behind the grieving stepmother act. Trish was after a cut of Jim Cole's estate.

"Not," Cindy said, "that there seems to be anything at all to inherit. Do the words *flat broke* mean anything to you? If not, try drowning in debt." She lifted her shopping bag. "Thanks for this, Merry. Tell your mom to call me sometime, and we can arrange our lunch date."

215

She walked out of the store.

Trish took a deep breath before turning a sad smile on me. "The poor girl. Such a tragedy the way her mother set her against her father."

I said nothing.

"You don't suppose what she said was true, do you? About nothing to inherit? Jim being"—she actually shuddered— "broke?"

"None of my business. As long as we're talking money, I trust you've made arrangements to pay Vicky Casey for the damage you caused at her bakery the other day."

"It's up to Louise to take care of it."

"I doubt that very much. You've been forbidden from going to the bakery, and I suggest you consider that limitation to apply to these premises also."

"What does that mean?"

"It means, get lost."

Trish stared at me through narrow dark eyes. "Don't make an enemy out of me, young woman."

"Not wanting to. Just politely asking you to leave."

She hesitated, and then she turned on her heel and did as I'd requested.

I let out a long breath and gripped the edge of the counter. Jackie put a set of Santa and Mrs. Claus dolls down while her customers continued to browse. "Wow, Merry, I didn't know you had it in you. You ordered someone to leave the store without her even breaking anything. Who was that person, anyway?"

"No one I hope to ever see again. She's Jim Cole's ex-wife. She's here to see what she can get from his estate." I thought about the expression on her face when Cindy told her there was nothing to inherit. Trish had, I thought, been genuinely surprised.

A woman burst through the doors, startling me out of my memories of Trish's behavior. The new arrival wore a pale pink skirt suit. A matching purse swung on her arm, and a string of pearls was around her neck. "Oh, my heavens! This is the most perfect store I've ever seen. Show me everything. Simply everything!"

I slapped my professional smile on and went to work.

The woman bought, and she bought heavily. She wanted dishes and linens for Easter dinner. Might as well get Christmas ones while she was here. That set of necklace and earrings would be perfect for her mother's birthday. The birthday wasn't until next February, but it never hurt to get things ahead of time, did it? As her son-in-law was so incredibly difficult to buy for, she'd get him one of those hand-carved charcuterie boards for Christmas. Her granddaughter was only eleven months old, but as she was clearly so far ahead of other children her age, she would be able to use the train set by Christmas time. Books would make good gifts for the other grandchildren. And as long as she was getting the holiday dishes for herself, another full set would be perfect for her friend Aggie. Poor Aggie didn't often have family to visit, so she didn't go to a lot of trouble. Perhaps the new dishes would inspire her to make an effort.

And . . .

On and on it went. At last, my head spinning, I was ringing up the purchases. The cash register was spitting out a receipt so long it threatened to trail along the floor, and Jackie was packing it all up.

"Can we help you get this to your car?" I asked when the woman in pink was digging through her gigantic purse in search of the card with which to pay the substantial bill—substantial enough that I could close the shop for the rest of the month if I so desired.

She stopped digging and eyed the stacks of boxes. She hesitated. I started to get a bad feeling about this. "I'm not so sure. My enthusiasm might have gotten the better of me. My husband will have something to say when he sees all this, but one doesn't get to Christmas Town every day." She sighed. "Do you happen to know if Santa Claus is around?"

"He keeps a low profile at this time of year," I said. "He'll be here in July for his summer vacation and again over the holiday season of course."

"Not until July?" Her expression dipped in such disappointment, I was afraid she was going to change her mind and decide not to take any of the goods. "I don't know if we'll be able to come back then. My husband likes to golf in the Hamptons in the summer months."

At that moment the door opened, and none other than my own father came in. It was a warm spring day, but he was dressed in one of his beloved ugly Christmas sweaters, this one featuring Rudolph's face and antlers, with a flashing red bulb as the nose. He wore red woolen pants and high black boots. His blue eyes sparkled, his gray hair was a bushy mess, and his beard needed a trimming. He patted his generous stomach and said, "Ho ho ho" to the woman.

She gasped.

Jackie gasped.

The other customers gasped.

I might have gasped myself. I know my father isn't Santa Claus, but sometimes, I do wonder.

"Looks like I'm in time to give you a hand, madam," he said. "Jackie, get the cart out of the storage room, will you?"

Jackie ran through the curtain into the back.

"Santa Claus?" the big spender asked as she handed me her credit card.

My dad winked at her. "That would be telling. Thank you, Jackie. I hope your car's not far, madam. I'm not as young as I once was, and I don't have any of my enthusiastic little helpers with me today."

The woman signed the credit receipt while Jackie stacked boxes onto the cart. When it was fully loaded, my dad maneuvered it out the door. Jackie walked beside it, her hand on the top, keeping it all steady. The woman, still gaping, followed.

A frenzy of shopping began.

There's nothing like watching people shop to get other people shopping, and Jackie and I were on the hop for the rest of the day. My dad did not come back.

When we'd finally waved the last of the customers, weighed down by their shopping bags, out the door, we turned the lock and flipped the sign to "Closed." Jackie leaned against the wall and said to me, "How did your dad—"

"Jackie, some things in life are better left unknown."

I took Mattie for a quick stretch in the alley and then spent some time on the store accounts. So much had been bought today, my shelves were decimated. I needed to get rush orders placed.

A good problem to have.

Finally, I switched out the lights, and Mattie and I walked home. Easter Weekend was coming up, and town would be busy. I was taking the entire day off on Saturday for Vicky's wedding, but Jackie and Melissa should be able to handle it. Sunday the store would be closed, and Alan and I were due at my parents for Easter dinner in the evening. Alan suggested we spend the night after the wedding at his place. We could enjoy the spring woods before dinner the next evening, and I was looking forward to that very much. Thinking of Vicky's wedding reminded me I hadn't decided what to wear yet. I was unofficially the maid of honor, but considering how small and casual the event was, I wouldn't need the equivalent of a big-sleeved, puffy pink dress. Perish the thought. It would be nice to get something new. Something springlike and cheerful.

I considered asking Vicky to accompany me, but decided not to. She had, as she said, more than enough on her plate right now. I'd ask Mom. Her taste tended toward the flamboyant, but I should be able to control her. I hoped so, anyway.

Mattie woofed quietly at a small, fluffy dog walking toward us. The other dog growled and lunged at Mattie, all teeth and aggression. Mattie simply looked bemused. The owner gave me an embarrassed shrug and said, "She's still in training. Sorry." They carried on.

The incident reminded me of Trish and Louise facing each other down at Victoria's Bake Shoppe, except in their case, both of them had been the small dog, eager to bring it on. Neither of them had been Mattie, wanting nothing more than to get home for dinner.

As we passed the town park, a man stepped out from behind a tree into the circle of light cast by the streetlight above. I was so startled, I gave a small gasp, and I stumbled. Mattie sniffed the man's shoes. The pink and blue lights of the town's holiday tree glimmered in the distance. No one was out walking, but cars passed slowly by, people heading home for dinner and a night in.

"Good evening," Kevin Farrar said.

"Goodness. You startled me," I said.

"Did I?" Notably he didn't apologize, as anyone would if such had not been their intention. "I'd have thought you'd be safe enough wandering the streets on your own at night, with a dog that size."

Mattie caught something in Kevin's voice, and he growled, the sound low in his throat. I didn't have to be a dog to catch it too.

"You're right," I said. "He's a good guard dog."

Kevin looked at Mattie. "So I see. He might lick an attacker to death."

"Nice talking to you." I pulled on the leash. "Come on Mattie. We're almost home."

At the magic word, Mattie forgot about imminent danger and started to walk away. I was about to follow when Kevin said, "I hear you've been asking about me."

"What?" I quickly went over my activities. I hadn't been asking around—not at all. I'd done research on the internet, but I found nothing that wasn't publicly available to anyone with the bare modicum of computer skills. I stopped walking and turned to face him. "You hear wrong."

"I'm a businessman. I've been working hard to make contacts all over this part of the state. I have feelers out to the neighboring town."

"You mean Muddle Harbor? I—" When Vicky and I had been in the café earlier, one of the visiting men mentioned investment opportunities in Rudolph. Jack Benedict implied shady things sometimes went on in Rudolph. I'd dismissed that comment out of hand as nothing but town rivalry. It was entirely possible Jack or someone else from Muddle Harbor was considering investing with Kevin. Had they told him we'd been in the café asking questions?

Had Kevin Farrar's guilty conscience immediately jumped to the conclusion that we'd been specifically asking about him?

"Why would that be a problem for you, Kevin?" I asked. "Your wife told me you own an investment company. I might have money to invest. I know people who do have money to invest."

He relaxed fractionally. "I wouldn't like to think you've been poking your pretty little nose into things that don't concern you, that's all."

Seeing we were no longer heading toward home, Mattie had come to sit next to me. He might not be an attack dog, but his bulk was still an enormous comfort to have at my side. Another car drove by. It was, I thought, extremely unlikely Kevin Farrar would attack me here, on the sidewalk, in the early evening. Nevertheless, I kept a firm hold of Mattie's leash with one hand, and put my hand on the phone in my pocket with the other. "Exactly what sort of things are you talking about?"

"My father-in-law died on your friends' property. Your friend, the chef, is still under suspicion. From what I hear, anyway."

"Sounds to me as though you don't hear much. The cops have moved on to other suspects."

Kevin blinked. "What sort of other suspects?"

"How about you, Kev? People believed Jim Cole was a wealthy man. Be nice to get an unexpected infusion of cash into this business of yours, wouldn't it?"

I braced myself for him to lash out, but if anything, he relaxed fractionally. He even grinned at me. "Would have been nice, yeah. Too bad that didn't happen. Guy was a waste of space, but I thought if it made Cindy happy to have her father back in her life, I'd go along with it. Turns out it didn't make her happy. Not at all. He wouldn't have hung around for long. Not once he realized she had nothing to give him. If you're thinking I killed him for his money, think again. I'll admit I asked him to invest in my business, but I didn't like his conditions. So I did some digging. I still have contacts in the banking world, and it didn't take much effort to discover the guy didn't have two nickels to rub together. Although he was still pretending he did. He couldn't have kept that up for much longer."

"I don't know why you're telling me this," I said.

"I'm a businessman. I have a reputation to maintain. Actually, I have a reputation to build, seeing as to how I'm new in your fair town. Jim's death had nothing to do with me, and I wouldn't want anyone to think it did. So, I'm asking you, politely, to stay out of it. In Rudolph or in Muddle Harbor."

"Good night," I said. I started walking, trying not to hurry toward the cheerful lights of the bandstand. Mattie trotted along behind me.

Kevin Farrar made no attempt to stop us, and he said nothing more.

\*   \*   \*

When at last we reached our house, Mrs. D'Angelo was sitting on her porch. She caught sight of us and jumped to her feet, waving and calling out. I waved back, but I said, "Let's walk some more, Mattie."

Not that I was trying to avoid my landlady (a foolish endeavor at the best of times), but I had a lot to think about.

I might be naive, but I considered Kevin's attempt to threaten me, if it could even be called that, so weak and foolish, it was hard to believe he might have killed his father-in-law. Kevin admitted he'd asked Jim for money. He would have checked into Jim's finances. Kevin had worked at an investment bank until recently, and he would likely have plenty of contacts in that world. Once Kevin realized Jim had no money, he'd have no reason to kill the man.

If Kevin hadn't killed Jim, someone else had. Why, I then had to wonder, was Kevin so eager to throw suspicion onto Mark? Could he be covering for someone? Cindy? Had Cindy killed her father and Kevin knew it, or did he suspect she had? She'd told me their only alibis were each other.

As we walked, I tried to remember exactly what I'd been thinking about when Kevin stepped into my path. Trish and Louise and their ridiculous, childish battle in the bakery. That was it. Thinking of that reminded me of Trish following Cindy into Mrs. Claus's and their not exactly joyful meeting.

After the two women left the store, I'd been so busy I hadn't had the opportunity to consider all of what happened between them, and what Cindy had told me. Jim Cole died without a will. Which didn't much matter as he didn't have anything to leave anyone.

Dusk was settling over town, and a couple of the brightest stars had come out. On the other side of a row of houses, past the town path, the dark waters of the lake lapped against the shore. The air was soft and full of the scent of new growth, plants pushing themselves up out of the slowly warming soil, buds opening on the trees. One of the neighbors had given his lawn an early cut, and the lovely smell of freshly mowed grass curled around me. Mattie walked contentedly at my side, sniffing at the occasional tree or fire hydrant, but not in a mood to stop for a closer inspection. At first, I'd kept myself on alert, peering into shadows, straining my ears, hoping I wasn't wrong about Kevin

Farrar and he wasn't following me with the intention of doing more than telling me to leave his affairs alone.

But I sensed nothing, and most importantly, neither did Mattie.

On such a lovely evening, my thoughts were focused on revenge, hatred, lies, and murder most foul.

I briefly considered Trish might have killed Jim for the money she believed he had. But, as Cindy pointed out, the couple were divorced, and Jim had a living child. Trish should not have had any expectations of inheriting anything.

Unless Jim had told Trish she was mentioned in his will. I reminded myself he was a not-nice man. On the other hand, no one claimed he was an idiot. He'd be unlikely to give a woman he was estranged from, and whose character he surely knew well, a reason to bump him off.

It was still possible Trish had killed him, though. Had she come to this area hoping to talk him into getting back with her? Had he laughed at her, mocked her, maybe flaunted his much younger girlfriend in front of her? And then, had Trish decided to kill him, inheritance or not?

The same logic applied to Louise. She believed Jim was, if not actually rich, then well-off. She wouldn't have stayed with him otherwise, and surely he knew that. Did he tell her she was his heir, to keep her hanging onto the relationship?

That was possible.

Had I been too quick to dismiss Kevin Farrar, Cindy's husband? He needed money. He told me he knew his father-in-law didn't have any money, but had he only learned after Jim's death about the true state of his finances?

And what about Cindy herself? She knew her father had nothing to leave her. Most likely she'd only recently learned that. Following his death, his lawyer would have been in touch with her and let her know the true state of affairs. She didn't seem all that bothered about it. She'd probably never expected anything from him in the first place. Which brought me to wondering how much anger she held against him for leaving her mother and herself to a life of poverty when he could have provided them with so much more.

*Enough anger to kill him?*

I didn't think so. Killing a father, estranged or not, is a big step. Cindy might have struck wildly at him, releasing years of pent-up rage, but I didn't believe she could hide what she'd done. Or even attempt to. She wouldn't have run away, leaving Mark to find the body. She would have confessed immediately and hoped the court would have some sympathy toward her. Then again, as I've said, I'm a lousy judge of character. She might well have done precisely that—killed him in a fit of anger.

I truly believed she was in the dark about what was going on with Kevin's business. Was she that naive, or simply that trusting? I have no more financial savvy than anyone else, and I'd realized pretty quickly Kevin was in a lot of trouble. I thought of the first Mrs. Cole saving carefully and watching every penny. A good lesson for a young girl to learn, but it might have made Cindy too trusting when it came to financial affairs.

Unless the business I'd found so easily was nothing but a front, and Kevin and Cindy were into something deeper and darker. Something they needed Jim's money (what money they incorrectly believed he had) to get them out of. Or deeper into.

I shook my head. Far too many instances of *unless* in this case.

My phone buzzed and I checked the display. Vicky.

"Hey, what's up?" she asked.

"Nothing much. Are you at home?" When I'd seen her name, my heart leaped into my throat, worried something bad had happened with the Jim Cole murder case, but as soon as I heard her voice, I relaxed. She sounded calm. Normal. "I've finished at the store. We had an amazing day. I'm walking Mattie now."

"I thought you might like an update on the Jim Cole case."

"Definitely. What's happened?"

"Diane Simmonds dropped by the house this morning. Around the time you and I were coming back from Muddle Harbor. Mark was in. She didn't come right out and say he was in the clear—you know her—but she pretty much implied it. She's building a case against Louise Ferguson."

"Wow. Why? How? What's she got?"

"All circumstantial so far, but they're digging further. Louise rather foolishly brought herself to police attention with that incident at my place. The police then looked more closely at her. She has a record of minor embezzlement as well as stalking an ex-boyfriend to the point he got out a restraining order against her. The cops in Syracuse found a witness who says Louise was furious with Jim for what she called 'holding out' on her. Which the so-called friend thinks means Louise thought he wasn't spending enough on her. Plus her alibi isn't holding up. No one can positively place her at the time of Jim's death or in the hour before or after. Plus, ta da . . .!"

"Spit it, Vicky."

"The friend told the cops Louise has another boyfriend on the side."

"That must keep her busy."

"He's someone her own age, according to the friend. Simmonds didn't say anything else about the other guy, or even if she's spoken to him, but Mark thinks she's thinking Louise might have decided to get rid of Jim so she could be with the other guy, and hopefully have Jim's money too."

"But Jim died without leaving a will."

"He did? How do you know that? My dad hasn't come back to me with that info yet."

"Cindy told me. She was in the store earlier, making friendly, hoping I have some influence with my mom—"

"As if."

"Precisely. Anyway, who came in when Cindy was there but none other than Trish herself. And not by coincidence either. I suspect she's been following Cindy, waiting for the right time to approach. Trish wanted to be all besties, but Cindy was having none of it." I told Vicky the rest of what happened.

"Jim Cole had no money and no will," she said when I'd finished. "Someone killed him for nothing. They are going to be seriously annoyed."

"We don't know that was the reason for the murder, Vicky. Don't forget that Jim was a reverse Santa Claus. He made enemies and spread ill will everywhere he went. But back to the subject at hand: if someone did kill him for what they thought he had, it would be unlikely to be Louise. She has no claim to anything of his, even less than Trish, who was a former wife."

"You know that. I know that. Did Louise? Maybe not. It's unlikely good old Jim said to her, "Love you, babe, but I'm not leaving you a red cent.""

"True. He probably did string her along. Can the police place Louise in Rudolph around the time?"

"Reading between the lines, Mark doesn't think so. Like I said, any evidence they have so far is circumstantial and based on a lot of hearsay. Her other boyfriend might have been in on it. That's just me guessing; Simmonds didn't say anything about him."

"Good to hear. I'm confident Simmonds will get her. Get them. She's a good detective and can be mighty determined when she sets her mind to something."

"My wedding can go ahead, worry free!" Over the phone I heard the sound of her hands clapping. "Mark's got workers coming next week to get started replacing the windows and the floorboards in what's going to be our living room. I'm working on the book proposal at the moment, so I'd better get back at it. I need to come up with synonyms for *delicious*. Try and think of some will you."

"Tasty. Yummy. Good."

"Be slightly more imaginative, please, Merry. Oh—Russ has agreed to take some photos for me at no charge. As a wedding present, he says. He's going to come into the bakery one day this week to do that."

"Sounds great. Good night."

"Good night."

I hung up. I walked home feeling as though a weight had been lifted from my shoulders.

# Chapter Nineteen

My mother had been surprised and pleased when I invited her to come dress shopping with me Tuesday morning. Which made me realize we hadn't been shopping together since I'd last been in need of adult supervision.

She hadn't been so pleased when I asked her to meet me at ten, when the stores opened. "Ten o'clock? You mean in the morning?"

"Yes, Mom. I mean ten in the morning. I've been taking a lot of time off from my own store, and I'll be missing the whole day Saturday. Jackie's getting delusions of grandeur, and I'm worried she's about to ask for another raise."

"If she does, tell her no."

"She'll threaten to quit."

"Let her threaten. She knows full well she'll never get another job where she's so indulged."

"Does everyone in town think I spoil Jackie?"

"Yes. Jackie most of all."

"Ten o'clock."

"If I must. We'll go for a nice lunch after."

* * *

My mom and I had fun. She didn't try—not too hard, any-way—to press an outfit that would be more suitable for a Met Gala on me. "Suitable for a garden party at Buckingham Palace," Mom instructed Jayne when we arrived on our mission.

"We're going to a wedding in Rudolph, New York," I said.

"The wedding of your closest and dearest friend in the world, Merry."

I soon found something I was delighted with. Light, color-ful, summery. I agreed to have coffee with Mom before going back to the store, although I had to tell her I didn't have time for lunch.

With Easter weekend approaching, the streets were busy with shoppers. Most of the store windows were decorated in themes of blue and pink; plenty of flowers for spring, and eggs and bunnies for Easter. The Easter Parade wagon rumbled toward us, filled with laughing children and smiling parents. As there was no snow, the traditional Christmas sleigh had been fitted with wheels, but it was still pulled by two large horses, their manes festive with blue and pink ribbons. Local farmer and Rudolph institution George Mann was at the reins. George had refused, absolutely and completely, to dress as the Easter Bunny.

"Shall we hop on the sleigh for the ride across town?" I sug-gested to Mom.

"No," she said flatly.

And so we walked. Once we were settled at a table by the window in Cranberries, she cradled her latte and asked, "How's Vicky's cookbook coming?"

"It's been slow. She's had so much on her mind lately, but now she's focusing again and getting it back on track."

"Good. She works so hard, she deserves it to be a grand success. I'm excited about buying it. I hope the bookstore will put on a major event."

"Are you intending to make any of the things in it?" I said with a smile, already knowing the answer.

"Of course not. It will be nice to display in the kitchen for the admiration of my friends when I tell them how close Vicky and I are."

"You're jumping the gun, Mom. She doesn't have a publisher yet. I sent emails to some of my publishing contacts in the city this morning, before meeting you, and I'm hoping someone will agree to have a look at her proposal. If they do, and if she gets the proposal finished, I'm sure they'll love it. Christmas cookbooks are hugely popular."

"Hopefully not too popular. It's a crowded field," said the woman who'd never opened a cookbook in her life. My dad has always been the cook in our family. "Vicky's book needs to have that something special to stand out from the rest."

"It will. Not only because of her baking, but the whole Christmas Town thing should help."

"There are only so many ways you can make a mince tart, dear."

"Vicky knows the best way. Why are you suddenly being down about this? A minute ago you were looking forward to displaying your own copy."

Mom peered at me from over the rim of her cup. "I'm sorry if I am. I'll admit I know absolutely nothing about the world of publishing in general, and publishing baking books in particular. But I do recall a number of years ago when a soprano of middling talent brought out a biography she'd spent years working on after she retired. Her book was published the very same week as a biography of a major baritone. Not only was he the better-known singer, but his life consisted of the stuff tabloids love. The soprano's book was all about her happy family and the joys of being part of the opera community. Her book was by far the better written, but it was a flop. His sat on the bestseller lists for a year."

"That wouldn't be the book you bought as a Christmas gift for everyone you know, would it? Because he had some nice things to say about you?"

She colored slightly. "I forget the details now. All I am saying, dear, is I wouldn't like Vicky to get her hopes up for a major success."

"Hopes are necessary, Mom. Look at you. You hoped to be an opera star. And thus you were."

She sipped her coffee. A light shone behind her eyes, and her grin was wicked. "So I was. And unlike the aforementioned soprano, I didn't see the good in everyone. The stories I could tell if I decide to write a book. Which I have no intention of ever doing."

* * *

That night I was curled up on the couch, searching for something to watch on TV. I felt restless, for no reason I could identify, so I wanted to find something I didn't have to pay much attention to. I settled on a baking competition show. A light rain had begun shortly after I got home; drops pattered on the windows, and wind rustled the still-naked branches of the trees. Mattie snoozed on the rug in front of the TV, and I enjoyed a glass of water. Earlier I'd microwaved my dinner.

Another exciting night in the life of Merry Wilkinson.

I soon got bored with the program. Some of the creations were so far beyond what the average baker could achieve they might as well have been made with magic. That got me thinking about Vicky's book. She was focusing on the sort of festive, holiday desserts any reasonably competent person could make at home with a bit of extra time and effort. I hoped she'd manage to get it finished. The book was sure to be a hit. I might even try my hand at making something from it myself, to take to a potluck or family dinner. My mom had pointed out that even if Vicky finished the book and it was as good as I expected, success was not guaranteed. Much of how well it did would depend on the competition, and new baking books were coming out all the time.

I shot upright.

Mattie jerked awake and barked.

*Competition. New baking books.*

Could it be?

I grabbed my iPad and made a quick check on the internet of something I needed to know.

*Yes, it could be.*

I grabbed my phone and called Vicky. It rang a few times, and then she answered, sounding sleepy. "What's up? It's kinda late, Merry."

"Is it? Sorry." I glanced out the window. All was dark.

"I'm in bed reading. About to switch out the light."

"Is Mark home?"

"Not yet."

"I'm coming over. I've thought of something that might be important."

"Missing-sleep important?"

"Potentially."

"I'll put the kettle on."

I told Mattie to guard the apartment, grabbed my purse and keys, and ran downstairs. Vicky's new house was within comfortable walking distance, but the rain was getting stronger, and I didn't want to take the time. I got my car out of the garage and tore down the street.

Streetlights cast pools of yellow onto the wet sidewalks. A few lights still shone from behind curtains on Lakeside Drive. New carriage lamps had been installed on the gateposts at the property at the end of the street and glowed with a welcoming yellow light. The gate was secured by a section of chicken wire loosely tossed around the frames on the top rail, but it wasn't locked. A small branch flopped across the top of the gate, blown there by the wind, a twig caught on one of the bars. I got out of the car opened the gate, went back to the car, drove through, got out of the car again, and shut the gate, securing it with the wire, got back into the car, and finally drove up the lane. The branch on the gate hadn't been disturbed, and the rain began to fall harder.

Vicky's Miata was parked in front of the closed garage doors, but Mark's car was gone. A light burned above the front door. The door was open, and Vicky and Sandbanks stood there. My friend was in her pajamas, a cute pants and T-shirt set featuring yellow cartoon characters. Her feet were bare, her toenails painted a sparkling dark purple.

"Tea's made," Vicky said. "What's so vitally important you've come out at this time of night? And in the rain."

As if to emphasize her point, the rain increased, and the wind picked up its pace. Branches growing too close to the house scratched against the walls and windows.

She stepped back and I came inside. Sandbanks sniffed my shoes and pant legs, catching up on the news from Mattie. I shook rainwater out of my hair. There wasn't yet a table in the entrance hall, so I tossed my bag onto the floor. "You told me you've had no more incidents of strange noises in the house since Jim Cole died, right?"

"Yes. Nothing. The police conclude he was responsible for all that nonsense, and Mark and I agree."

"Maybe. Maybe not. Is it possible someone else was poking around here, and his death scared them off?"

"Anything's possible, Merry. I'm just happy they've stopped. Whoever they were."

"Stopped. For how long will it stay stopped? The person might get their nerve up again and come back when the attention dies down."

Vicky twisted the lock on the door behind me, and we walked together down the long hallway to the kitchen. A teapot emitting aromatic steam sat in the center of the table, along with two cups and containers for milk and sugar.

Vicky plopped herself into a chair. "Tea?"

"Sure."

Sandbanks gave me a final sniff and wandered out of the room. Vicky poured the tea and passed me a cup.

I cradled the warm cup in my hands. "With all that's been going on, the Jim Cole murder in particular, we've lost sight of a minor issue that might turn out to be not so minor. Someone tried to break into the bakery a few days ago, right?"

"Yes. The alarm went off, the police were called. Whoever tried to break in was long gone by the time the cops arrived, and they hadn't gotten inside."

"The police said there hadn't been any other break-and-enter attempts on Jingle Bell Lane that night."

"The person got scared off."

"That word again. I can't stop wondering if that incident could be somehow related to what was going on here earlier. Did the police have anything more to report about it?"

"No," Vicky said. "They took fingerprints around the door but found nothing other than those of me and my staff. And, by the way, yours. Some scratches in the doorframe where the person tried to wedge the door open. That must have been what set the alarm off. They told me to let them know if it happened again. As though I might forget to call. "

"The attempts to get into this house were pretty clumsy, along with noises in the night, which you'd think any barely competent wanna-be thief would try to avoid. When the cops searched the house and property after Jim's death, they found signs of previous attempted break -ins, right?"

"Recent ones, yes, but they couldn't say how recent. This house has always been a magnet for bored kids."

"But now someone's living here. That should be enough to end the spooky element kids are looking for. No other houses on this street have reported incidents."

"I don't know about that, but so what?"

"Hear me out. Let me hear my own self out. This is all just coming together in my mind. Why would your bakery be the target of a break-in? What do you have worth stealing?"

"I have a great deal of expensive equipment, Merry."

"Yes, you do. The stoves, the fridges, high-end industrial mixers and such. Not the sort of thing a midnight prowler can carry away without making a lot of commotion and needing a moving truck. Baking trays and cake pans. Flour and sugar. Not usually the object of random theft, compared to say the jeweler's or the electronics store."

"Those places probably have better security than the bakery."

"Maybe. How about this house? You guys have a TV and your own computers, but you haven't fully moved in yet. No art on the walls, for example. No heirloom silver. No one would think you or Mark have much worth stealing. You're just a young couple starting out, without all the stuff older people accumulate." I thought of my parents' house. My mother's jewelry, mementos of her travels, the gifts she'd been given by adoring fans or fellow artists.

"Your point is?"

"What do you have in this house, and in your place of business, no one else has?"

"Sandbanks?"

"Recipes."

"What?"

"The recipes you're developing for your book. The notes you're making about them. You have the outline of the book on your laptop, but most of the recipes themselves are on paper, right?"

"Yeah. I always work off paper when I'm following a recipe. I can fasten the page to something metallic at eye level, rather than trying to scroll through a screen. I can make notes with a pencil in sticky hands I wouldn't want to touch a device with. What of it?"

I said nothing. I watched my friend process all I'd been saying. "The recipes are on my laptop though," Vicky said at last. "All of them. It's backed up to the cloud regularly. My latest notes might not be recorded right away, but anything that recent would still be in my head. If someone stole my recipe folder or the computer, all I'd have to do would be download them again. Why then—" The light dawned. "Someone wants my recipes to put out a book of their own."

"That's what I believe. Recipes can't be copyrighted, right? I checked into that before calling you."

"It's possible but difficult to do. There must be hundreds, thousands, of recipes for chocolate cake out there in the world, and all anyone has to do is make a simple change to make the recipe their own. Like ask for a quarter teaspoon of salt instead of a half. Plenty of recipes float around between friends and within families; no one can trace where it began ,to make a claim on it. If the recipe is completely unique and can be proven to be so, it can be copyrighted, but that's hard to prove and harder to do. None of mine are anything like that. Most of my recipes are old favorites updated. My mince tarts, for example, are my grandmother's recipe. Half the women on my mother's side of the family make them exactly the same way."

"Who's lately been showing an excessive amount of interest in your baking, Vicky? Who's been trying to analyze your pastry? Who's been hanging around your place watching what people are ordering? Who asked me what my favorite and least favorite desserts of yours are, as though she was doing a survey or something?"

"Brittany Pettigrew. She who wants to be the pastry chef of the Muddle Harbor Café."

"Bingo."

"She asked what's your least favorite thing I make? What did you say?"

"I don't think that matters right now, Vicky. Brittany makes no secret of her ambition to be a pastry chef, and not just a pastry chef, but one of great renown. She doesn't want to go to the trouble to learn the necessary skills. She wants to do it all right now. She wants to have it all right now. Her own aunt told us Brittany wants to do things the quick and easy way because that's the way it worked when she was the popular girl at school. Yes, she can make a few standard things herself, like the blueberry pie she brought out at the café, but she has nowhere near enough to put in a book, and no amount of small-school popularity is going to come to her aid this time. When you interviewed her, she told you she was planning on writing a holiday-themed baking book, but only after you mentioned you were working extra hard because of your own book. Was that true, or did she suddenly decide to do it because you put the idea in her head? Regardless, she intends to use your recipes. To do that, she has to get her hands on them."

Vicky thought for a long time. "You might be onto something, Merry. If so, she's been scared away from the house by the police attention around the death of Jim Cole, but she'll likely be back."

"I think it's more than that, Vicky. I think Brittany killed Jim."

"Why? What possible reason would she have to do that? Did they know each other?"

"Not that I'm aware, but I don't think it matters. Jim Cole was looking for a way of overturning his aunt's will. That's the game he was playing, anyway. Did he know he was wasting his time and money, but didn't care? That's possible. Lawsuits were as much an addiction for him as gambling is for some people. He was compelled to keep doing it. Then again, he was out of money, and although his late cousin wasn't wealthy, Emmeline's estate would have realized some value from the sale of this house. She intended to leave all of it to a women's charity, not to her only surviving relative.

"As has been pointed out, this house is now legally yours and Mark's. I don't know enough about the laws of inheritance to know if you could be forced to sell the house back to the estate if the will was overturned, but that doesn't matter. Jim never showed the slightest bit of interest in the house before Emmeline died, so I consider it unlikely he wanted the house itself. He wanted the money you paid the estate for it. The only chance he had of overturning the will was if he could prove Emmeline was not in her right mind. One way of doing such would be to show that she was mentally unable to take responsibility for her own property. Specifically, the upkeep of this property. Simmonds found pictures of the exterior of the house and the grounds on his phone. Pictures taken the day he died, at night and not exactly showing the place in its best light. Jim Cole was obviously here once. No doubt about it. As for the other times? I don't see it. He wouldn't have needed to come into the house for the proof he was after, and even if he did, all he had to do was knock on the door and ask to see the old family home one last time. He would have had no reasonable explanation to give you for wanting to take pictures of the desolate garden late at night. So, he came without asking permission or letting you know he was here. I speculate he saw Brittany creeping around at the same time, trying to actually get into the house. Did he attempt to blackmail her? He wasn't above doing that. Did he suggest they join forces, and something went wrong? Possible."

"Can you prove any of this?"

"Not a single word. But we have enough to have a chat with Detective Simmonds in the morning. Once she starts pulling on one thread, she'll eventually unravel the entire ball of wool."

Our tea sat between us, ignored. From the other room came the sound of Sandbanks snoring with great enthusiasm.

A bell rang. I just about leaped out of my skin. "What was that?"

"The doorbell. Mark had it installed yesterday." Vicky stood up. "He must have forgotten his keys. No one would be calling at this time of night without texting first."

"I'm going home," I said. "You get up first, so why don't you call Simmonds in the morning and arrange a time for us to talk to her?"

"Will do."

We walked down the hallway together. The window set into the front door showed nothing but darkness and rain beyond. Vicky stretched her hand toward the lock.

Mark worked at the Yuletide Inn. The inn was on the outskirts of town, several miles from here. Mark would not walk to work. Vicky's car had been the only one in the driveway when I arrived, and the garage was currently stuffed full of moving boxes and construction equipment. Mark must have driven to work. Surely, he, like everyone else in the world, kept his house keys on the same chain as his car keys.

"Wait!" I yelled.

Vicky half turned at the same time as she twisted the lock. "What?"

I tried to shove my friend out of the way, get to the opening door, but I was too late. Brittany Pettigrew stepped into the hall. Her dark hair was dotted with rain, her eyes glowed with satisfaction, and she gave us a big smile. She held a chef's knife in her right hand.

# Chapter Twenty

Vicky and I stared at the intruder. Brittany smiled back at us. Rainwater puddled on the floor around her.

Vicky was first to recover her wits. "Hi, Brittany. Sorry, but this isn't a good time for a visit. You know what it's like—what time we bakers have to get up in the morning to get the bread dough rising. Merry's leaving."

"I don't make bread," Brittany said. "That's next on my list to learn."

"A good skill to have." Vicky stretched her arm toward Brittany. Brittany slapped it away with her free hand. She held up the other, the one holding the knife. "I'm sick and tired of fooling around. I tried to do this the nice way, but I've run out of patience. Give me the recipes you're developing for your book, and I'll leave you alone."

"Not likely," Vicky said.

"Maybe we can talk it over," I suggested.

"Nothing to talk over," Vicky said.

Brittany held the knife in front of her face. Madness gleamed in her eyes. The door behind her was open, and the rain continued to fall. Her foot was only inches away from my bag. The bag I'd tossed onto the floor, the one containing my phone.

"Mark will be home soon," Vicky said.

"He'll be delayed tonight. He has a flat tire to deal with." Brittany made a cutting motion with the knife. The light from the hall lamp gleamed off the blade. It looked as though it had been sharpened recently. "Recipes?"

"Say I give them to you. Then what?" Vicky's voice was perfectly calm, a woman in control, not bothered in the least. But her hands were clenched at her sides, and her shoulders stiff with tension. "You have to know I'll call the police soon as you leave and tell them you broke into my home and threatened us."

"I didn't break in," Brittany said. "You unlocked the door when I politely rang the bell. I tried breaking in before, though. The boards over those old windows are a heck of a lot stronger than they look."

"A technicality," Vicky said. "I am asking you to leave. Please do so."

"I tried climbing a branch to get to the second floor. Branch broke, so I didn't try that again. I might have broken my neck."

"That would have been most unfortunate," Vicky said.

"Vicky," I said, "let her have what she's after and be on her way. What does it matter? Recipes can't be copyrighted."

"You won't call the cops." Brittany ignored me. "Not if you don't want your boyfriend charged with murder."

"What does that mean?" Vicky said. "You just told me you cut Mark's tires. He'll have to call a tow truck, and he'll have witnesses."

"Not the murder of you, you idiot. I need you alive in case something's wrong in one of those recipes."

Involuntarily I took a step back. My mind raced as I attempted to assess the situation. Two of us. One of her. Brittany had a knife, and she looked as though she had no compulsion against using it. Mark's complete set of chef's knives—minus the one he'd taken outside when he found Jim Cole's body—was in the kitchen, but I'd never get to them in time. Sandbanks was unlikely to come to our aid. He was losing his hearing in his old age. He was still snoring happily, dreaming of when he'd been a carefree young puppy bounding across the lawn in pursuit of squirrels.

"I can get him arrested for killing that Jim Cole," Brittany said. "I have pictures of Mark crouching over Jim Cole's body. Pictures of him holding a rock. He looks angry. Angry enough to kill."

"Mark never touched that rock," Vicky said.

"Photographs don't lie," Brittany said. "Isn't that what people say?"

Brittany was not a very clever criminal. The only reason she'd gotten away with the death of Jim Cole, so far, was because she hadn't been on anyone's radar for the killing. It was nothing but a coincidence that she'd crossed Jim Cole's path that night. However—whyever—he died, she had been hiding in a clump of bushes when Mark found Jim. She took pictures, thinking she might have an opportunity to use them some day. She'd kept the pictures, foolishly not realizing those pictures could be used against her in court to place her at the scene. Mark hadn't touched the rock that killed Jim, meaning if Brittany had such a photo, she'd photoshopped it into his hand. Probably exaggerated the anger in his features too. No sloppy, amateur photoshopping job would fool police experts for more than a couple of minutes. By then, however, it might be too late for us.

"We can't let that happen, Vicky," I said. "Give her the recipe book." I stared at Vicky as hard as I could, trying to send a message. *Give the book to Brittany now, and let the police take care of her.*

Vicky gave me a nod. "Okay. I hate the very idea. But I'll do it. For Mark. How do I know you'll destroy the pictures of Mark and Jim?"

"I give you my word," Brittany said.

Vicky snorted. "Like that's worth a lot."

"Up to you to find out." Brittany used the knife to indicate the dark hallway. "Get them. I'll keep an eye on your meddlesome friend here, in case you try a fast one."

Vicky led the way to the kitchen. Brittany jerked her head at me to follow. I did so, and she fell into step behind me. Brittany was a good bit taller than me, and she was able to hold the knife comfortably against the side of my neck. I did not like the feeling of it resting there.

"My recipe book's in the back of that drawer," Vicky said.

"Get it," Brittany ordered.

Vicky opened a drawer and crouched down. The shelf was full of pots and frying pans. No way would Vicky keep papers in there.

It was up to me to distract Brittany while Vicky searched for whatever she was after. "Why did you kill Jim Cole?" I asked.

"I didn't mean to kill him. I didn't even know him. He should have minded his own business, but he wouldn't do that. He saw me trying to find a way into your house. He scared the daylights out of me when he snuck up behind me and asked what I was doing. I told him it was none of his business." Her voice began to rise. "It wasn't! He was a dirty old man, creeping around in the dark, trying to look in the windows. I told him to get lost, and he laughed at me. He called me a silly little girl and told me to run along."

"It's in here somewhere." Pot lids clattered as Vicky shoved them aside. "I hid the book when I realized someone was trying to get it."

Brittany stepped to one side, so she could look directly at my face. She was no longer watching Vicky. She didn't relax her grip on the knife, though. I tried not to glance in the direction of Mark's knives—too far away, and Brittany stood between me and them. She'd be on me before I could grab one.

"He started to get mad, told me to be quiet." Brittany wanted me to believe what she was telling me. "He pushed me and I fell. He didn't even check to see if I was okay. He was just going to walk away, expecting me to do what he said. That wasn't going to happen."

The sound of their argument must be what Vicky and I heard shortly before Mark's car pulled up to the house. What our nervous, too-alert nerves told us was a ghostly moan had been either Jim hushing Brittany or her falling to the ground when he pushed her.

"He laughed again and turned his back on me. I had to stop him from telling you what I was doing. So I picked up a rock and hit him." For the first time, Brittany's voice faltered. "I . . . I didn't mean to kill him. I wasn't going to kill him, but I wasn't going to let some stupid old man laugh at me and ruin my plan."

"I understand," I said in what I hoped was a calm, reasonable tone of voice. "He was not a nice person."

"I would have called for help—I would have. I was going to. I got out my phone, but I heard a car, and a few minutes later I heard Mark coming out of the house. He went around the other side. I hid and waited until he came out of the trees at the back, and he saw the old man. He crouched over the guy, and then he called for help. So it was okay for me to leave, right? I didn't want to get involved. I'd parked my car on the street, so I cut through the trees and hopped over the fence. I went straight home. I heard the next day that he'd died. The old guy. I was sorry about that, but it wasn't my fault. He had a heart attack or something."

"I understand," I said. And I did understand. Nothing would ever be Brittany's fault.

Vicky rose up in one long, swift graceful movement, a cast iron frying pan clutched in both hands. She swung the frying pan at Brittany's head. Brittany was facing me, but she must have read something on my face. She whirled around and saw the pan coming just in time. She lifted her left arm to protect herself as she jumped out of the way. The frying pan struck her arm, but not hard enough to disable her. She fell against the counter, but she managed to keep her grip on the knife in her right hand. She screamed and slashed wildly in the air. She was between me and the knife block, but the path to the hallway was clear.

"Forget her. Let's go!" Vicky grabbed my arm and dragged me after her. Together, we flew down the hallway. The front door stood open, the black-and-white-checked tiles in the entranceway slick with rainwater.

Unfortunately, Vicky and Mark hadn't furnished this part of the house yet. Nothing like a solid candlestick or sturdy lamp I could wield as a weapon. I tried to grab for my purse, but Vicky still had a firm grip on my arm, and she pulled me out the door. We tumbled down the steps, into the driving rain and the howling wind and the pool of yellow light cast by the lamp above the door.

Inside the house, Brittany yelled for us to come back. "I'm not going to hurt you! All I want is those recipes. I'll mention you in the acknowledgements in my book."

"You could have just given her your file," I said to Vicky.

"How naive can you be? She isn't going to let us live, Merry. Brittany wants to be the baking queen. Only room for one baking queen around here." We started to sprint down the driveway, but Vicky stopped short with a yelp of pain. She swore heartily and staggered against me. I looked down. She was in her bare feet, and the driveway was made of rough, sharp-edged gravel.

"This way." I ran to the grassy verge and slipped behind an oak tree that had likely been planted when the house was first built. Vicky limped after me, her face twisted in pain. We crouched down, and I dared to take a peek around the tree.

Brittany stood on the steps. She was dressed in black jeans and a black T-shirt, and her long black hair streamed around her. Her face was twisted in rage and frustration, and her dark eyes blazed fire. Drops of water dripped through the holes and cracks in the porch roof and fell on her head and shoulders. Her knife was clenched firmly in one hand. As I watched, she rotated the other shoulder. She winced, feeling the result of the contact with Vicky's frying pan. To my intense disappointment, the arm was still usable, and she pulled her phone out of her pocket and switched on the flashlight app.

I cursed. My own phone was in my purse, which was on the floor in Vicky's foyer.

Brittany came cautiously down the steps. She shone her light on the ground in front of her, and took a few steps forward.

"We have to get to the street," Vicky whispered.

I studied the ground around us. Broken twigs; rotten, split wood; dead and brutally sharp pine needles; tough weeds; stray pieces of gravel; jagged-edged rocks; random bits of roof tiles or plywood window coverings that had flown off in storms over the years. Even glimmers of glass, likely from bottles left when kids partied on the property.

"You won't be able to make it on those bare feet," I said. "Stay here. Stay quiet. I'll make a run for it."

"It's me she's after now," Vicky said.

"I'll distract her. If she follows me, get to the house. Lock the door and call 911."

"I can't—"

"You can," I said. I've seen enough movies and TV shows to know how to distract a pursuer. I crouched down, trying to keep as much of myself behind the tree as possible. I held my breath as a wave of light passed over the ground in front of us. It moved on.

"You shouldn't try to hide from me," Brittany said. "I don't want to kill you, Vicky, but I will if you keep playing games. Actually, maybe I will kill you. Then I can go into the house and take as much time as I need to search for your recipe book. I know what it looks like, see. I saw it on the desk when you interviewed me that time. You should have given me the job. All I wanted was to learn to bake like you. Later, when I thought about it, I decided I didn't mind not getting the job. I don't need you. You might be content to live here, in this little backwoods town where you grew up. But not me. I'm going to make it in the world."

Brittany's words washed over me; her light continued to play across the tangled bushes and tough vines. I patted the ground around me and came in contact with a stone about the size of a golf ball. It would do. I gripped it, balancing the weight. Vicky's aunt Marjorie hadn't been the only one who'd played softball for

Rudolph High. I'd been the pitcher on the team. Not a particularly good pitcher, but that hadn't much mattered as we hadn't been a very good team. Except, of course, for Vicky, who regularly hit home runs and caught flyballs in midfield. I took a breath, straightened up, pulled my right arm back, and threw the stone across the driveway with all the strength I could muster. It crashed into the bushes, making a satisfying amount of noise as it did so. Brittany's light swung away, and she ran across the driveway.

I also ran. I didn't worry about making noise as I crashed through bushes, shoving aside grasping branches, tripping over rocks. I called for help as I went.

The beam of light followed me. I heard Brittany shouting and the sound of splashing water as she ran through puddles forming on the driveway.

I'd gone about twenty yards when I reached what had once been a rose garden surrounded by a boxwood hedge. The hedge was overgrown, the rose bushes nothing but sharp thorns and choking vines. I wouldn't be able to push my way through them fast enough. The hedge disappeared into the darkness to my left; the driveway lay to my right. I didn't know how far the rose garden extended or if I'd be able to find my way off the property from there. I considered hiding in the darkness, hoping Vicky had been able to reach the house and a phone.

The beam of light touched the edges of the hedge. It swept to the left, back and forth, up and down. Searching, probing.

I was out of time. I had to get back onto the driveway, where I could run flat out to the street and then to the nearest house, and hope I could move faster than Brittany.

I broke out of the concealing safety of bushes and trees and hit the open driveway. In the darkness, I couldn't see when I stepped onto the wet gravel ,and I hit it too hard. My feet slipped out from under me, and I crashed to the ground with an involuntary cry. I landed, hard, on my back. My head shook and my teeth rattled. I stared up into a sky full of reaching branches. Water dripped onto my face.

Twigs snapped, branches were pushed aside, and I knew I had to move.

I got to my feet as quickly as I could. Fortunately, nothing seemed to be broken. The light reached the edges of the driveway. And then it went out.

I breathed. My heart pounded. I could see absolutely nothing. The sudden appearance and disappearance of even that bit of light had destroyed what night vision I might have been able to attain.

Then again, if I couldn't see, neither could Brittany.

I slowed, trying to hurry without making any noise. I knew she was behind me, her own footsteps crunching gravel and splashing through puddles, the gasping of her breath.

Lights came into sight. Light from the new carriage lanterns, recently installed, casting a warm glow onto the ground around them. Beyond them the powerful streetlights and a row of houses.

I'd make it. I was in front of Brittany, and I'd soon reach the street. It wasn't too late. People would still be up. Hopefully, a car would be coming down the road, bringing people home from a night out. Vicky would have called 911. I listened for sirens but heard nothing.

All was quiet. No one out walking their dogs or enjoying a late night stroll. Not in this rain.

The gates were closed. My heart sunk as I realized that by the time I got the gates open, with all the noise that entailed, she'd be on me.

I turned around. Brittany Pettigrew stood a few yards away, staring at me without expression. The knife was still in one hand. A long, thick branch lay on the ground about a foot in front of me. I didn't dare bend over to grab for it.

"I haven't done anything to you," I said. "Ever. Vicky will have made it back to the house. She'll have called for help."

Brittany said nothing, she simply swung the knife back and forth, back and forth.

I felt behind me. My hand fumbled for the latch to the gate. Instead, it found the branch looped over the top, the one I'd seen earlier. I thanked my lucky stars I hadn't removed it and tossed it aside. I closed my fingers around it. It was slick with rain, but I held on tight and lifted it away from the gate.

A thin, sodden twig against a kitchen knife. It wouldn't be much of a fight, but I'd do what I could.

"Let it go, Brittany," came a voice out of the darkness. "You've lost."

Vicky stepped forward. She'd put on a pair of flip-flops, likely the first shoes that came to hand.

Brittany swung around. "No. No. I can't. I won't. I told everyone I'm going to be a big TV star and have my own baking show. No one believed me, but I'll show them. I'll show them all.

"I've called the police. They're on their way. Put down the knife, and we'll go up to the house and wait for them, why don't we? We're getting wet out here."

Brittany screamed. She charged at Vicky, lifting the knife high. I also screamed as I threw the only weapon I had—a twig. It hit Brittany in the back of the neck, and she yelped as she staggered and swatted at it with her free hand.

Vicky moved in, trying to grab for the knife hand, but Brittany dodged out of the way. Vicky danced backward, taking herself out of range. Brittany's attention no longer on me, I swooped down and snatched the substantially larger branch off the ground. Brittany and Vicky faced each other. Vicky's hands were up. Brittany took a step toward her. Vicky stepped back. I gripped my branch in both hands. If I whacked Brittany over the head, the branch would be as likely to snap in half as do any damage, so instead I went in low. She was totally focused on Vicky now, leaving me forgotten. I shoved the branch between Brittany's legs and twisted, hard, putting most of the force on her right knee. She screamed and collapsed.

Vicky placed one foot on the enraged woman's knife arm and said, "Don't you dare move."

And then I heard it. Sirens coming our way.

# Chapter
# Twenty-One

"I've seen some strange excuses for murder in my time," Detective Diane Simmonds said, "but never over a recipe for mince tarts."

"It wasn't the recipes," I said. "Jim Cole mocked Brittany. She didn't like that. She didn't intend to kill him, but having killed once and apparently gotten away with it, I've no doubt she would have killed us—Vicky and me—for the recipes."

"Why?" Alan asked. "Why were they so important to her? I mean . . . yeah, Vicky's a great baker, but so are a lot of people."

"A simple matter of pure entitlement," I said. "Her aunt Janice told us Brittany was feted as the prettiest girl at school; that her father indulged her in everything, largely because of her looks, and her mother pretended not to notice. That sort of attention has got to do a number on one's head. When she left high school, she was just another moderately pretty small-town girl with no particular talent and no work ethic. Her longtime boyfriend dumped her as soon as he went into the wider world. I suspect she took the job at her aunt's café because it was the easiest thing to do while she waited for fame and fortune to come her way. It's possible she did some baking at home—indulgent fathers like that sort of thing from pretty daughters. At a guess, I'd say she saw some TV cooking show and decided that would be her route to the life she believed she deserved. Starting with a job as a pastry chef at Victoria's Bake Shoppe. And then, she couldn't even get that."

"Because I wasn't hiring a pastry chef," Vicky said. "Ironically, I would have taught her some of my techniques and practices if she'd come to work for me and showed enthusiasm and interest. But she wasn't prepared to put in the time."

"As we saw when we were at the Muddle Harbor Café, she considered waitressing and bussing to be beneath her."

"As for the other matter," Mark said, "do you believe what she said about Cole? That it was an accident, and she intended to call 911, and then I showed up, so she left it to me to do that?"

"Doesn't matter what she said," Simmonds said. "She's more than welcome to claim it was an accident in court. But she didn't call for assistance. She didn't come forward to tell us what she knew. She allowed another person—several other people in fact—to fall under suspicion for murder. At a considerable waste of police time and resources, I might add."

We were in the kitchen of my apartment. The teapot had been refreshed several times, and bottles of beer brought out of the fridge. Vicky and I had changed out of our wet clothes and were wrapped in sweaters and thick blankets against the cold that seemed to have penetrated into our very bones. Ranger bounced around the apartment, sniffing everyone and begging them to play. Mattie sat next to Simmonds, staring up at her with adoration; Sandbanks had immediately fallen asleep.

While Vicky had kept an eye—and a foot—on Brittany, I ran to the gate. I struggled to get it open with my shaking hands and frantic breathing, but then the police were all around me, streaming onto the property, with their powerful flashlights and strong voices, and once again sirens and flashing lights disturbed the peace of Lakeside Drive.

Mark arrived home from work as the police were hauling Brittany to her feet and bagging the knife. He'd watched in disbelief as she, screaming accusations and still demanding Vicky hand over the recipes, was taken away. He immediately called Alan, who likely broke a good number of speed limits getting there.

Detective Simmonds drove up moments later to see the four of us standing in a circle as the rain fell, and Vicky and I briefly related what had happened. The medics wanted to take Vicky to the hospital to have her feet treated, but she refused on the grounds that she didn't want to miss any part of what I had to say. Instead, Mark called Michelle, Vicky's mom, who was an ER nurse, and asked her to come around. The medics decided that would do.

Simmonds hadn't allowed us back into Cole House. Vicky protested, loudly and firmly, that Sandbanks couldn't be left, so an officer was dispatched to get the old dog.

Roused from his nap, he sniffed eagerly at the boots of all the new arrivals. Vicky fell to her knees and wrapped the big furry body in a hug.

"We might need to get ourselves a new guard dog." Mark laid his hand lightly against Vicky's back. He closed his eyes, and I knew he was thinking of how close he'd come to losing her.

Vicky let out a yelp of pain as she put pressure on her feet, and Mark hurried to help her. "I'm glad Sandbanks slept through it all," she said. "He would have wanted to say hi, and Brittany might have turned her anger on him."

"Vicky and Merry need to get into dry clothes," Alan said. "And Mark and I need to get out of the rain."

"Can we go to my place?" I asked the detective. "We'll wait for you there."

"Go ahead," Simmonds said. "Brittany had been in the house, so the forensics team need to go over it before I can let anyone back in." She'd glanced up at the cloud-covered sky. "Not a nice night to be gathering outdoor evidence."

* * *

Mattie was delighted to have all these unexpected visitors, canine as well as human. Mrs. D'Angelo, dressed in her nightgown and housecoat, streaks of white face cream still evident, ran up the stairs after us, demanding to know what was going on. One of her "contacts" on Lakeside Drive had immediately put out the word of police activity *once again* at Cole House.

My father called shortly thereafter, also wanting to know what was going on.

"You can tell Mom," I said, after reassuring him we were all fine, "she solved the case."

"She'll be delighted to hear it. Will she know how she accomplished that?"

"I'll tell her in the morning. 'Night Dad."

"Good night, honeybunch. Call if you need anything."

Michelle arrived with a bag full of bandages, antiseptic wipes and ointment; the moment she came through the door, she dropped to her knees in front of Vicky's chair.

"They look worse than they are," Vicky said.

"That's good to know," Michelle said, "because they look mighty bad."

Vicky yipped and yelped, and Alan, Mark, Mrs. D'Angelo, and I winced in sympathy, as Michelle carefully extracted thorns, dirt, bits of gravel, and who knows what else from her feet, and dabbed antiseptic on the cuts.

"You'll be limping up the aisle," Michelle said as she secured the last bandage, "but most of this should heal quickly, provided you keep off your feet."

"I can't keep off my feet. You know what my job's like, Mom."

"We can get some padded mats for you to stand on at the bakery," Mark said. "That'll help."

"You must have been in terror for your very lives," Mrs. D'Angelo said with an unsuitable degree of pleasure, "to allow that to happen." She'd settled comfortably in an old, overstuffed chair, a castoff from my parents' house. A cup of tea rested on the table beside her, and her ever-present phone was in her lap.

"Can't talk about it," I said. "Police orders."

"You can tell me, dear."

I smiled sweetly.

Michelle was checking the last of her bandages and putting her equipment away when Detective Simmonds rang the down-stairs bell.

The moment she walked in, she ordered Mrs. D'Angelo out of my apartment. My landlady made a key-locking-lips gesture and said, "My lips are sealed, Detective. I know how to keep highly sensitive details to myself."

"Out!"

Mrs. D'Angelo sighed heavily. "Very well. I can see this is on a need-to-know basis. Merry, I expect the full story in the morning. My friends are depending on me." She left, head held high, closing the door behind her with a slam of righteous indignation.

Simmonds crept across the room. She put her ear to the door, waited about twenty seconds, and threw the door open. Mrs. D'Angelo put her hands to her heart and jumped back. "Good heavens, Detective. You startled me. I seem to have left my . . . my . . ."

"Good night, Mabel," the detective said. "Shall I call an officer to sit with you for the rest of the night?"

"No. No. Not necessary. Until tomorrow, Merry." She bustled off.

"You might as well have let her stay," Alan said. "You know she'll beg Merry for every little detail in the morning, and what information she doesn't get, she'll make up."

"Be that as it may, I don't want a potential court case confused by gossip and hearsay," Simmonds said. "I'm not much of a tea person, and I have a long night ahead of me. Any chance of a coffee, Merry?"

"I'll get it," Alan said.

# Chapter
# Twenty-Two

I dropped into the bakery on Thursday. Vicky had to keep off her damaged feet as much as possible, but she limped into the restaurant to join me over coffee and a sandwich. She insisted her feet were healing rapidly, and she'd be right as rain to walk up the aisle on her wedding day. She also told me she and Mark had decided to sell the house.

"Sell it? Are you sure, Vicky?"

"Mark and I talked it over. A lot. It was always his dream to have a big old house with a huge property. Not mine, but I want him to be happy, and he was so thrilled when we got it. Most of that thrill's gone." Her face twisted. "I mean, a man died there. Mark found the body in our yard. A woman tried to kill me on that property. You and me. I'm not worried about the history of the house—Emmeline and her sisters and all that. But . . . I can't forget that I was frightened in that house. I don't want those memories coming back on dark winter nights when Mark's working late. Do you understand?"

"Totally. Mark's okay with this?"

She threw me that great big Vicky smile. "Turns out that while I was wanting Mark to be happy, he was wanting me to be happy. He says that even before the confrontation with Brittany, he was beginning to think buying a big old house with lots of history and not much livability might have been a matter of biting off more than he can chew. But he didn't tell me because he thought I loved the house."

You're putting it back on the market, then?"

"Might not have to. Sue-Anne called us. She says the town's thinking of buying it and turning it into a museum to do with the history of Rudolph. We shouldn't be completely relying on the Christmas Town thing to keep our town going. She said it's time to think outside the Christmas box."

"Sounds like something my dad would say."

"It probably was. Sue-Anne isn't known for original ideas. My own dad might have had something to do with it too. Charles Cole never specified what would happen to the trust he set up to maintain the house once he had no further heirs. Dad says if we call the house the Charles Cole Museum, the town can possibly take over the trust. It's not a lot, but enough they can do some repairs, keep the heat on, that sort of thing. Sue-Anne also mentioned that the Rudolph Gardening Club have long wanted to get their hands—or I should say trowels—into the Cole House garden and restore it to its former glory."

"Where are you going to live in the meantime?"

"It won't all happen right away. As you know, the town council never rushes into anything, although they eventually do whatever your dad tells them to do. We have time to look for a place. We're thinking a nice modern bungalow on a small lot not far outside town."

"Sounds like a great idea," I said.

# Chapter
# Twenty-Three

Vicky and Mark's wedding might have been small, but it was truly marvelous. My friend looked absolutely stunning in the dress we'd chosen for the church service. She'd planned to match the dress with a pair of sky-high stiletto heels. Instead, at her mother's insistence, she wore hastily purchased, thick-soled flats that covered the few remaining bandages on her feet. She clutched a small bouquet of spring flowers and spoke her vows clearly and with emphasis. Mark was dressed in a perfectly cut gray suit, the tie matching Vicky's lock of pink hair. As he said his own vows, the look he gave her lit up the church.

Alan held my hand and gave me a smile, almost as warm as Mark's. In the pew in front of us, Michelle wept and Tom Casey beamed.

My mom got to her feet in a river of silver and approached the front of the church. I leaned around Alan and looked at my dad. He was wearing a suit, nice although considerably out of date, and beaming with pride. "What's this?" I whispered.

"Michelle and Aline's secret surprise," Dad said.

My mother began to sing Habanera, an aria from *Carmen*.

*Love is a rebellious bird*
*That no one can tame*

That piece of music is sometimes used at weddings, although the lyrics aren't entirely suitable. Which doesn't really matter as it's in French. I only know this because of the number of times that aria has been sung in our house and the intense discussions between my mother and her fellow singers about it.

The service was short but sweet, and we emerged into the bright spring sunshine, got into our cars, and headed for the Yuletide Inn, where photographs would be taken in the garden prior to going in for dinner.

"Do you remember our wedding, Noel?" my mom asked. My parents were traveling to the reception with Alan and me. Vicky had initially suggested having Sandbanks, Mattie, and Ranger form part of the bridal party, but Mark and I didn't think that was such a great idea. Sandbanks could be incontinent at times; Ranger's enthusiasm would be guaranteed to get the better of him; and Mattie's sheer size might present an obstacle to the older of Vicky's relatives as they entered or left the church.

Instead, the three dogs were at Alan's place. Vicky and Mark would be spending the night in the bridal suite of the hotel.

Grace Olsen and the staff at the Yuletide Inn had gone above and beyond to give Vicky and Mark an evening to remember. The tables looked beautiful, the food was fantastic, and when we got up to dance, the music was played by a DJ who knew how to accommodate all tastes and age groups.

Russ Durham asked me for a dance. It was a slow one, and we moved into position. On the far side of the room, I saw Alan approach Michelle Casey, and her accept with a smile.

"As much as I wanted a dance with you," Russ said, "I have an ulterior motive. I figured this would be a good time for an update. Your mom will have my head if she finds out I'm talking shop at Vicky's wedding."

"Update away," I said. "It will be our secret."

"No doubt you heard Brittany's been charged with the murder of Jim Cole and the attempted murder of you and Vicky."

"Detective Simmonds came to the store to tell me so in person."

"I've had a busy week, digging into all the angles of this story. It's going to be a big one."

"Already is." *The Gazette* had gone all out with a front-page feature spreading into the back pages, about Cole House itself. Russ conducted in-depth interviews with people acquainted with the story of the house and its history. Old photos of the mansion in its full grandeur and of the family in happy days had been found in the paper's archives and printed anew.

"I was happy to get the chance to do a story on the house. It's an important piece of Rudolph history, and it deserves to be remembered. Because I'm such an outsider," he said in his deep Louisiana accent, "I can do more with that history than someone for whom it's always been nothing more than a place for high school kids to party and try to scare each other. I do have one piece of information that might be new to you."

"What?"

"Miss Emmeline Cole was nowhere near as poverty-stricken as people believed."

"Meaning?"

"She had considerable wealth in her own name. Her fiancé, Arnold MacLeish, died December twenty-fourth, 1983. A couple of weeks before his death, he changed his will, leaving everything to her, obviously expecting her to become his wife shortly. His parents, who seem to have liked Emmeline very much, never contested that will. If anything, they believed she should have what he wanted her to have. As well as enough money to provide her with an adequate, although not lavish income, for the remainder of her days, she inherited stock valuing ten thousand dollars. That was in 1983."

"And . . . ?" I wondered where this was going. Ten thousand dollars wasn't a life-changing amount of money. Not even in 1983.

"After his death, Emmeline became a recluse. With some of what she'd inherited from her fiancé, plus what she had from her own family, she bought a small house in Rochester, where she remained for the rest of her days. From that point on, she lived her life much as Miss Haversham did. She never traveled; didn't give parties; rarely, if ever, went to restaurants. She didn't collect rare art or books. She had few friends, no children of her own, and no contact with her only surviving relatives: her cousin, Jim Cole, or his daughter, Cindy. She served on some charitable committees, but nothing that involved her going out in public. Thus she had no need to sell Cole House, which she still owned, or the stock MacLeish left her. Did I mention that her fiancé was an executive in a burgeoning computer company you might have heard of? Its name is Apple."

"You mean she got Apple stock from him? Ten thousand dollars' worth of stock? What would that be worth today?"

"Upward of ten million, I believe."

I trod on Russ's foot. He grinned down at me. "Yup."

"Do you think she knew that?"

"Oh yes. She definitely knew. Emmeline was no Luddite. She had modern computer equipment in her house. She kept up with the news and her charitable causes. She tracked the stock market regularly. She knew. She didn't need the money—that's all. So she never sold any of the stock, and dividends were automatically reinvested to buy more stock.

"How do you know this?"

"When Jim started trying to overturn her will, Emmeline's lawyer, Tom Casey, alerted the Rochester police and asked them to take an interest in Emmeline's death, wondering if there was anything suspicious about it."

"Was there?"

"Nothing indicates so. But their investigation into her finances and her computer habits turned up what I just told you."

We resumed our dance. "The charity for homeless women is in for a substantial windfall."

"That they are."

I started to laugh. We flew around the room, and I laughed and laughed. People stopped dancing to look at me. Alan thew a puzzled look at Russ as he and Michelle danced past us.

"What's so funny?" Russ asked.

"Jim Cole. Trying to get his hands on that run-down old house. If he'd pretended to be a slightly nicer man; if he'd shown some friendship to his older, reclusive cousin. If he'd visited her now and again. Offered to take her on outings or help with her shopping. He could have been in line for a cut of ten million bucks."

"Considering what I've learned about Emmeline Cole, that would only have worked if he was genuinely a nice man. She was no fool."

I stopped once again. I looked across the room. Vicky and Mark were dancing together now, looking as though nothing in

the world existed but each other. My mom was regaling the table
of Vicky's siblings and their spouses with tales of her glory days.
Tom Casey and my dad were chatting. Both men had ties askew
and drinks in hand.

"Tom Casey had to know that all along."

"Of course he did. An inkling anyway, although likely not
the total amounts. His father was the Cole family lawyer, and
then Emmeline's. He wasn't going to tell anyone, Merry. Not
until the estate was settled. Attorney client privilege and all that.
I'm going to get another drink. Want one?"

"Sure."

We went to the bar, and Russ got a bourbon on the rocks for
himself and a glass of white wine for me. Alan thanked Michelle
for the dance and joined us. He slipped his arm around me. I
suspect he didn't entirely trust Russ. When I first came back to
Rudolph to open Mrs. Claus's Treasures, Russ and I had eyed
each other as potential mates. Alan, who I later found out had
long adored me from afar (foolish man), had seen what was happening. Sparks had not flown between Russ and me, and I'd
finally realized Alan was the one I wanted to be with.

I hugged Alan in return.

"You two had a long talk," he said.

"I learned some interesting things. Tell you later."

"As for the murder itself," Russ said. "Turns out the house
itself had nothing do with the death of Jim Cole. Rather ironic,
don't you think, that with all the enemies he's made over the
years, he died because he happened to cross paths late one night
with a disturbed young woman he didn't even know. I can't
print much of this yet, but Diane gave me a heads-up. Brittany's
going to plead to involuntary manslaughter for Cole. She'll
claim he snuck up on her, made threats against her, and she

defended herself. She says she didn't know he was badly hurt, and when Mark showed up moments later—"

"Not moments," I said.

"Whatever. She left, assuming Mark would call for help."

"Will that defense hold?"

"It might, Merry. A young woman alone on a dark, spooky property at night. A man not known for minding his own business. Her lawyer will make a big deal out of Cole's reputation. On the other hand, she was where she was not supposed to be, and she had no legitimate reason to be there. The police got DNA off the fence around the property, following the death of Jim Cole. Years of people climbing the fence and getting splinters in fingers, or scraping their legs, etcetera. Most of it they weren't able to match with anyone, but they have at least two very recent samples. Only after Brittany was arrested were they able to identify those two samples as hers. Not only DNA, but she snagged her clothes on a nail one night, and the torn fabric has been matched to a shirt found at her house. Enough evidence to prove she didn't wander onto the property on that one occasion, only to be accosted by Jim Cole, but had been there, uninvited, several times, in an attempt to access the house and to deliberately frighten the inhabitants."

"Did she confess to the frightening bit?" Alan asked.

"It was, according to her, nothing but a joke. She says she was angry at Vicky for not hiring her and wanted to get back at her. So she wanted to make Vicky think the house was haunted. She tried breaking in but was unsuccessful, which would account for some of the noises Vicky and Mark heard. The night Jim Cole died, Brittany knew Vicky had company, and thought she'd scare you both by knocking on doors and windows and the like. She was hoping you'd flee, leaving the door unlocked, and she could walk right in."

Alan shook his head and said nothing.

"One more thing . . ." Russ grinned at us.

"It's like pulling teeth," I muttered.

"Brittany's fingerprints match a set found on the back door of the bakery following the attempted break-in. Diane's going to testify that this shows a pattern of stalking and harassment, which ultimately resulted in a man's death."

Some of this I'd heard from Diane Simmonds over the few days following Brittany's arrest, but it was nice to have it confirmed and to know the police were gathering hard evidence.

Vicky and Mark joined us. They were both out of breath, red-faced, breathing deeply, and glowing with joy. "Okay," Vicky said, "this looks like a seriously serious discussion. Why aren't you partying? Alan, dance with me. Mark, you take Merry. Sorry, Russ—you're on your own."

"One more quick question," Alan said. "What's Brittany have to say about the attack on Vicky and Merry?"

"She's likely going to plead not guilty. Say it was all a misunderstanding. Vicky and Merry panicked and ran off into the night, and worried for their safely, Brittany followed them."

I snorted.

"Will that one hold?" Alan asked.

"Highly unlikely. She brought a knife with her, for one thing. Rather than park in Vicky's driveway, the way a regular visitor would, she hid her car on a back street and, once again, climbed over the fence."

"All's well that ends well," Vicky said. "Now, I want to dance."

\* \* \*

"I am not going to be able to decide," my dad said to me as we were lining up for the midnight dessert buffet. "Everything looks better than the next." He patted his ample stomach. "Do you think it would be rude to ask for a doggie bag?"

"Yes," I said. I myself was having trouble deciding between the key lime pie and the triple-layer sprinkle cake. The lemon sorbet looked delicious, and it would have fewer calories, but it was a special occasion after all. Maybe just this once, the pie *and* the cake.

"I had an interesting phone call today," Dad said.

"Do tell."

"Janice Benedict, from Muddle Harbor."

That came as a surprise. "What did she want?"

Dad helped himself to a bowl of chocolate mousse. I served myself pie, congratulating myself on only taking one dessert.

Dad jerked his head to indicate an empty table. We took our plates and sat down.

"Janice said the animosity between Rudolph and Muddle Harbor has gone on long enough. After you and Vicky visited, she got to thinking about her grandmother and her great- aunt, Iris and Ethel, and how the two sisters never visited or even spoke to each other in their later years."

"That is sad, but Janice isn't related to anyone we know, is she?"

"No. But she feels partly responsible for what happened with Brittany. It was her, Janice believes, who put the idea into the girl's head about getting a job at Vicky's, and everything flowed from there. Brittany was grumbling and complaining, as Janice said was normal with her, about the Muddle Harbor Café being beneath her. So Janice said something along the lines of, 'Go to Rudolph then, if you're so special.'"

"It's hardly Janice's fault what Brittany did with that sugges-tion." I cut a sliver of pie and popped it into my mouth. Delicious.

"I know, and Janice knows that too. But she wants to talk, and I want to listen. She has an idea of maybe, at first, using Vicky's place to provide cakes and pies for the café. Particularly around the holidays. Janice freely admits baking isn't one of her skills, and the woman she was using as her supplier before she hired Brittany has decided to retire."

"It's a start," I said. "What about Jack Benedict and Randy Baumgartner? How are they likely to feel about a . . . lessening of hostilities ,shall we say, between our two towns?"

Dad grinned over a spoon piled high with chocolate mousse. "Janice says it's long past time to let the two old fools stew alone in their resentment. Janice plans to run in the next mayoral race. She's got some promising ideas, and I'd like to give her the benefit of my experience to help her develop them. I'm going to Muddle Harbor on Tuesday for lunch at the café. I've long said we in Rudolph would be happy to share our success with Muddle Harbor, if they'd let us."

I toasted my dad with the last slice of key lime pie. "If anyone can do it, Dad, I know you can. Just one thing: don't commit Vicky to anything. I suspect she'd going to be even busier than she usually is for the next while."

\* \* \*

At the end of the evening, most people had left, the DJ had packed up his equipment, and the staff were discreetly clearing the tables. Vicky's feet were propped up on a chair. She'd taken an extra dose of painkillers so she could dance up a storm and enjoy her own party, but tomorrow her feet would be killing her.

Russ, Alan, and Mark had dispensed with jackets and ties altogether, and I'd kicked off my shoes. We sat around a table, enjoying one last drink before heading off into the night.

I stood up, picked up a discarded dessert spoon, and tapped the side of my glass. When I had everyone's attention, I cleared my throat and said, "I have one last gift for Vicky."

"Not for me?" Mark asked with a twinkle in his eye.

"Only indirectly."

Vicky threw a questioning look at Alan, and he shrugged. "I've no idea what she has in store. I never do." He took my hand and held it lightly.

"I got a phone call from Roy McDonald this morning."

"And he is . . .?" Mark asked.

"An editor at one of the biggest publishing houses in the United States. Specifically the editor in charge of their lifestyle and home imprint."

Vicky's feet dropped to the floor. "He wants to see my book! That is so great. Thank you, Merry." She turned toward Mark, her eyes shining. "Did you hear that? He wants to see my book." Her face fell. "It's not finished yet. How long do I have before getting it to him? Will he wait or give up on me and go on to someone else?"

"He doesn't want to *see* your finished book, Vicky." The first couple of days after the injuries to her feet, Vicky had been unable to stand for long periods of time, and she insists she can't bake sitting down. Instead, she sat at her desk in the bakery office, supervised her staff, worked on the accounts, and finally, finally got enough of her book proposal finished to send to me. I sent it to my most promising contact in publishing, and to my considerable surprise, he got back to me almost immediately. Normally, publishing works at a glacial pace, but Roy must have seen something he immediately liked.

"Not yet," I said. "He wants to give you a contract. Now. Based on what I told him about it, and about you and your proposal. He's ready to start to negotiate and give you an advance."

She fell back against her chair. "An advance. Did you hear that, Mark? An advance. On my book."

He grinned at her. "I heard, babe."

"You'll need an agent," I said. "And to that effect, as the second part of my gift, I've arranged for one of the top cookbook agents in New York to talk to you."

She started to get to her feet, but Mark put a hand on her arm. "Careful there."

Vicky dropped down. The enormous grin began to fade, replaced with total panic. "Does that mean I have to . . . finish the book?"

"Yes, Vicky," I said. "It means you have to finish the book."

# Recipes from *Year-Round Holiday Favorites from America's Christmas Town* by Vicky Casey

## Traditional Holiday Shortbread

These shortbread cookies are very traditional and a huge hit at Victoria's Bake Shoppe. Shortbread is one of the easiest cookies for the home baker to make, as it has few ingredients and simple instructions. This recipe is best suited for baking in a slab and then cutting into squares and rectangles, not for cutting prior to baking with cookie cutters.

### Ingredients

2 cups cake flour
¾ cup + 1 tablespoon cornstarch
¼ teaspoon salt
1 cup unsalted butter, room temperature
⅓ cup granulated sugar
¼ cup confectioners' sugar (aka icing sugar)

### Instructions

In a medium bowl, whisk together the flour, cornstarch, and salt until well blended.

In a stand mixer set on medium speed, or with a handheld mixer, beat the butter until creamy. Beat in the granulated sugar until light and fluffy, about 2 minutes, scraping down the sides and bottom of the bowl as necessary. On low speed, add the flour mixture in two or three additions until it forms a soft dough. Wrap the dough with plastic wrap and chill for approximately 30 minutes.

Preheat the oven to 350°F.

On a lightly floured piece of parchment paper, roll the dough out to a ¾-inch-thick slab,

Transfer, parchment and all, to the baking sheet, and bake until lightly golden and firm to the touch, about 40 minutes. Slip the parchment paper with the shortbread onto a hard surface. Immediately sprinkle the shortbread heavily with the confectioners' sugar. While still warm, cut the shortbread into 1- or 1½-inch pieces. Let cool completely.

Cookies will keep in an airtight container for about a week.

# Coconut Sugar Cookies

Coconut flakes give these basic sugar cookies a nice modern touch. Great for making with kids who want to cut out the shapes and decorate with colored sugar or sprinkles before baking.

## Ingredients

7 ounces sweetened flake coconut
3¾ cups all-purpose flour
1½ teaspoons baking power
¼ teaspoon salt
1 cup unsalted butter, room temperature
1½ cups sugar
2 large eggs, room temperature
1½ teaspoons vanilla extract
Plain or colored sugar or sprinkles for decorating

## Instructions

Place coconut in a food processor and grind until fine.

In a small bowl, mix flour, coconut, baking powder, and salt together.

Combine butter and sugar in a stand mixer or with a handheld mixer, and mix until pale and fluffy.

Add eggs and vanilla, and combine.

Add flour mixture and combine. Do not overmix.

Wrap dough in plastic and place in refrigerator for 2–24 hours.

Preheat oven to 350°F.

On a floured surface, roll out dough to approximately ¼ inch thick, and cut into shapes.

Place cookies on baking sheet or silicone mat, approximately 1 inch apart.

If desired, sprinkle lightly with plain or colored sugar or sprinkles.

Bake for 10–12 minutes, until edges are golden brown.

Cookies will keep in an airtight container for about a week.

# Curried Butternut Squash Soup

As well as baking favorites, Vicky's cookbook includes some of the recipes she makes for hungry holiday shoppers, take-out orders, and catering. This is a great soup for using up what you have in the way of end-of-harvest-season produce, so you don't need to stick to the measurements provided. Feel free to adjust to your heart's content.

1 butternut squash, peeled and chopped
2 large sweet potatoes, peeled and chopped
2 large or 3 medium potatoes, peeled and chopped
1 onion, peeled and chopped
1 slice of hot red pepper, finely chopped (as desired)
Salt and pepper
1 tablespoon curry powder
½ tablespoon cumin powder
2 tablespoons vegetable oil
½ tablespoon dried rosemary
2 cups vegetable stock.

Toss squash, sweet potatoes, potatoes, onions, and hot pepper into a roasting pan. Sprinkle with salt and pepper. Mix spices and herbs in a small bowl, and add to vegetables. Sprinkle with vegetable oil and toss thoroughly.

Roast in 350°F. oven for about 1 hour.

Put vegetables in a stock pot and add stock. Bring to a boil, then lower heat and simmer for about 20 minutes. Puree in a blender or with an immersion blender.